U0057513

觀光英語

TRAVEL ENGLISH

朱靜姿◎著

Welcome to the "Travel English".

This is a conversational and reading oriented program which designed to help the readers who are planning to travel overseas either they are going with a group tour or by themselves to improve their English conversation and reading skills. It also provides lots of useful information about traveling aboard which is good for readers' reference.

It is our sincere belief that "Travel English" will provide the readers the most useful and valuable point of views to study English and to prepare for traveling around the world.

Many thanks and may your adventure overseas provide enjoyment and happiness beyond your dream and return home from a rewarding journey.

Zoe Chu
Vancouver

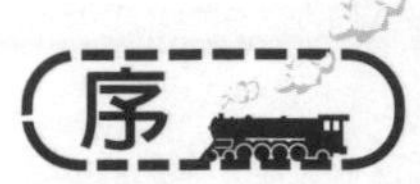

許多人在學習英文的過程中，會碰到最大的困難與障礙，那就是找不到一個能讓他們開口說英文的好環境來練習說英文，以至於一直都沒有勇氣開口說英文，即使認識許多的單字，對於文法也了解不少，可惜就是無法將這些所學到的英文單字與文法，應用到最基本且簡單的日常生活會話上。

這樣的聾啞英文學習法，阻礙了英文學習者用英文流暢表達自我意念的能力，進而失去了把英文學習好的自信心。

本書出版的目的是希望能幫助大家了解如何使用簡單明瞭的英文與他人溝通，並訓練發展英文學習者的會話技巧，進而建立自信，在出國旅遊的途中，敢開口說英文，即使只是一個單字、一句簡單的片語或是比手劃腳，都能輕鬆地表達自我與他人侃侃而談。

不管你是有錢又有閒的旅客，或是花了一段時間努力工作存了一筆旅費，就等放年假出國旅遊的旅客，還是那種超幸福的、即將拿著父母親提供的學雜費出國遊學或是留學的學生，當打包好行李，來到機場準備登機時的那一刻，那種既興奮又令人期待的滿足感，眞的是人生中最過癮的一件事。

只是接下來，到了國外，可就不能像是在家鄉那麼樣的逍遙自在了，因爲要過海關；要克服語言障礙；要調時差；要適應不同氣候、

環境與文化上的差異；要能吃得慣國外的食物（萬一找不到中式餐飲時），更要隨時注意自身與財物的安全。

因此，要享受一個美好又有品質的旅遊，出國前要先做些功課，以下是一些不錯的建議：

1.要提升自己的英文會話能力，畢竟英文目前還是世界共通的國際語言。當然啦，如果本身還會其他國的語言那就更好了。在國外時，千萬不要害怕自己英文不好而不敢開口說英文，其實只要是一個簡單的單字，或是片語再加上肢體語言以及臉上的表情都是很好的溝通工具，可以令人輕易理解的，搞不好還會遇到個會與您說中文的老外喔！只要你肯開口，加上隨機應變的能力，一定可以享受到意想不到的旅遊樂趣。

2.平時多了解一下世界各地的地理位置、不同的文化歷史背景、飲食習慣、藝術、宗教信仰、治安問題、氣候變化等等，多加強這方面的知識，當你下次有機會旅遊時，一定會讓你不虛此行，滿載而歸的。

在國外旅遊時，會遇到千變萬化的場合與狀況，本書"Travel English"《觀光英語》，則提供了讀者一些不可錯過的絕佳學習英文的思考方向。由於之前作者已出版了一本"Practical Hotel & Restaurant English"《實用餐旅英文》，因此，有關住宿飯店與餐廳飲食部分，本書則不再重複。

感謝Celia Chang的校稿，以及兩位優秀的年輕插畫者：Part 1 Speak Up由林正庭（Teddy）所繪製，Part 2 Reading由熊任恩（Bear）所繪製。

最後，祝各位讀者旅途愉快，滿載而歸。

朱靜姿 Zoe Chu

於溫哥華

Part 1 Speak Up
插畫者
林正庭 Teddy（Klimt）
自畫像

Part 2 Reading
插畫者
熊任恩 Bear
自畫像

本書特色 About Travel English

"Travel English"《觀光英語》一書，總共分成兩部分，Part 1 Speak Up在於強調英文口語會話的訓練，Part 2 Reading在於強調英文閱讀能力的訓練，這兩部分皆以有關旅遊方面的英文爲基礎，提供讀者一些旅遊時經常需要用到的英文用語及常識，幫助各種類型的環遊世界旅程更加地暢行無阻，愉快自在。

Part 1 Speak Up

1. Tongue Twister

說英文前先唸一唸英文繞口令，讓自己的舌頭做一下暖身運動，有助於說英文時更加「輪轉」。本單元有錄製語音CD。

2. Tourists Speak Up

本單元匯集了旅客在旅遊途中經常會使用到的各種情況的實用英文句。

3. Flight Attendants, Immigration Inspectors, Customs Inspectors, Clerks, Rental Agent, Doctors... Speak Up

本單元根據實際上的需求，依據在旅途上一定或是可能會遇到的各行各業及各式各樣的人士與旅客之間的互動而產生的各類問答英文實用句。

4. Teddy Bear Speak Up

兩位可愛的年輕人，他們之間逗趣以及無厘頭的說話方式，讓學習英文增添許多樂趣，從他們的對話中可以學到非常多的口語英文與俚語喔。

5. Conversations

編寫了各種逼眞實用之旅遊情境英文會話，以供讀者學習旅遊中的應對技巧。本單元有錄製語音CD。

6. Useful Information

提供讀者許多有關旅遊的中英文對照的有用常識與資訊，以幫助讀者在旅途中能更暢行無阻。

7. Quizzes

小考！自我評量！

8. Answers

答案。可即時知道自我評量之結果並予以修正。

Part 2 Reading

Reading部分，內容包括了機上各種廣播詞、進海關要如何填寫報關單、拉斯維加斯的簡介、海外旅遊時寫張Post Card給好友們、閱讀一個歐洲旅行團的每日行程表、海外旅遊的安全指示、閱讀一些旅遊景點的標示以及海外旅遊經驗分享等等。

Table Of Contents

Part 2 Reading

WORLD MAP

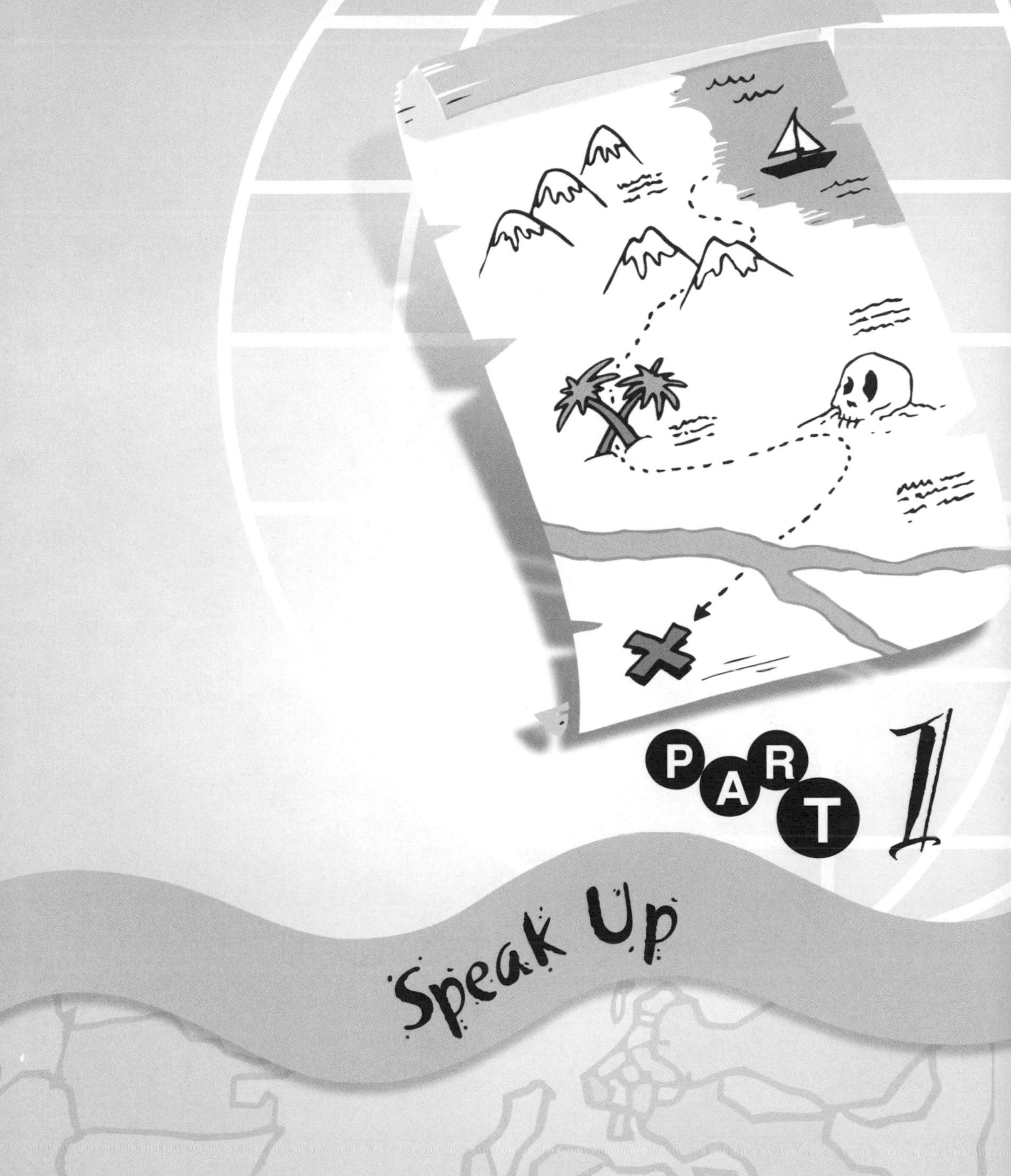

PART 1

Speak Up

Travel English

Unit 1

Fun Geography Challenges

Betty bought butter, but the butter Betty bought was bitter.

Tourists Speak Up

What is world's largest continent? **(Asia)**

Which is the largest country in the world? **(Russia)**

Which is the second largest country in the world? **(Canada)**

Which country has the most people in the world? **(China)**

What are the 2 major rivers in China? **(the Yellow, the Yangtze)**

What's the highest mountain in the world? **(the Himalayas)**

Name the mountain in Switzerland. **(the Alps)**

The 2000 Olympic Games were held in___________. **(New Zealand)**

Where were 2004 Olympic Games held? **(Athens, Greece)**

Where can you ride a camel across? **(Sahara Desert)**

Where is the Eiffel Tower located? **(Paris, France)**

Where is the Leaning Tower of Pisa located? **(Italy)**

Where is Big Ben located? **(London, England)**

Where is the Empire State Building located? **(New York)**

The Grand Canyon is located in which state? **(Arizona)**

What tropical rain forest comprises the largest land area?

(Amazon rain forest)

Is the Yangtze the longest river in Asia? **(Yes)**

Which is the longest river in the world? **(Nile)**

Where does Dalai Lama come from? **(Tibet)**

What's the highest capital in Asia? **(Tibet)**

What's the highest capital in the world? **(La Paz-Bolivia)**

Which is the largest ocean in the world? **(Pacific)**

What's the capital city of Taiwan? **(Taipei)**

What's the tallest building in the world? **(Taipei 101)**

Where can we visit pyramids? **(Egypt)**

In what country do the people worship cows? **(India)**

How many states are there in the USA? **(50)**

Which country celebrates Christmas in summer? **(Australia)**

In what countries do people use chopsticks?

(Taiwan, China, Japan, Korea)

What countries should I go for a good SPA resort?

(Indonesia or Thailand)

How many Disney are there in the world? **(4)**

And where are they? **(Los Angles-California, Orlando-Florida, Tokyo-Japan, Paris-France)**

What do you want to see in your trip to ___________?

I want to see pyramids in my trip to Egypt.

Where did you spend your last holiday and what did you enjoy most about it?

I spent my last holiday in _______________.

What's your favorite country for **a holiday / honeymoon**?

France is my favorite country for honeymoon.

How many continents did he cycle cross?

Practice asking and answering questions from the sentences above.

Teddy Bear Speak Up =_=; 0_O

To travel around the world 環遊世界

Buddy 好朋友；老兄；老弟

Teddy: What's up, man? =_=

Bear: As soon as I have enough money I'm going to travel around the world. ^O^

Teddy: Wow! What a great idea, buddy. Why don't you bring me with you? A_A

Name some places 講些地名

Dude 男人；男孩（美國俚語）

You are telling me 這還用你說

Teddy: Can you name some places that you really want to visit in the world? =_=

Bear: I really want to visit the Disney World in Orlando, the casino hotels in Las Vegas, the Great Wall in China, the pyramids in Egypt, the Canadian Rockies in Canada, the Leaning Tower in Pisa, the Waikiki's white sand beach in Hawaii, the Niagara Falls, the Cancun city in Mexico and.... How about you, dude? 0_O

Teddy: Umm.... Taipei 101 in Taiwan. You know, it's the tallest building in the world. =_*

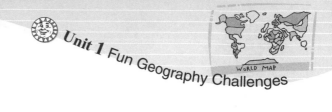

Bear: Mm.... You are telling me! @_@

Find a partner for Teddy & Bear role playing game.

Conversations

In the Travel English Class

Ms. Chu: Good evening, everyone. Welcome to the Travel English class. We are going to have lesson 1, the Fun Geography Challenges for tonight. Before the class, let's play a game to challenge the geography. Are you ready?

Students: Yeah...

Ms. Chu: Great! Now, you have to keep that in mind. You'll be divided to 2 teams. One is the "Ice Field Team" and the other is the "Ocean Team". Take turns, each team has to choose a question sheet from the box on the podium and read it loudly to the other team. Your team will get one point if you answer the question correctly. Let's start from the "Ice Field Team".

Teddy: "Name a city in Australia."

Sasa: Sydney.

Becky: "What's the second biggest city in America?"

Bear: Los Angeles.

Wing: "Name the biggest city in England."

Angel: London.

Kate: "A country or a place that has water all around it."

Alien: Island.

Jason: "How many countries are there in the world?"

Jean: About 200.

Lena: "What's the most important part of a city?"

Freddie: Downtown.

Lorne: "What's your favorite city in Europe?"

Rita: Paris.

Stella: "What's the capital city of Japan?"

Vincent: Tokyo.

Andy: "What city is also called 'The Big Apple' ?"

Ivy: New York.

Anne: "Name 2 mountains in the world."

Jack: The Alps and the Rockies.

Sam: "What's the longest river in Asia?"

Emily: The Yangtze River.

Grace: "The Grand Canyon is located in which state?"

Marco: Arizona.

Ms. Chu: Wow, you guys are just incredible. Keep going!

Chitchatting

Ms. Chu: The Pacific is the world's largest ocean, larger than all the landmasses combined.

Teddy: It's said, "The Earth's landmasses make up only a third of the planet's total surface." Is it true, Ms. Chu?

Ms. Chu: Yes, that's right. If you add up all of the Earth's landmasses,

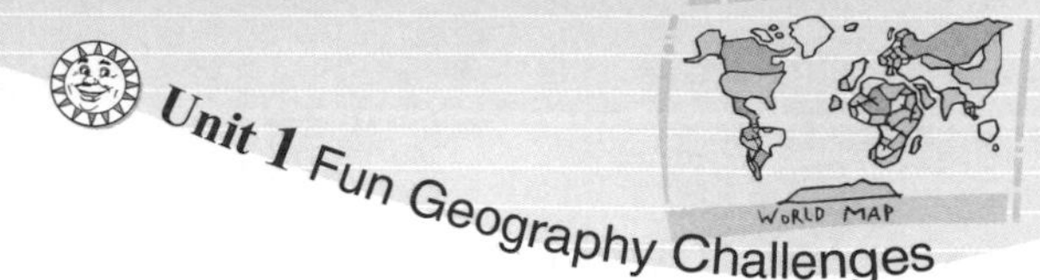

they make up about 196,950,000 square miles only.

Bear: What's the other two-thirds?

Ms. Chu: The other two-thirds are covered by water. Primarily, they're oceans, rivers, lakes, and seas.

Teddy: Which is the longest river in the world?

Bear: I know. It's Nile.

Ms. Chu: Yeah! It is Nile in Africa.

Bear: Are there any rivers in Antarctica?

Ms. Chu: Good question! Actually, rivers and lakes are found everywhere except Antarctica.

Teddy: We are planning to travel around the world someday. What would you suggest us to prepare before that?

Ms. Chu: If you guys really want to travel around the world someday, I suggest you better do a little study of the land, waters, climate, people, and history of the world. Don't be a geography ignoramus.

1. Now is your turn to practice the dialogues with a partner.

2. Use the sentences from "Tourists Speak Up" or "Teddy Bear Speak Up" to create some new dialogues.

Useful Information

North America 北美洲國家及各主要城市

United States of America (USA) 美國

Anchorage 安克拉治 / Boston 波士頓 / Chicago 芝加哥 / Honolulu 檀香山 / Los Angels 洛杉磯 / Miami 邁阿密 / New Orleans紐奧良 / New York 紐約 / San Francisco 舊金山 / Seattle 西雅圖 / Washington 華盛頓

Canada 加拿大

Calgary 卡加立 / Montreal 滿地可（蒙特婁）/ Ottawa 渥太華 / Quebec 魁北克 / Toronto 多倫多 / Vancouver 溫哥華

South America 南美洲國家及各主要城市

Argentina 阿根廷

Buenos Aires 布宜諾斯艾利斯

Peru 秘魯

Lima 利馬

Mexico 墨西哥

Mexico City 墨西哥市

Brazil 巴西

Rio de Janeiro 里約熱內盧

Asia 亞洲國家及各主要城市

Bengal 孟加拉

Dacca 達卡

Brunei 汶淶

Burma 緬甸

China 中國

Canton 廣東 / Hong Kong 香港 / Macau 澳門 / Peking 北京 / Shanghai 上海

Japan 日本

Nagoya 名古屋 / Sapporo 札幌 / Okinawa 琉球 / Osaka 大阪 / Tokyo 東京

Guam 關島

Korea 韓國

Seoul 漢城

India 印度

Delhi 德里 / Mumbai (Bombay) 孟買

Indonesia 印尼

Denpasar 峇里島 / Djakarta 雅加達 / Surabaja 泗水

Malaysia 馬來西亞

Kuala Lumpur 吉隆坡 / Penang 檳城

Maldives 馬爾地夫

Myanmar (Burma) 緬甸

Rangoon 仰光

Nepal 尼泊爾

Kathmandu 加德滿都

New Guinea 新幾內亞

Pakistan 巴基斯坦

Karachi 喀拉蚩

Philippines 菲律賓

Cebu 宿霧 / Manila 馬尼拉

Singapore 新加坡

Srilanka 斯里蘭卡

Colombo 可倫坡

Taiwan 台灣

Chiayi 嘉義 / Chinman 金門 / Hualian 花蓮 / Kaohsiung 高雄 / Penghu 澎湖 / Taipei台北 / Taichung台中 / Tainan台南 / Taitung 台東

Thailand 泰國

Bangkok 曼谷 / Chinman 清邁 / Phuket 普吉島

United Arab Emirates 阿拉伯聯合大公國

Abu Dhabi 阿布達比 / Dubai 杜拜

Vietnam 越南

Ho Chi Minh 胡志明市 / Nanoi 河內

Europe 歐洲國家及各主要城市

Austria 奧地利

Vienna 維也納

Belgium 比利時

Brussels 布魯塞爾

Bulgaria 保加利亞

Sofia 索菲亞

Czech 捷克

Prague 布拉格

Denmark 丹麥

Copenhagen 哥本哈根

England 英國

London 倫敦 / Manchester 曼徹斯特

Finland 芬蘭

Helsinki 赫爾辛基

France 法國

Nice 尼斯 / Paris 巴黎

Germany 德國

Berlin 柏林 / Frankfurt 法蘭克福 / Hamburg 漢堡 / Munich 慕尼黑

Greece 希臘

Athens 雅典 / Corfu (Kerkyra) 科孚

Iceland 冰島

Reykjavik 雷克雅未克

Ireland 愛爾蘭

Dublin 都柏林

Israel 以色列

Jerusalem 耶路撒冷

Italy 義大利

Florence佛羅倫斯 / Naples 那不勒斯 / Rome 羅馬 / Venice 威尼斯

the Netherlands (Holland) 荷蘭

Amsterdam 阿姆斯特丹

Norway 挪威

Oslo 奧斯陸 / Tromso 特朗瑟

Poland 波蘭

Warsaw 華沙

Portugal 葡萄牙

Lisbon 里斯本

Russia 俄羅斯

Moscow 莫斯科

Scotland 蘇格蘭

Edinburgh 愛丁堡

Spain 西班牙

Madrid 馬德里 / Barcelona 巴塞隆納

Sweden 瑞典

Stockholm 斯德哥爾摩

Switzerland 瑞士

Geneva 日內瓦 / Lucerne 盧森 / Zurich 蘇黎世

Turkey 土耳其

Istanbul 伊斯坦堡

Yugoslavia 南斯拉夫

Belgrade 貝爾格萊德

Oceania 大洋洲國家及各主要城市

Australia 澳洲

Brisbane 布里斯本 / Cairns 凱恩斯 / Canberra 坎培拉 / Melbourne 墨爾本 / Perth 伯思 / Sydney 雪梨

New Zealand 紐西蘭

Auckland 奧克蘭 / Christchurch 基督城

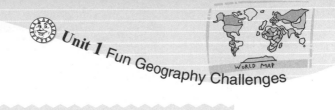

Africa 非洲國家及各主要城市

Egypt 埃及

Cairo 開羅

Morocco 摩洛哥

Casablanca 卡薩布蘭卡

South Africa 南非

Cape Town 開普敦 / Johannesburg 約翰尼斯堡

the Antarctic 南極洲

the Geography 地型

Ocean 海洋 / Sea 海 / Beach 海邊 / River 河流 / Creek 小溪 / Lake 湖泊 / Canyon 深峽谷 / Cliff 懸崖；峭壁 / Cave 洞穴 / Limestone Caves 石灰岩洞 / Stalactitle 鐘乳石 / Reef 暗礁 / Shore 岸 / Waterfall 瀑布 / Swamp 沼澤 / Island 島 / Mountain 山岳 / Hill 小山；丘陵 / Volcano 火山 / Valley 山谷 / Forest 森林 / Desert 沙漠 / Ice Field 冰原 / Glaciers冰河 / Delta三角州

All about Tourist Attractions 觀光勝地

Amusement parks 遊樂場

Disney Land (Los Angeles) / Disney World (Orlando)

Beaches 海邊

Miami South Beach (Miami) / Waikiki Beach (Hawaii)

Canals 運河

Casinos 賭場

Atlantic City (New Jersey) / Las Vegas (Nevada)

Cruise 客輪

Dog sleighs 由狗拉的雪橇

Hot springs 溫泉

Ice fields 冰原

Columbia Ice Field (Canada)

Lakes 湖泊

Buntzen Lake (Vancouver) / Lake Louise (Canadian Rockies)

Limestone caves 石灰岩洞

Stalactitle 鐘乳石

Monorails 單軌鐵路

Seattle Monorail (Seattle)

Museums 博物館

National parks 國家公園

Canadian Rockies (Canada) / Yellow Stone National Park (USA)

Gondolas 纜車

Outlet 工廠直營的名牌商店區

Parks 公園

Queen Elizabeth Park (Vancouver) / Stanley Park (Vancouver)

Public markets 公眾市場

Pike Place Market (Seattle)

Pyramids 金字塔

Snow mobil 雪車

Square 方形廣場

Pioneer Square (Seattle) / Time Square (New York)

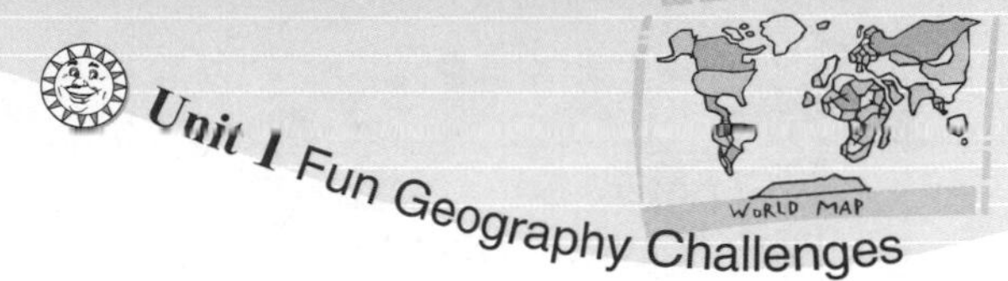

Suspension bridges 吊橋

Capilano Suspension Bridge (Vancouver) / Lynn Canyon Suspension Bridge (Vancouver)

Towers 塔

CNN Tower (Toronto) / Space Needle (Seattle)

Trolley 有軌電車

Oceans 海洋

Antarctic Ocean 南極海 / Arctic Ocean 北極海 / Atlantic Ocean 大西洋 / Pacific Ocean太平洋

Seas 海洋

Aegean Sea 愛琴海 / Baltic Sea 波羅的海 / the Caribbean 加勒比海 / East China Sea 東海 / English Channel 英吉利海峽 / Gulf of Mexico 墨西哥灣 / Gulf of Thailand 暹羅灣 / the Mediterranean 地中海 / North Sea 北海 / Philippine Sea 菲律賓海 / Sea of Japan 日本海 / South China Sea 南海 / Tasman Sea 塔斯曼海

Rivers 河流

Amazon River 亞馬遜河 / Colorado River 科羅拉多河 / Congo River 剛果河 / Danube River多瑙河 / Mekong River 湄公河 / Mississippi River 密西西比河 / Missouri River 密蘇里河 / Murray River 墨瑞河 / Nile River 尼羅河 / Rhine River 萊茵河 / Rio Grande River 里約格蘭德河 / St. Lawrence River 聖羅倫斯河 / Seine River 塞納河 / Thames

River 泰晤士河 / Yangtze River 揚子江（長江）/ Yellow River 黃河 / Yukon River 育空河

Mountains 山岳

the Alps 阿爾卑斯山脈 / the Andes 安地斯山脈 / the Appalachians 阿帕拉契山脈 / the Atlas 亞特拉斯山 / Cook 庫克山 / Everest 聖母峰 / Fuji 富士山 / the Himalayas 喜瑪拉雅山脈 / Kilimanjaro 吉力馬扎羅山 / Kosciusko 科修斯古山 / Matterhorn 馬特合恩峰 / McKinley 麥金利山 / Pikes Peak 派克峰 / the Rockies 落磯山脈 / the Urals 烏拉山脈

Deserts 沙漠

Arabian 阿拉伯沙漠 / Australian 澳洲大沙漠 / Death Valley 死亡谷大沙漠 / Gobi 戈壁大沙漠 / Kalahari 喀拉哈里沙漠 / Mojave 摩哈比沙漠 / Sahara 撒哈拉沙漠 / Takla Makan 塔克拉馬干沙漠

Words & Phrases

continent	n.	洲
located	adj.	坐落的；位於的
leaning	n.	傾斜
Olympic Games	ph.	奧林匹克
held（hold過去式）	v.	舉行
New Zealand	n.	紐西蘭
Athens	n.	雅典

Greece	n.	希臘
camel	n.	駱駝
Sahara Desert	n.	撒哈拉沙漠
Empire State Building	ph.	帝國大廈
Grand Canyon	ph.	大峽谷
Arizona	n.	亞利桑那州
tropical rain forest	ph.	熱帶雨林
comprise	v.	包含
Amazon	ph.	亞馬遜河
Dalai Lama	n.	達賴喇嘛
Tibet	n.	西藏
highest	adj.	最高的
capital	n.	首都
La Paz	n.	拉巴斯
Bolivia	n.	玻利維亞
longest	adj.	最長的
largest	adj.	最大的
tallest	adj.	最高的
Taipei 101	n.	台北101
pyramid	n.	金字塔
Egypt	n.	埃及
worship	v.	崇拜
cow	n.	母牛
India	n.	印度
chopsticks	n.	筷子
geography	n.	地理學

challenge	v.	向…挑戰
keep in mind	ph.	記住
podium	n.	講台
point	n.	比賽分數
you guys		你們大家
incredible	adj.	難以置信的
keep going	ph.	繼續保持
chitchat	v.	閒聊

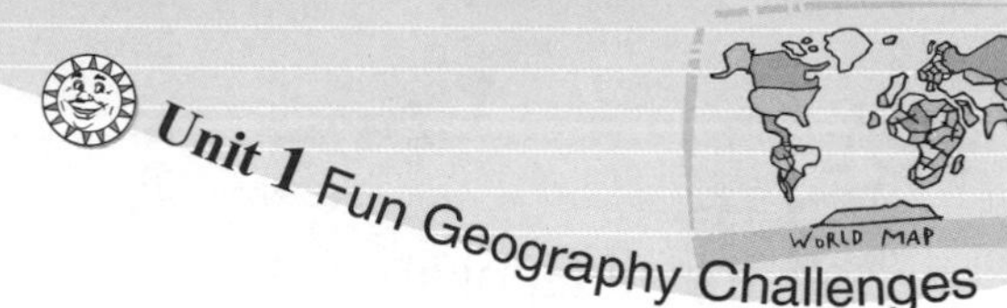

landmasses	n.	大陸
combined	adj.	相加的
it's said		據說
make up	ph.	組成
third	adj.	三分之一的
planet	n.	行星
surface	n.	表面
add up	ph.	把…加起來
square mile	ph.	平方英哩
two-thirds	adj.	三分之二的
primarily	adv.	主要地
Nile	n.	尼羅河
Africa	n.	非洲
Antarctica	n.	南極洲
except	prep.	除了
suggest	v.	建議
have better	ph.	最好
climate	n.	氣候
history	n.	歷史
ignoramus	n.	無知的人

1. Answer the questions.

(1) Which is the largest country in the world?

(2) Which is the second largest country in the world?

(3) Which country has the most people in the world?

(4) What's the highest mountain in the world?

(5) Where were 2004 Olympic Games held?

(6) Where is the Leaning Tower of Pisa located?

(7) The Grand Canyon is located in which State?

(8) What tropical rain forest comprises the largest land area?

(9) Which is the longest river in the world?

(10) Where does Dalai Lama come from?

(11) Which is the largest ocean in the world?

(12) What's the tallest building in the world?

(13) Where can we visit pyramids?

(14) How many states are there in the USA?

(15) Which country celebrates Christmas in summer?

2. Answer the following questions.

(1) Name some continents in the world.

(2) Name some country in Europe.

(3) Name some cities in Asia.

(4) Name some rivers in the world.

(5) Name some mountains in the world.

1. Answer the questions.

(1) Russia is the largest country in the world.

(2) Canada is the second largest country in the world.

(3) China has the most people in the world.

(4) The Himalayas is the highest mountain in the world.

(5) 2004 Olympic Games were held in Athens, Greece.

(6) The Leaning Tower of Pisa is located in Italy.

(7) The Grand Canyon is located in Arizona.

(8) Amazon rain forest comprises the largest land area.

(9) Nile is the longest river in the world.

(10) Dalai Lama comes from Tibet.

(11) Pacific is the largest ocean in the world.

(12) Taipei 101 is the tallest building in the world.

(13) We can visit pyramids in Egypt.

(14) There are 50 states in the USA.

(15) Australia celebrates Christmas in summer time.

2. Answer the following questions.

(1) North America, South America, Europe, Asia, Africa, Oceania, and the Antarctic.

(2) Austria 奧地利 / Belgium 比利時 / Bulgaria 保加利亞 / Czech 捷克 Denmark 丹麥 / England 英國 / Finland 芬蘭 / France 法國 / Germany 德國 / Greece 希臘 / Iceland 冰島 / Ireland 愛爾蘭 / Israel 以色列 / Italy 義大利 / the Netherlands (Holland) 荷蘭 / Norway 挪威 / Poland 波蘭 / Portugal 葡萄牙 / Scotland 蘇格蘭 / Spain 西班牙 / Sweden 瑞典 / Switzerland 瑞士 / Turkey 土耳其 / Yugoslavia 南斯拉夫

(3) Canton 廣東 / Hong Kong 香港 / Macau 澳門 / Peking 北京 / Shanghai 上海 / Nagoya 名古屋 / Sapporo 札幌 / Okinawa 琉球 / Osaka 大阪 / Tokyo 東京 / Seoul 漢城 / Delhi 德里 / Mumbai (Bombay) 孟買 / Denpasar 峇里島 / Djakarta 雅加達 / Surabaja 泗水 / Kuala Lumpur 吉隆坡 / Penang 檳城 / Rangoon 仰光 / Kathmandu 加德滿都 / Karachi 喀拉蚩 / Cebu 宿霧 / Manila 馬尼拉 / Colombo 可倫坡 / Chiayi 嘉義 / Chinman 金門 / Hualian 花蓮 / Kaohsiung 高雄 / Penghu 澎湖 / Taipei 台北 / Taichung 台中 / Tainan 台南 / Taitung 台東 / Bangkok 曼谷 / Chinman 清邁 / Phuket 普吉島 / Abu Dhabi 阿布達比 / Dubai 杜拜 / Ho Chi Minh 胡志明市 / Nanoi 河內

(4) Amazon River 亞馬遜河 / Colorado River 科羅拉多河 / Congo River 剛果河 / Danube River 多瑙河 / Mekong River 湄公河 / Mississippi River 密西西比河 / Missouri River 密蘇里河 / Murray River 墨瑞河 / Nile River 尼羅河 / Rhine River 萊茵河 / Rio Grande River 里約格蘭德河 / St. Lawrence River 聖羅倫斯河 / Seine River 塞納河 / Thames River 泰晤士河 / Yangtze River 揚子江（長江）/ Yellow River 黃河 / Yukon River 育空河

(5) the Alps 阿爾卑斯山脈 / the Andes 安地斯山脈 / the Appalachians 阿帕拉契山脈 / the Atlas 亞特拉斯山 / Cook 庫克山 / Everest 聖母峰 / Fuji 富士山 / the Himalayas 喜瑪拉雅山脈 / Kilimanjaro 吉力馬扎羅山 / Kosciusko 科修斯古山 / Matterhorn 馬特合恩峰 / McKinley 麥金利山 / Pikes Peak 派克峰 / the Rockies 落磯山脈 / the Urals 烏拉山脈

Unit 2

Flying Around The World

Tongue Twister

She says she should sit.

Passengers Speak Up

On the flight

May I have more nuts?

Well, what do you have?

What have you got?

Yes, rum and coke, please.

Could you bring me some water, please?

Beef, please.

May I have some red wine?

Can I have Scotch and water?

Can I have another Scotch and water?

Can I have some more juice?

Could I have some Chinese tea?

May I have a pillow?

Could you bring me a blanket, please?

When do you serve dinner?

When does the in-flight movie start?

Do you sell duty-free on the plane?

When do you start duty-free service?

Can I save my dinner for later?

Which is the movie channel?

Could you tell me how to fill out this form?

Can you help me with this form?

How long is the flying time?

How much longer is the flight?

What time will we be landing?

May I recline my seat?

Transferring

Where is the transfer desk?

Where is the transfer counter?

Where should I take my connecting flight?

I'm transferring to Seattle.

I'm transferring at Hong Kong.

Can I take a connecting flight here to New York?

I have to transfer to TB002.

I missed my connecting flight.

When will the next flight leave?

What time do I board again?

How long should I wait?

Practice asking and answering questions from the sentences above.

Flight Attendants Speak Up

Would you like something to read?

Could you put your bag under the seat, please?

Could you put your bag in the overhead cabinet during take-off, please?

Could you put your tray table up, please?

Could you put your seat up, please?

Fasten your seat belt, please.

Fasten seat belt while seated.

Dinner will be served in 10 minutes.

Would you like a drink before your meal?

Can I get you something to drink?

Would you care for a drink?

We have milk, juice, soda, beer, wine, whiskey, and cocktails.

Would you like chicken, fish, or beef?

Would you like chicken or fish for dinner?

Which would you like for dinner, fish, chicken, pork, or beef?

Have you finished?

Would you like some coffee or tea?

With sugar and cream?

Coffee? Chinese tea?

Some more coffee?

Some more tea?

May I clear the table?

May I take away your tray?

Could you close the window blind, please?

Would you like some instant noodles?

Practice asking and answering questions from the sentences above.

Teddy Bear Speak Up =_=;0_O

See someone off 送行

Give someone a ride 載人一程

Teddy: Is your brother going to see you off at the airport? =_?

Bear: Of course, buddy! He's going to give us a ride to the airport. ^.^

Pop the trunk 用駕駛旁的按鈕來打開汽車行李箱

Load the luggage 放行李

Teddy: Could you pop the trunk for me? =_=

Bear: No problem! Let me help you load the luggage into the trunk. 0_O

Take off 起飛

Taxing 滑行

Flying 飛行

Landing 降落

Bear: Hey! What time does the plane take off? 0_O

Teddy: It takes off at 10:30. = =

Non-stop flight 直達（到達目的地的飛行中不做任何停留）

Direct flight 直飛（到達目的地的飛行中不需換機）

Transfer 轉機

Connecting flight 接駁班機

Stop-over 短暫停留

Transit passengers 過境旅遊

Transfer passengers 轉機旅客

You can say that again 你可以再說一次（你說的沒錯）

Dude 男人；男孩（俚語）

Teddy: Are we taking the non-stop flight or we have to change planes? =_?

Bear: It is a direct flight meaning we don't have to transfer to a connecting flight or to recheck-in, but we have to stop over in Tokyo. 0_O

Teddy: To be brief, we are transit passengers not transfer passengers. ^o^

Bear: You can say that again, dude. ^O^

First class 頭等艙

Business class 商務艙

Economy class 經濟艙

Fly (take) 搭

Upgrade 升等

Cool 好酷

Teddy: Are we flying economy class? =_?

Bear: Yes, what do you expect? 0_?

Teddy: It'll be so cool if we could be upgraded to first class! ^o^

Bear: Stop dreaming, man. @_O

Check-in 登機手續

Teddy & Bear: We'd like to check-in, please. =_= , 0_O

Ground staff: Certainly, sir. n_n

A window seat 靠窗座位

An aisle seat 靠走道座位

Ground staff: Would you like a window seat or an aisle seat? n_n

Teddy: A window seat, please. =_=

Preference 偏愛

Over the wing 靠機翼的

Ground staff: Do you have any seats preference? n_n

Bear: No, but give me any seats not over the wing and away from the toilet. 0_O

Traveling together 一起旅行的

Seat together 坐在一起

Ground staff: Are you traveling together? n_n

Teddy & Bear: Yes, we would like to be seated together, please. =_= , 0_O

Boarding pass 登機證 (flight, flight number, gate number, and seat number)

Teddy: What do we need to get on the plane? =_?

Bear: Passport and boarding pass. 0_O

Boarding gate 登機門

Follow the sign 跟著指標

Bear: Where is the boarding gate? @_@

Teddy: We can just follow the signs. ^_^

Upright position 豎直；垂直

Ops 驚嘆聲

Bear: Hey! You have to keep your seat in upright position during take off. 0_O

Teddy: Ops! Sorry! I almost fall asleep. 9_9

Turbulence 亂流

What the hell 搞什麼鬼（台語：哇勒）

Bear: Are you scared of turbulence? 0_O

Teddy: Not at all, actually, I quite enjoy the way of shaking in the air. Ha...ha... ^0^

Bear: What the hell! x_x

Recline 座位可活動後仰

In-flight movies 飛行中放映的電影

Bear: I'm full. I want to recline my seat for a rest. 9_9

Teddy: I want to watch the in-flight movie. ^_^

Jet-lagged 有時差現象的

Won't = Will not

A long fly 長途飛行

Ruin 搞毀

Bear: I wish we won't be tired and jet-lagged after a long fly. 0_>

Teddy: Yeah...Feeling sleepy in the daytime will ruin our holiday. =_<
By the way, are there any midnight tours? =_=

Find a partner for Teddy & Bear role playing game.

See someone off at the airport

Justin: Bye, Honey. Have a nice trip to New York.

Joyce: Thanks. As soon as I arrive at the hotel, I'll give you a call.

Justin: OK, but remember I'm going to attend a two-day meeting in Taichung tomorrow and stay overnight there.

Joyce: Well, if you are not at home when I call, I'll leave a message on the answering machine to let you know that I've arrived safely.

Justin: Great. What time do you expect to get there?

Joyce: Mm...If the airplane arrives on time, I'll be at the hotel around 11:30 in the morning. It's about 11:30 at night your time.

Justin: All right. Call me when you know the time of your flight back, and I'll pick you up at the airport.

Joyce: Thank you. Hon. Don't forget to eat breakfast before you go to work.

Justin: Don't worry. I won't forget. Enjoy your trip.

Check-in (1)

Erin: Hi! I'd like to check-in, please.

Ground staff: Certainly, ma'am. May I see your passport and ticket, please?

Erin: Here you go.

Ground staff:	You are going to Vancouver today.
Erin:	Yes.
Ground staff:	How many pieces of luggage do you have?
Erin:	I have two pieces of luggage to check-in and a carry-on.
Ground staff:	Did you pack the luggage yourself?
Erin:	Yes!
Ground staff:	Has it left your sight at anytime since your arrival at the airport?
Erin:	No!
Ground staff:	OK! Please put your luggage on the scale.
Erin:	Sure.
Ground staff:	Would you like a window seat or an aisle seat?
Erin:	Could I get a window seat, please?
Ground staff:	Sure.
Ground staff:	OK, here are your baggage claim tags, boarding pass, and passport. Your seat number is A12, and your plane leaves at 6:50pm from gate D68.
Erin:	Which way is to gate D68?
Ground staff:	Go straight this way, follow the signs and you will find the way to gate D68.
Erin:	Thanks a lot.
Ground staff:	You're welcome. Have a nice flight.

Check-in (2)

Joshua:	Hi! Should I check in here for flight TB 1030 to Vancouver?

Ground staff: Yes, sir. May I have your ticket and passport, please?

Joshua: Here you go.

Ground staff: How many bags do you have?

Joshua: I have two suitcases.

Ground staff: Would you mind putting them on the scale?

Joshua: No.

Ground staff: I'm sorry, sir. One of your bags is 5 kilograms overweight.

Joshua: What should I do now?

Ground staff: Well, you can pick some stuff out of your suitcase and take them with you as hand-carry luggage.

Joshua: OK. Thanks a lot.

On the plane (1)

Joshua: What time do you serve dinner?

Attendant: We are preparing it now. It shouldn't be too long.

Joshua: Thanks.

(Dinner is served)

Attendant: Can I get you something to drink?

Joshua: Yes, a coke with rum, please.

Erin: Could I get some orange juice, please?

Angus: May I have some red wine?

Attendant: Here you go. Would you like chicken or beef for your dinner?

Joshua: Chicken, please.

Erin: Could I have vegetarian dish?

Attendant: Wait for one second, please?

Angus: I'll have beef, please.

Attendant: Would you like some coffee or Chinese tea?

Joshua: Coffee, please.

Erin: Some Chinese tea, please.

Angus: No, thanks. Can you take away my tray?

Megan: Excuse me. I'm cold. Can I get a blanket, please?

Eric: Excuse me. My headphones don't work. Can you exchange them for me, please?

Attendant: Here you go.

Eric: What in-flight movies do you have?

Attendant: You can read our in-flight magazine to check it out.

Eric: Thanks.

On the plane (2)

Lillian: Excuse me, my friend is sick. Do you have any medicine for airsickness?

Attendant: Yes, he looks pale. How do you feel, sir?

Andrew: I feel like throwing up. Can you give me another airsickness bag?

Attendant: Certainly, sir. I'll also bring you some medicine for airsickness and some water.

Andrew: Thank you.

Attendant: You are welcome.

1. Now is your turn to practice the dialogues with a partner.

2. Use the sentences from "Flight Attendants Speak Up", "Passengers Speak Up", or "Teddy Bear Speak Up" to create some new dialogues.

Useful Information

Signs in the Airport 機場內的標誌

Arrival 入境

Departure 離境

International flights 國際航線

Domestic flights 國內航線

Airport terminal 機場大廈

Terminal 1 第一航廈

Check-in 報到登記

Boarding gate 登機門

Flight information board 飛機資訊顯示版

Flight schedule monitor 飛機班次顯示銀幕

Duty free shop 免稅商店

Custom 海關

Immigration 移民局

Waiting lounge for transit (Transit lounge) 過境室

Transfer counter 轉機櫃檯

VIP lounge 貴賓室

Foreign passport holders 持外國護照旅客

Visitors 觀光旅客

Baggage claim 領行李處

Baggage carousel 行李轉盤

Currency exchange 外幣兌換

Elevator 電梯

Lost & Found 失物招領

Visitor information 旅客詢問處

Emergency exit 緊急出口

Parking 停車場

Ground transit 地面的轉乘處

Airport shuttle 機場接駁車

Seats 機上座位

A window seat 靠窗的座位

An aisle seat 靠走道的座位

A middle (center) seat 中間的位子

Two seats together 兩個在一起的位子

A seat close to the front 前面的座位

A seat close to the back 後面的座位

A seat over the wing 靠機翼的座位

A seat behind the bulkhead 在這個隔間的第一個座位

A seat near the lavatory 靠近廁所的座位

A seat away from the lavatory 遠離廁所的座位

A seat by the emergency exit 靠近緊急出口的座位

First class 頭等艙

Business class 商務艙

Economy class 經濟艙

Cabin Interior 機內設備

Storage bin 行李放置處

Overhead cabinet (Overhead bin, Overhead compartment) 頭頂置物箱

Seat-back 椅背

Armrest 扶手

Tray table 折疊餐桌

Seat belt 安全帶

Movie screen 電影銀幕

Headset (Headphone) 耳機

In-flight magazine 機內雜誌

Blanket 毛毯

Pillow 枕頭

Recline button 座位可活動後仰的按鈕

Window shade (Window blind) 窗戶遮蓋

Air conditioning 冷氣空調

Lavatory 洗手間

Airsickness bag 嘔吐袋

First aid kit 急救箱

Smoke detector 煙霧偵測器

Emergency door 緊急出口

Life vest 救生衣

Buckles 釦環

Tabs 拉環

Straps 帶子

Mouthpiece 吹口

Seat control panels 座位控制板

Reading light switch 閱讀燈

Attendant call button 服務鈴

Attendant call cancel 服務鈴取消

Headphone jack 耳機插座

Volume control 音量控制鈕

Channel selector 頻道選擇鈕

Signs on the Flight 機艙內的標誌

Fasten seat belt 繫上安全帶

No smoking 禁煙

Occupied 廁所有人

Vacant 廁所無人

Return to your seat 請回到座位

(EXIT) Emergency exits 緊急出口

(O_2) Oxygen mask 氧氣面罩

Air Crew 組員稱謂

Captain 機長 / First officer 副機師 / Flight engineer 機上工程師 / Chief purser 空服長 / Purser 座艙長 / Flight attendant 空服員 / Cabin crew member 空服員 / Stewardess 空姐（非正式說法）/ Steward 空少（非正式說法）/ Ground staff 地勤人員

Safety Equipment Demonstration on the Flight 機內安全示範

Fasten seat belts.

繫上安全帶。

Slip the live vest over your head.

立刻從頭上穿上救生衣。

Bring the waist strap around your waist.

將腰帶環住腰部。

Connect and tighten the clip by pulling it outward.

向外拉使夾子緊緊連接。

Pull the red tabs firmly downwards to inflate.

要充氣時將紅色的垂片穩穩地向下拉。
Blow into one of those mouthpieces to inflate it further.
進一步的充氣要將氣吹入吹口。

Food and Drinks on the Flight 飛機內的食物與飲料

Food 食物

Nuts 堅果；花生 / Beef 牛肉 / Fish 魚 / Pork 豬肉 / Chicken 雞肉 / Omelet 蛋捲 / Chinese breakfast 中式稀飯早餐 / Turkey sandwich 火雞肉三明治 / Instant noodles 速食麵

Drinks 飲料

Milk 牛奶 / Orange juice 柳橙汁 / Apple juice 蘋果汁 / Pineapple juice 鳳梨汁 / Tomato juice 番茄汁 / Coke 可樂 / Diet Coke 健怡可樂 / 7-up 七喜 / Sprite 雪碧 / Ginger ale 薑汁汽水 / Perrier 礦泉水 / Beer 啤酒 / Red wine 紅酒 / White wine 白酒 / Whiskey 威士忌 / Scotch 蘇格蘭威士忌 / Martini 馬丁尼 / Gin Tonic 琴湯尼 / Bloody Mary 血腥瑪莉 / Screwdriver 螺絲起子 / Vodka lime 伏特加萊姆 / Vodka rum 伏特加蘭姆 / Coffee 咖啡 / Tea 茶 / Chinese tea (Oolong tea) 烏龍茶

Flight Information 飛行資訊

Outside air temperature 機外溫度

Ground speed 相對地上的飛行速度

Altitude 高度

Longitude 經度

Latitude緯度

Distance to destination 離目的地的距離

Local time at origin 出發地的目前時間

Local time at destination 目的地的現在時間

Estimated arrival time 預估的到達時間

IDL (international date line) 國際換日線

In-flight Magazine 機上雜誌

In-flight movie 飛行中放映的電影

In-flight music 飛行中放映的音樂

Duty-free shopping list 免稅商品表

Menu 菜單

Baggage Allowance 免費托運行李限額

Free baggage allowance on trans-Pacific flights to the USA and Canada is a maximum of two and each is no more than 32 kilograms.

經太平洋飛往美國與加拿大的免費行李最多兩件，每件不可超過32公斤。

Luggage 行李（不可數名詞）

Baggage 行李（不可數名詞）

Suitcases 手提箱（可數名詞）

Carry-on (Carry-on luggage, hand-carry luggage) 隨身行李

Baggage tag 行李牌

Baggage claim tag 行李提領單

Words & Phrases

landing	n.	降落
transfer	v.	轉換
connecting flight	ph.	轉搭的班機
would you like...		你想要…嗎
have a nice trip	ph.	祝旅途愉快
as soon as	ph.	一…就馬上…
attend	v.	參加；出席
stay overnight		停留一夜
answering machine	ph.	電話答錄機
luggage	n.	行李
pack	v.	裝箱；打包
sight	n.	視覺
ground staff	ph.	地勤人員
scale	n.	磅秤
baggage claim tag	ph.	行李提領單
boarding pass	ph.	登機證
passport	n.	護照
gate	n.	登機門
suitcases	n.	手提箱
kilogram	n.	公斤
overweight	adj.	超重
hand-carry luggage	ph.	手提行李

vegetarian	n.	素菜
throw up	ph.	吐
airsickness bag	ph.	嘔吐袋

1. Complete the sentences.

(1) Well, what _________ you have?

(2) _________ have you got?

(3) Could you _________ me some water, please?

(4) Can I have some ________ juice?

(5) _________ do you serve dinner?

(6) __________ is the transfer counter?

(7) Where should I__________ my connecting flight?

(8) I _________ transferring at Hong Kong.

(9) When does the next flight __________?

(10) Would you like ____________ to read?

(11) Could you put your bag ___________ the seat, please?

(12) Could you put your tray table ________, please?

(13) Fasten seat belt ________ seated.

(14) Would you like chicken, fish, ________ beef?

(15) Which ________ you like for dinner, fish, chicken, pork, or beef?

2. Asking questions.

(1) ____?

I have two pieces of luggage to check-in and a carry-on.

(2) ____?

I'd like an aisle seat, please.

(3) ____?

Yes, a coke with rum, please.

(4) ____?

We'll start duty-free service in 20 minutes.

(5) ____?

I feel like throwing up.

1. Complete the sentences.

(1) Well, what **do** you have?

(2) **What** have you got?

(3) Could you **bring** me some water, please?

(4) Can I have some **more** juice?

(5) **When** do you serve dinner?

(6) **Where** is the transfer counter?

(7) Where should I **take** my connecting flight?

(8) I **am** transferring at Hong Kong.

(9) When does the next flight **leave**?

(10) Would you like **something** to read?

(11) Could you put your bag **under** the seat, please?

(12) Could you put your tray table **up**, please?

(13) Fasten seat belt **while** seated.

(14) Would you like chicken, fish, **or** beef?

(15) Which **would** you like for dinner, fish, chicken, pork, or beef?

2. Asking questions.

(1) How many pieces of luggage do you have?

(2) Would you like a window seat or an aisle seat?

(3) Can I get you something to drink?

(4) When do you start duty-free service?

(5) How do you feel, sir?

Welcome to the United States of America

Unit 3

Going Through Immigration And Customs

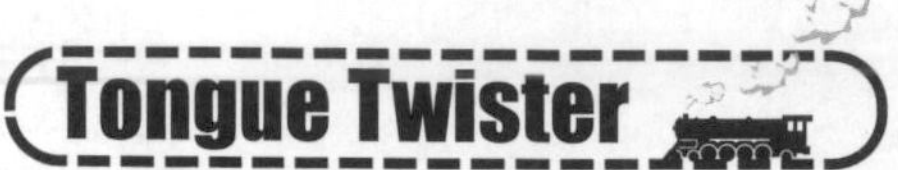

Do tongue twisters twist your tongue?

Tourists Speak Up

At immigration

This is my passport, customs declaration form and I-94 (disembarkation card).

I'm here for sightseeing.

Just for sightseeing.

I'm here on holiday.

I'm here on vacation.

I'm here on business.

I'm here to study English.

I'm here for studying.

I've got a student visa.

I'm here to attend **a college / an university**.

I'm here to study at **a college / an university**.

I've come to visit some friends and relatives.

I've come on business.

I've come to study English.

I've come to see a friend.

I'm returning home.

I'm just passing through.

I'm just transferring.

I'll be staying for 2 weeks.

About 3 months.

I'll be here for a couple of years.

I'm going to stay at a local hotel.

I'll stay at my friend's house.

I'll be staying with my uncle's family.

I'll be staying with a friend in Vancouver.

Baggage claim

Would you please show me the baggage claim area for TB Flight 002?

Where is the baggage claim area?

Where is the carrousel for TB Flight 002?

Where can I get my baggage?

Where can I pick up my baggage?

Where are the luggage carts?

At customs

I have nothing to declare.

Yes, I carry 1 carton of cigarettes and 1 bottle of whiskey.

These are gifts for my friends.

This is a gift.

It's for my personal use.

These are my personal belongings.

Just some clothes and my personal belongings.

Do I have to pay tax on them?

Where is the taxi stand?

Practice asking and answering questions from the sentences above.

Immigration Inspectors Speak Up

Passport, please.

May I see your passport, please?

What's the purpose of your visit?

Are you traveling alone?

Are you traveling with a group?

How long have you been away from **Canada / the United States**?

How long will you be **in the United States / in Canada**?

How long do you plan to stay?

How long are you going to stay?

Where are you be staying?

Where are you going to stay?

What's your local address?

Do you intend to work in the United States?

How much money are you carrying?

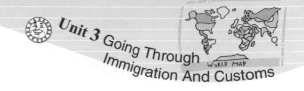

How much money do you have with you?

May I see your return ticket?

Do you have your return ticket?

OK. You can go through now.

You may go through now.

You can pass through.

Enjoy your visit.

Have a pleasant stay.

Have a good visit.

Practice asking and answering questions from the sentences above.

Customs Inspectors Speak Up

Do you have anything to declare?

Have you got anything to declare?

Do you have anything special to declare?

Anything special to declare?

Are you carrying any food, plant, seed, tobacco, or alcohol?

Do you carry any cigarettes or liquor?

Do you carry any cigarettes or alcohol?

Do you have any tobacco or spirits?

Do you have any fruit or vegetables?

Do you have any fruit?

You are not allowed to bring in any fruit or meat.

What do you have in the bag?

What have you got there?

What's in your suitcase?

Please open your suitcases.

Open the bag.

Pay the duty at the window over there.

Practice asking and answering questions from the sentences above.

Teddy Bear Speak Up =_=;0_O

I-94 (disembarkation card) 美國入出境表（入境申請表）

Customs declaration form 海關申報表

Teddy: Could you show me how to fill out I-94 and customs declaration form? >~<

Bear: That's easy. Just copy mine. Hey...You should write your own name not my name. @_@

Teddy: Oh... =_!

The purpose of visit 此行的目的

Sightseeing 觀光

Officer: What's the purpose of your visit? n_n

Bear: Just for sightseeing. 0_O

A couple of 兩個

Officer: How long will you be staying? n_n

Teddy: A couple of months. =_=

Baggage claim area 行李領取處

Baggage carrousel 行李旋轉盤

Luggage carts 行李推車

Bear: Let's go get our baggage at the baggage claim area. 0_O

Teddy: Look! The monitor shows our baggage is on carrousel 2. ^o^

Bear: Great. I'll be waiting here for our baggage and you go get a luggage cart. ^.^

Declare 申報

1 carton of cigarettes (tobacco) 一盒香煙（菸草）

Liquor (alcohol; spirits) 酒精飲料（酒精；烈酒）

Inspector: Anything special to declare? n_n

Bear: We carry 1 carton of cigarettes and 1 bottle of liquor? 0_O

Inspector: OK! You're fine. You can pass through. n_n

Car rental counters 租車公司櫃檯

Escalator 電扶梯（手扶電梯）

Bear: Excuse me. Where is the car rental counters? 0_?

Clerk: Go down the escalator and you'll see the signs along the way. Just follow the signs. n_n

Bear: Thanks. 0_O

Find a partner for Teddy & Bear role playing game.

Conversations

At immigration inspection (1)

Vivian: Good evening, sir.

Immigration Officer: Passport, please?

Vivian: Here you go.

Immigration Officer: What's the purpose of your visit to the United States?

Vivian: I'm here on vacation.

Immigration Officer: Are you traveling alone?

Vivian: Yup.

Immigration Officer: How long are you staying?

Vivian: About 2 weeks.

Immigration Officer: Where are you going to stay?

Vivian: I'll stay with my friend in Napa Valley.

Immigration Officer: Do you intend to work in the United States?

Vivian: No.

Immigration Officer: May I see your return ticket?

Vivian: Sure. Here you go.

Immigration Officer: OK! Enjoy your visit!

Vivian: Thank you.

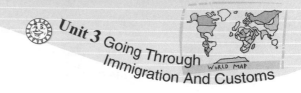

At immigration inspection (2)

Immigration Officer: What's the purpose of your visit?

Peter: I'm here on business.

Immigration Officer: What do you do?

Peter: I'm a sales director with Teddybear Company.

Immigration Officer: How long do you plan to stay?

Peter: About 10 days.

Immigration Officer: OK. You may go now.

Peter: Thank you.

At customs inspection (1)

Customs Inspector: Do you have any fruit?

Vivian: No.

Customs Inspector: Anything special to declare?

Vivian: No.

Customs Inspector: Do you carry any cigarettes or liquor?

Vivian: Yes, I carry 1 carton of cigarettes and 1 bottle of Gin.

Customs Inspector: That'll be fine, then. What's in your suitcase?

Vivian: Just some clothes and my personal belongings.

Customs Inspector: What have you got there?

Vivian: That's a gift.

Customs Inspector: OK. You may go.

Vivian: Thank you.

At customs inspection (2)

Customs Inspector:	Open your suitcase, please.
Victor:	Yes, ma'am.
Customs Inspector:	What's this white powder? Is this drugs?
Victor:	No, this is the medicine for my cough. I've got the prescription from my doctor. See, here it is.
Customs Inspector:	OK! What are those?
Victor:	Those are gifts.
Customs Inspector:	What's the total value of these gifts?
Victor:	About 2 hundred and fifty dollars. Do I have to pay tax on them?
Customs Inspector:	No, You don't have to pay.
Victor:	Can I close my suitcase now?
Customs Inspector:	Yes, and you can go through now.
Victor:	Thank you, ma'am.

At lost and found counter

Angela:	I can't find my baggage. My baggage is missing.
Staff:	Do you have an air ticket and claim tag?
Angela:	Here is my claim tag and my ticket.
Staff:	Would you please fill out this form?
Angela:	Sure. Do I have to come back here for my baggage?
Staff:	No, we'll send it to you.
Angela:	Oh! That's great.
Staff:	Where would you like your baggage delivered?

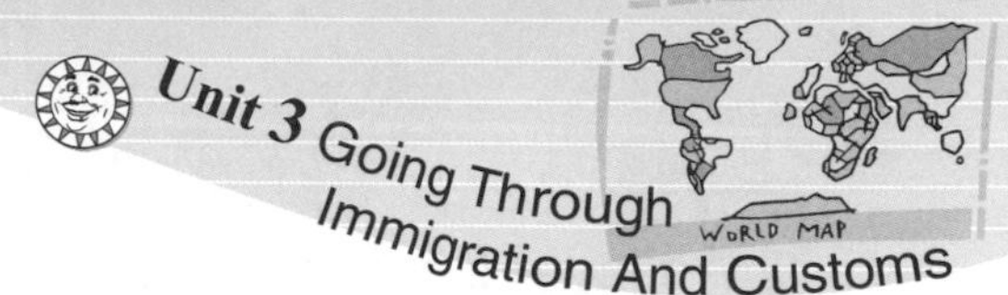

Angela: Hyatt Hotel downtown. How soon could you deliver my baggage?

Staff: Hopefully by tomorrow evening.

Angela: OK. Please send my baggage to me as soon as possible.

1. Now is your turn to practice the dialogues with a partner.

2. Use the sentences from "Tourists Speak Up", "Immigration Inspectors Speak Up", " Customs Inspectors Speak Up", or "Teddy Bear Speak Up" to create some new dialogues.

Useful Information

Useful Information

Signs at the Immigration / Passport Control 入境檢查指標

Welcome to the US (Canada) 歡迎到美國（加拿大）

Welcome home 歡迎回家

Citizens 公民

Permanent residents (Green card holders) 永久居民（美國的綠卡持有者）

Visitors 觀光客

Things You Need When Going through Immigration / Customs 入境檢查及過海關必備品

Passport (Uncovered) 護照（拿掉封套）

I-94 Arrival / Departure form (disembarkation card) 入境 / 出境表（入

境美國才需要。入境美國時，移民局官員會撕去上半聯，並將下半聯訂於旅客的護照上，出境美國時要將下半聯還回去）

Customs declaration form 海關申報表

Return ticket 回程機票

Arrival Terminal 入境航空站

Airport shuttle 機場接送旅客的車輛

Baggage claim area 行李領取處

Car rental counters 租車櫃檯

Coffee shop 咖啡館

Currency exchange 外幣兌換

Customs 海關

Ground transportation 地面交通運輸

Immigration 移民局

Limousine bus (limo) 機場接送旅客的小型巴士

Lost and found 失物招領處

Parking lot 停車場

Passport control 出入境護照檢查管理處

Porter 機場行李搬運員

Restrooms 洗手間

Taxi stand 計程車招呼站

Terminal shuttle 機場巴士

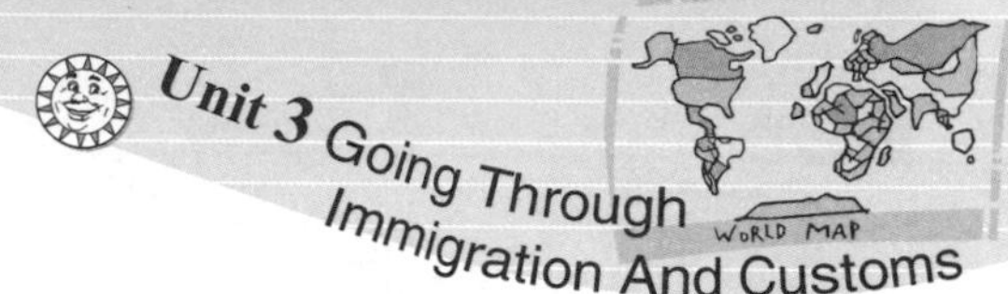

Words & Phrases

immigration	n.	移民局；移民
customs declaration form	ph.	海關申報表
I-94	n.	美國入出境表
disembarkation	n.	登陸；上岸
sightseeing	n.	觀光
student visa	ph.	學生簽證
relative	n.	親戚

passing through	ph.	過關
transfer	v.	轉換
a couple of	ph.	兩個
baggage claim area	ph.	行李領取處
carrousel	n.	行李旋轉盤
baggage	n.	行李
luggage cart	ph.	行李推車
customs	n.	海關
declare	v.	申報
carton	n.	紙盒
cigarette	n.	香煙
personal belongings	ph.	私人攜帶物品
purpose	n.	目的
customs inspector	ph.	海關檢查員
tobacco	n.	菸草
alcohol	n.	酒精
liquor	n.	酒精飲料
spirit	n.	烈酒
Napa Valley	n.	美國加州葡萄酒產地
intend	v.	意圖
return ticket	ph.	回程機票
medicine	n.	藥
cough	n. v.	咳嗽
prescription	n.	處方籤
lost and found	ph.	失物招領處

1. Give 10 reasons about the purposes of your visit to the United States.

(1)____.

(2)____.

(3)____.

(4)____.

(5)____.

(6)____.

(7)____.

(8)____.

(9)____.

(10)_______________________________________.

2. What things are there at arrival terminal? (Give 10 of them)

(1) ___________________________.

(2) ___________________________.

(3) ___________________________.

(4) ___________________________.

(5) ___________________________.

(6) ___________________________.

(7) ___________________________.

(8) ___________________________.

(9) ___________________________.

(10) ________________________________.

1. Give 10 reasons about the purposes of your visit to the United States.

(1) I'm here for sightseeing. (Just for sightseeing.)

(2) I'm here on holiday. (I'm here on vacation.)

(3) I'm here on business.

(4) I'm here to study English.

(5) I'm here to attend a college (an university).

(6) I'm here to visit my uncle.

(7) I've come to see a friend.

(8) I'm traveling with a group.

(9) I'm returning home.

(10) I'm just passing through. (I'm just transferring.)

2. What things are there at arrival terminal? (Give 10 of them.)

(1) Airport shuttle 機場接送旅客的車輛

(2) Baggage claim area 行李領取處

(3) Car rental counters 租車櫃檯

(4) Coffee shop 咖啡館

(5) Currency exchange 外幣兌換

(6) Customs 海關

(7) Ground transportation 地面交通運輸

(8) Immigration 移民局

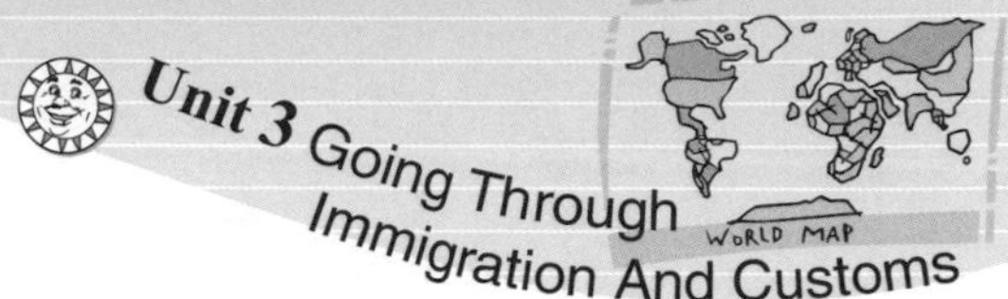

(9) Lost and found 失物招領處

(10) Restrooms 洗手間

Unit 4

Renting A Car

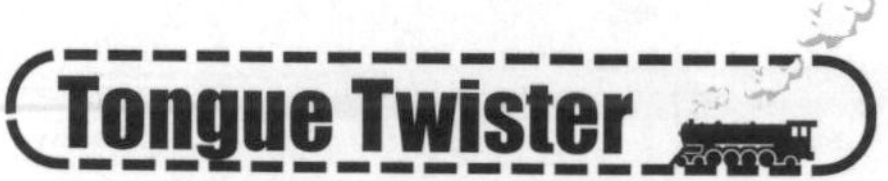

Tongue Twister

A big black bug bit a big black bear. But where is the big black bear that the big black bug bit?

Tourists Speak Up

Renting a car

Where can I rent a car?

Are there any rent-a-car companies around here?

Do you have any downtown locations where I can pick up the car?

I've made a reservation two days ago.

My reservation number is TBUSA22.

I'd like a full-size car.

What kind of cars do you have?

I'd like one with an automatic transmission.

Do you have a compact car available now?

I want to rent a car for 1 month.

Just for one day.

What is the rate?

How much does it cost per day?

What are the rates per day?

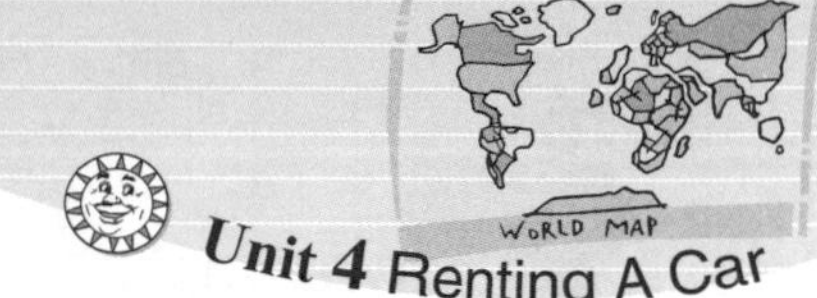

Do you have a special weekly rate?

Do you have any promotional rates for the weekend?

Do you have any special deals this week?

Is the mileage free?

Is the rate with unlimited mileage?

Does the car have air conditioning?

Does the rate include insurance?

Does the rate include gas?

I need insurance.

I'd like full coverage.

How much does it cost for adding an additional driver?

I'll take that one.

I'll pick it up at the airport at 8:00 on Saturday morning.

When do I have to return the car?

How much is the drop-off charge?

Do you have airport shuttles?

What's the extra charge if I don't return it on time?

I'm here to pick up my car.

Let me go check the car to make sure there aren't any scratches and dents on the car.

How do I open the hood?

Asking the directions

Excuse me, could you tell me where am I on this map?

Can you show me on the map where I am?

Which way is **north** / **south** / **east** / **west**?

What's the name of the street?

Do you have any idea where this address is?

Do you know the way to Central Park?

Can you tell me the way to...?

How do I get to...?

Am I on the right road to...?

How far is the next village?

Is there a way with little traffic?

How long does it take by car?

Parking

Where can I park?

May I park here?

How long can I park here?

What's the charge **per hour** / **per day**?

Gasoline

We need to stop for some gas (gasoline).

Where's the nearest gas (gasoline) station?

Full tank, please.

Give me 10 liters of gas, please.

Practice asking and answering questions from the sentences above.

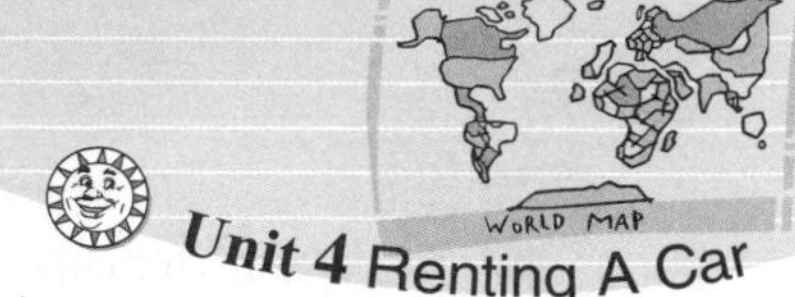

Rental Agents Speak Up

Do you have a reservation?

Do you have a confirmation number?

Are you 25 years old or older?

What kind of cars do you want to rent?

What type of cars would you like?

We have economy, compact, mid-size, and full-size.

It's $25.00 plus tax per day with unlimited mileage.

How long do you want it?

How many days do you want to rent the car?

That'll be an extra 5 dollars per day per person.

Do you need insurance coverage?

What kind of insurance coverage would you like?

May I see your driver's license and a credit card, please?

The car needs to be back with a full tank of gas to avoid any refueling service charge.

You can drop it off at any of our branch locations.

Have a nice trip.

Practice asking and answering questions from the sentences above.

Teddy Bear Speak Up =_=;0_O

Age requirements for renting a car 租車年齡限制

Teddy: Oh man! There is age requirement for renting a car. We are both only 25 years old. >~<

Bear: Don't worry, man! We are just qualified. ^o^

Additional drivers 增加額外駕駛

Teddy: Who will be the additional driver? Are you? =_?

Bear: What's the difference? 0_?

Full coverage (Full insurance) 保全險

How come 為什麼

Bear: We need full coverage. 0_O

Teddy: How come? =_?

Bear: Um... Oh... Because I don't trust your driving skills. A_A

Teddy: Hey, are you my friend? ~_~

Unlimited mileage 無限制英哩數

Out of your mind 你瘋啦

Teddy: Cool! We've got the unlimited mileage. Why not just drive it 24 hours a day? He... he... A_A

Bear: Are you out of your mind? X_X

Hitchhiker 想搭便車的人

Next one will be better 下一個會更好

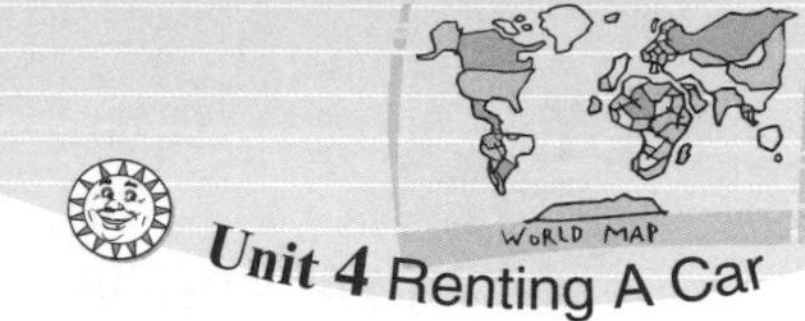

Nope 不（口語）

Teddy: Look, the hitchhiker over there looks pretty sexy. Want to pick her up? ^o^

Bear: Nope. That one is not my type. Maybe next one will be better. V_V

Tow away zone 違規停車拖吊區

Teddy: Hey, that's a tow away zone. We can't park here. >~<

Bear: The parking lot is so full. What the &*%$#@.......! ~"~

Drive on the right 右邊駕駛

Drive on the left 左邊駕駛

Would rather 寧可…

Bear: I'm glad we can drive on the right in America and in Canada.0_O

Teddy: But when you drive in Japan you have to drive on the left. =_=

Bear: On the left...? I would rather join a group tour, then. 0_!

Pull over 把…開到路邊

Speed 超速

Cop 警察

Teddy: Hey! Slow down! Don't let the cops pull you over for speeding.

Bear: Holly cow!... There's one just behind us....

Find a partner for Teddy & Bear role playing game.

Conversations

Renting a car by phone

Reservation: Good morning, Teddybear Car Rental. My name is Everly. How may I help you?

Catherine: Yes. I would like to rent a car for tomorrow.

Reservation: What kind of car would you like?

Catherine: Do you have an economy car available for tomorrow?

Reservation: Yes. We have a Toyata Echo available for tomorrow. How long will you be renting the car?

Catherine: How much is the rate for 3 days.

Reservation: It's $28.00 plus tax per day with unlimited mileage or $18.00 plus tax per day with an addition of 15 cents per mile.

Catherine: OK. I'll take the one with unlimited mileage.

Reservation: Great. May I have your name, please?

Catherine: Yes. It's Catherine Lee.

Reservation: Which location and what time would you like to pick up the car?

Catherine: I'll pick up the car at the airport at 10:00 in the morning.

Reservation: Great. Your confirmation number is TBUSA22. Just go to the counter and our agent will help you with your car.

Catherine: Thanks.

Renting a car

Rental Agent: Good morning, sir. My name is Rita. How may I help you?

Anthony: Yes, I'd like to rent a car. What kind of cars do you have?

Rental Agent: We have a compact car, a full-size car, a mini-van, and a luxury car.

Anthony: Do you have a convertible available now?

Rental Agent: Yeah...! What do you think about this one? (pointing to a car on the picture)

Anthony: Wow! It's awesome. What is the rate?

Rental Agent: Our price for a convertible is 50 bucks per day with unlimited mileage.

Anthony: OK! I'll take it.

Rental Agent: How long do you want it?

Anthony: For 5 days.

Rental Agent: OK! May I see a valid driver's license and a major credit card, please?

Anthony: Sure. Here you go.

Rental Agent: Are there any additional drivers?

Anthony: How much do you charge for adding an additional driver?

Rental Agent: That's an extra 5 bucks per day per person.

Anthony: 5 bucks per day? Um... No, thanks. I don't think we need it.

Rental Agent: Do you need insurance coverage?

Anthony: Yes, I would like full coverage, please.

Rental Agent: That's an extra 20 bucks per day.

Anthony: No problem.

Rental Agent: Where would you like to return the vehicle?

Anthony: I'll return the car at the airport. How much is the drop-off charge?

Rental Agent: It's free of charge.

Anthony: Great!

Rental Agent: This is your car rental contract. Please sign here, here, and here.

Anthony: Sure.

Rental Agent: Here are the keys, your driver's license and credit card. Someone will show you to the car. The car needs to be back with full tank of gas by 11:00am on Saturday.

Anthony: Thanks.

Rental Agent: You're welcome.

Checking the car

Anthony: Let me go check the car to make sure there aren't any scratches or dents on the car.

Rental Agent: Is everything OK, sir?

Anthony: Yes. Everything seems to be fine. It's a nice car.

Rental Agent: Have a nice trip, sir.

Anthony: Thanks.

1. Now is your turn to practice the dialogues with a partner.

2. Use the sentences from "Tourists Speak Up", "Rental Agents Speak Up", or "Teddy Bear Speak Up" to create some new dialogues.

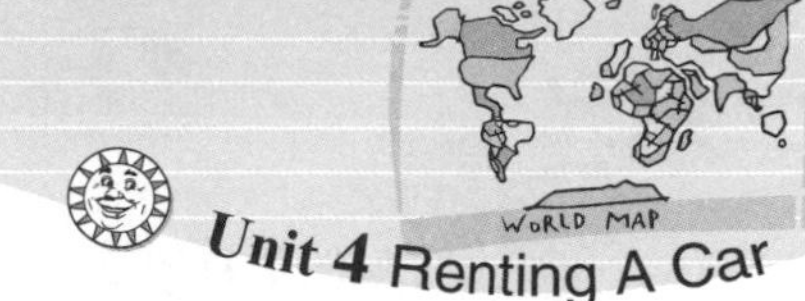

Useful Information

Rent-A-Car Companies 租車公司

Avis	www.avis.com
Budget	www.budget.com
Dollar	www.dollarcar.com
Hertz	www.hertz.com
National	www.nationalcar.com

Motel Chains 汽車旅館

Best Western

Comfort Inn

Days Inn

Econo Lodge

Holiday Inn

Motel 6

Ramada

Shilo Inn

Traveler's Inn

Renting a Car 租車

Things you need when renting a car 租車時必備物品

All drivers of the vehicle must present and provide a valid driver's license (international driver license) and major credit card in their name.

所有駕駛人必須到租車現場，並提供有效的駕照（國際駕照），及本人的信用卡。

All drivers of the vehicle must be 25 years of age or older.

所有駕駛人必須要年滿 25歲或以上。

Types of vehicles 車輛的種類

Economy 經濟型 1,300cc - 1,600cc

Compact 小型車 1,600cc - 1,800cc

Mid-size 中型車 2,200cc - 2,600cc

Full-size 大型車 2,600cc 以上

Luxury 豪華型

Premium 頂級型

Convertible 敞篷車

Mid-size SUV (Sport Utility Vehicle) 中型休旅車

Standard SUV (Sport Utility Vehicle) 標準休旅車

Full-size SUV (Sport Utility Vehicle) 大型休旅車

Pickup 小卡車

Mini van 小型箱型客貨車

12 passengers van 12人座箱型客貨車

Manual-shift car (Manual car) 手排車

Automatic car (Automatic transmission car) 自排車

Sports car 跑車

Four-wheel drive car 四輪傳動車

Sedan 轎車

Coupe 雙門小轎車

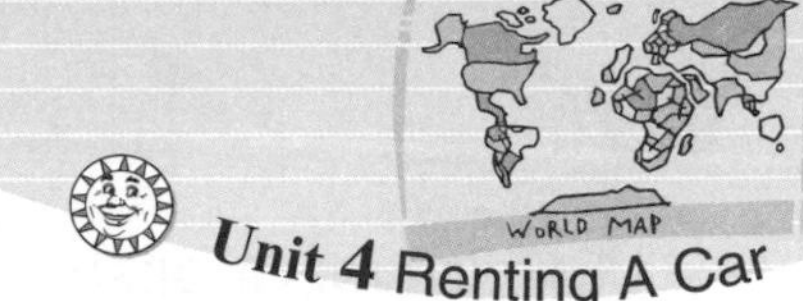

Hatchback 後車門往上開的斜背式汽車

Car Parts 車零件

The front 前面

Roof 車頂

Windshield 擋風玻璃

Windshield wiper 擋風玻璃的雨刷

Hood 引擎車蓋

Headlights 前照燈

Bumper 保險桿

Turn signal 方向燈

The back 後面

Rear window 後窗玻璃

Trunk 汽車車尾行李箱

Fender 汽車防護板

Taillight 車尾燈

Wheel 車輪

Tire 輪胎

License plate 汽車牌照

Things in the car 車裡的配備

Accelerator 油門

Air conditioning 空氣調節

AM / FM stereo system 調幅調頻立體音響系統

Anti-theft system 防盜系統

Anti-lock brakes 防煞車鎖死

Automatic overdrive 自動加速

Compact disc and cassette player 光碟機及錄音帶放音機

Convenience of remote keyless entry 中控遙控鑰匙

Cruise control 定速操縱器

Dual airbag protection 兩個安全氣囊

Front wheel drive (4x4 only) 前輪帶動

Horn 喇叭

Map lights 閱讀燈

Power driver seat 電動座椅

Power locks 中控門鎖

Power mirrors 電動後照鏡調整開關

Power sterling 動力方向盤

Power windows 電動車窗

Powerful v6 engine 六氣缸引擎

Car Breakdown 車壞了的說法

The car has broken down.

車壞了。

I've run out of gasoline (petrol).

車沒油了。

The engine won't start.

車引擎不動了。

The engine is overheating.

車引擎過熱。

I've got a flat.

車爆胎了。

I have a flat tire.

車爆胎了。

The battery is dead.

電瓶沒電了。

These wipers don't work.

雨刷壞了。

The windshield is cracked.

擋風玻璃破掉了。

There is something wrong with **brakes** / **carburetor** / **exhaust pipe** / **radiator** / **a wheel**.

煞車 / 汽化器 / 排氣管 / 散熱器 / 車輪 有問題。

Please charge the battery.

請將電池充電。

The battery needs to be charged.

這個電池需要充電。

I need a tow trunk (breakdown van).

我需要一部拖車。

Can you send a mechanic?

可以幫忙找個修車技工嗎？

Options for Fuel Policy 加油的選擇

Option One 選擇 1

Pay in advance for the fuel and bring the car back empty.

取車時因爲油箱是滿的，可先付油料費，還車時油箱可以是空的。

Option Two 選擇 2

Bring the car back with a full tank of gas to avoid any refueling service charge.

取車時油箱是滿的，還車時油箱也必須是滿的，以免要付油料費。

Option Three 選擇 3

Pay only for the gas you use, based on the renting location's per-gallon (per liter) refueling service charge.

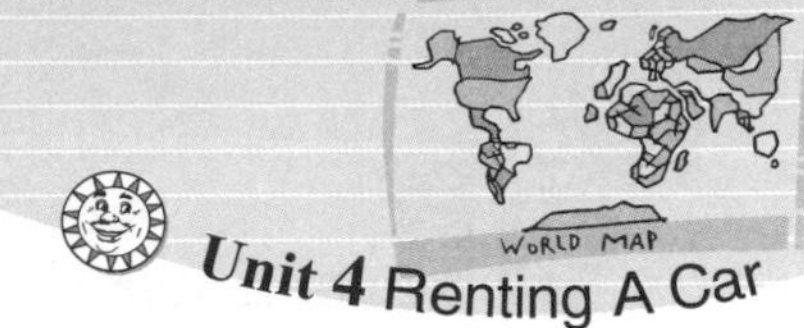

用多少付多少，根據租車地點的油價依加侖（公升）來計價。

Gasoline 汽油

Gasoline (Gas) 汽油

Petrol 汽油（英國）

Super 特級的

Premium 優質的

Regular 普通的

Lead free 無鉛的

Diesel 柴油

Liter 公升

Gallon 加侖

1加侖 = 3.785升（美制）

1加侖 = 4.546升（英制）

Self = Self service 自助式（自助式油價較低）

Full = Full service 有服務員服務（非自助式油價較高）

Tips for Worry Free Driving 不用擔心車子出狀況的提示

Check battery 檢查電池

Check brake fluid 檢查煞車油

Check power steering fluid 檢查動力轉向油

Check engine oil 檢查引擎油

Check coolant reservoir 檢查冷卻劑水箱

Check the air pressure in the tires 檢查輪胎的胎壓

Check the spare tire 檢查備胎

Check all running lamps, brake lights, back-up lights, and turn signals 檢查所有在運轉的燈，包括煞車燈、倒退燈以及方向燈

Check the windshield washer and fluid 檢查雨刷及雨刷水

Check all the belts 檢查皮帶

Check for any fluids leaking from under the vehicle 檢查車子下方是否有油滴漏

Traffic Signs 交通號誌

❶ BIKE ROUTE

❷ DEAD END

❸ DETOUR

❹ DO NOT ENTER

❺ DO NOT PASS

❻ EXIT

❼ LANE CLOSED

❽

❾

❿ NO TURN ON RED

⓫

⓬ ONE WAY

⓭ R R

⓮

⓯ SPEED LIMIT 60

⓰ STEEP HILL

1. Bike route 腳踏車專用道
2. Dead end 死巷
3. Detour 繞道
4. Do not enter 禁止進入
5. Do not pass 禁止超車
6. Exit 出口
7. Lane closed 車道封閉
8. No left turn 禁止左轉
9. No right turn 禁止右轉
10. No turn on red 紅燈禁止右轉
11. No U turn 禁止迴轉
12. One way 單行道
13. Railroad crossing 鐵路平交道
14. School student crossing 注意學童穿越
15. Speed limit 60 限速60英哩
16. Steep hill 斜坡

17. Stop sign 停車（車子要完全停止，安全的情況下再開走）
18. Stop sign (4 ways) 停車（四面來車，先到的車先停、先走，車子要完全停止喔！）
19. Slippery when wet 天雨路滑
20. Towing zone 禁止停車區
21. Wrong way 禁止進入
22. Yield 讓
23. Parking (One hour) 一小時停車區
24. No parking 禁止停車

Words & Phrases

rent a car	ph.	租車
downtown location	ph.	市區位置
reservation	n.	預訂
automatic transmission	ph.	自排汽車
promotional rate	ph.	促銷價
special deal	ph.	特價
free mileage	ph.	不受限的英哩數
unlimited mileage	ph.	無限制的英哩數
gas	n.	汽油
full coverage	ph.	全險
additional driver	ph.	添加額外駕駛人
drop-off charge	ph.	不在原租車地還車的費用
airport shuttle	ph.	機場接駁車

scratch	n.	擦傷
dent	n.	凹痕
hood	n.	引擎蓋
village	n.	村莊
parking	n.	停車
gasoline station	ph.	加油站
full tank	ph.	滿油箱
liter	n.	公升
confirmation number	ph.	確認號碼
driver's license	ph.	駕照
avoid	v.	免除
refuel	v.	補給燃料
buck	n.	元
vehicle	n.	車輛

1. Unscramble the dialogue.

(1) Yes. It's Catherine Lee.

(2) It's $28.00 plus tax per day with unlimited mileage or $18.00 plus tax per day with an addition of 15 cents per mile.

(3) Do you have an economy car available for tomorrow?

(4) Good morning, Teddybear Car Rental. My name is Everly. How may I help you?

(5) How much is the rate for 3 days.

(6) OK. I'll take the one with unlimited mileage.

(7) Yes. We have a Toyata Echo available for tomorrow. How long will you be renting the car?

(8) Yes. I would like to rent a car for tomorrow.

(9) Great. May I have your name, please?

(10) What kind of car would you like?

2. Write 10 sentences about car breakdown.

(1) ______________________________.

(2) ______________________________.

(3) ______________________________.

(4) ______________________________.

(5) ______________________________.

(6) ______________________________.

(7) ______________________________.

(8) ______________________________.

(9) ______________________________.

(10) ______________________________.

1. Unscramble the Dialogue.

(4) Good morning, Teddybear Car Rental. My name is Everly. How may I help you?

(8) Yes. I would like to rent a car for tomorrow.

(10) What kind of car would you like?

(3) Do you have an economy car available for tomorrow?

(7)Yes. We have a Toyata Echo available for tomorrow. How long will you be renting the car?

(5) How much is the rate for 3 days.

(2) It's $28.00 plus tax per day with unlimited mileage or $18.00 plus tax per day with an addition of 15 cents per mile.

(6) OK. I'll take the one with unlimited mileage.

(9) Great. May I have your name, please?

(1) Yes. It's Catherine Lee.

2. Write 10 sentences about car breakdown.

(1) The engine won't start.
車引擎不動了。

(2) I've got a flat.
車爆胎了。

(3) The battery is dead.
電瓶沒電了。

(4) These wipers don't work.
雨刷壞了。

(5) The windshield is cracked.
擋風玻璃破掉了。

(6) There is something wrong with brakes.
煞車有問題。

(7) There is something wrong with transmission.
變速箱有問題。

(8) The engine is overheating.

車引擎過熱。

(9) I've run out of gasoline (petrol).

車沒油了。

(10) There is something wrong with the radiator.

散熱器有問題。

KB-1024
KB-1024
KB-1
Unit 5
Public Transportation

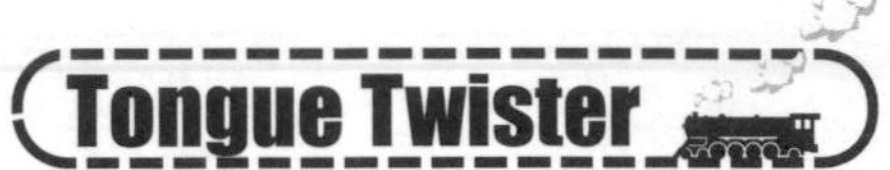

Two crazy cooks took a look at a cookie cookbook.

Excuse me. Could you tell me how to get to Time Square?

Excuse me. Could you tell me where I am now on this map?

Subway / Sky train

Excuse me. How do I get to the nearest **subway / sky train** station?

Where is the nearest **subway / sky train** station?

Where is the **subway / sky train** entrance?

Where is the **subway / sky train** station?

Which exit should I take for Central Park?

Does this train stop at Main Street Science World?

Where do I change trains to go to Coquitlam?

Where's the ticket machine?

Taxi (cab)

Where can I get a cab?

Can I get a taxi around here?

Please get me a taxi.

What's the fare to the international airport?

Take me to **this address / the airport / the railway station / the town center / the Holiday Inn**, please.

Would you start the meter, please?

Could you drive more slowly?

I'm in a hurry.

Turn **left / right** at the next corner, please.

Go straight ahead, please.

Please stop here.

Let me get off here.

Stop at the corner, please.

Stop in front of the hotel, please.

Do you have special night fare?

Keep the change.

Could you help me carry my luggage?

Could you give me the receipt, please?

Would you wait for me, please?

Bus

Where is the bus stop?

May I have a bus route map, please?

I'd like a bus pass.

I'd like a booklet of bus tickets.

Which bus should I take to go to Stanley Park?

Which bus goes to Hollywood?

Which tram (streetcar) goes to the centre of town?（英式講法）

Where can I get a bus into town?

Where is the terminus?

How often does the bus run for Manhattan?

How often do the buses to the airport run?

Is there a bus going to the museum?

How long will it take?

Do I have to change buses?

What time does it arrive in Seattle?

How much does the bus fare cost to Whistler?

How long does the bus take to New York from Philadelphia?

Could you tell me when to get off?

I want to get off at the next stop.

I'm getting off.

Train

Where is the railway station?

Two round-trip tickets to Boston, please.

How much is a round-trip ticket to Cambridge?

What time does the next train leave?

Is there a **dinning car / sleeping car** on the train?

What platform does the train for Bonn leave from?

Your train will leave from track 8.

Will the train leave on time?

May I have a timetable?

Do I have to change train?

Is it a through train?

Does the train stop at Hamburg?

How long does the train stop here?

Can I stop over on the way?

Boat

When does the boat for Bowen Island leave?

When does the cruise for Alaska leave?

Where's the embarkation point?

Practice asking and answering questions from the sentences above.

Teddy Bear Speak Up =_=;0_O

Monthly pass 月票

Day pass 一天有效票

Buck 元

Teddy: How much does a monthly pass cost?

Bear: I'm not quite sure. But I know that one-day pass costs only 8 bucks and is valid for one day's unlimited travel. 0_O

Coach (long-distance-bus) 巴士（美國）；長途公車（英國）

Bear: When's the next Coach to London?

Clerk: It's 4:30.

One-way 單程

Round-trip 來回

Teddy: We want two tickets to Vienna, please.

Booking Clerk: One-way or round-trip?

Teddy: Round-trip, please.

Platform 月台

Teddy: Is this the right platform for the train to Vienna?

Clerk: Yes. It is.

Dining car 餐車

Teddy: Can we get some snakes and drinks from the dining car?

Clerk: Yes, you can get snakes and drinks from the dining car when it isn't being used for main meals. There's also an attendant comes around with a cart with snakes, soft drinks, and coffee.

Teddy & Bear: Whoo... Sweet!

Sleeping car 臥車

Berth 臥鋪

Lower berth 下鋪

Upper berth 上鋪

Teddy: Here we are. This is the sleeping car. ^o^

Bear: Which is my berth? 0_O

Teddy: I'd like the lower berth. =_=

Bear: I want the lower berth, too. I don't like the upper berth, either. O_O

Teddy: Be quiet and rest, man! ...%&#$@&... ~"~

A through train 直達火車

A local train 當地火車

Teddy: Is it a through train? =_?

Bear: No. >~<

Teddy: Do we have to change trains? =_?

Bear: Yes, we have to get a local train. 0_O

Sufficient time 足夠的時間

Bear: Is there sufficient time to change? 0_?

Teddy: I'm not sure. But we've got to run, anyway. =_=

Find a partner for Teddy & Bear role playing game.

Conversations

Taking a bus (1)

Bus Drive: Good morning!

Celia Good morning! Does this bus go downtown? (Do you go downtown?)

Bus Driver: Yes. You're on the right bus to downtown.

Celia: How much is the fare to downtown?

Bus Driver: It's 2 dollars.

Celia: How many bus stops are there to Roberson Street?

Bus Driver: It's the sixth stop.

Celia: Could you tell me when to get off?

Bus Driver: No problem.

Celia: Thank you.

Bus Driver: You're welcome.

Bus Driver: Here we are. Downtown Roberson.

Celia: Thanks a lot.

Bus Driver: Watch your step, please.

Taking a bus (2)

Cathy: Is this the bus to Chinatown?

Karen: No, you need to take # 20.

Cathy: Do you know how often does the bus come?

Karen: You can check the bus schedule here on the bus stop. Let me see... Oh! The bus schedule for Monday says the bus comes every 20 minutes. I think the bus should come in the next 10 minutes.

Cathy: Thanks a lot.

Karen: Don't mention it.

Taking the sky train (subway)

Nancy: Excuse me. Do you know where the nearest sky train station is?

Ellen: I'm going there, too. You can come with me.

Nancy: Oh! Great.

Ellen: There's the ticket machine. You can go get a ticket.

Nancy: How much is the fare to North Vancouver?

Ellen: You pay two zones to go, which is 3 dollars.

Nancy: Do I have to change trains?

Ellen: Yes, you take the westbound train to Waterfront station and get off. Follow the signs to switch to a sea bus to go to North

Vancouver.

Nancy: Do I have to buy another ticket for the sea bus?

Ellen: No, you don't have to. You can use the same pass and it is valid for 90 minutes.

Nancy: Thank you very much for the help.

Ellen: You're welcome.

Taking a taxi

Richard: Put my baggage in the trunk, please.

Taxi Driver: Yes, sir.

Taxi Driver: Where to, sir?

Richard: To the airport, please.

Taxi Driver: Yes, sir.

Richard: How long does it take to go to the airport?

Taxi Driver: It's rush hour now. The traffic is very heavy. I think it'll probably take more than 30 minutes.

Richard: I've got to be at the airport by 8:00. Can we make it?

Taxi Driver: I'll try.

Richard: Hurry up, please.

Taxi Driver: Here we are. It's 7:59. We are just in time.

Richard: Great! How much do I owe you?

Taxi Driver: It's 15 dollars, sir.

Richard: Here is a twenty. Keep the change.

Taxi Driver: Thank you, sir.

1. Now is your turn to practice the dialogues with a partner.

2. Use the sentences from "Tourists Speak Up" or "Teddy Bear Speak Up" to create some new dialogues.

Useful Information

Things on a City Street 市區街道上有…

Block 四面圍有街道的街區

Bus 公車

Bus stop 公車站牌

Crosswalk 行人穿越道

Fire hydrant 消防栓

Intersection 十字路口

Mail box 郵筒

Metro entrance 地下鐵入口（法國巴黎）

The MRT (the metro rapid transit) entrance 捷運入口（台灣台北）

Newstand 報攤

Office building 辦公大樓

Parking lot 停車場

Parking meter 停車收費器

Pedestrian 行人

Sea bus entrance 渡輪入口（加拿大溫哥華）

Sidewalk 人行道

Sky train entrance 架空列車入口（加拿大溫哥華）

Street light 街燈

Street sign 路標

The subway entrance 地下鐵入口（美國紐約）

Telephone booth 電話亭

Terminus 終點站

Traffic light 紅綠燈；交通號誌

Tram (streetcar) 有軌電車（英國）

Trash can 垃圾桶

Taxi (cab) 計程車

Underground entrance 地下鐵入口（英國）

Public Transportation Service 公共運輸服務

Bus 公車

Cruise 客輪

Ferry 渡輪

Hydrofoil 水上飛機

Metro 地下鐵（法國巴黎）

The MRT (the metro rapid transit) 捷運（台灣台北）

Sea bus 渡輪（加拿大溫哥華）

Sky train 架空列車（加拿大溫哥華）

Subway 地下鐵（美國紐約）

Taxi (cab) 計程車

Train 火車

Tram (streetcar) 有軌電車（英國）

Underground 地下鐵（英國）

Trains 火車

International express trains

國際線直達快車

Long distance inter-city trains

長距離的城市與城市間的火車

Short distance inter-city trains

短距離的城市與城市間的火車

Intermediate to long-distance trains (Germany)

中距離到長距離的火車（德國）

Fast trains (connecting the biggest towns)

快車（連結最大的市鎮）

Fast trains (stop at big and medium towns)

快車（停靠大的與中型市鎮）

Medium-distance trains (not stopping at small stations)

中距離火車（小站不停）

Local trains (stopping at all stations)

當地火車（每站都停）

Other Terms 其他專有名詞

Dinning car 餐車

Sleeping car (compartments with wash basins and 1, 2, or 3 berths)
臥車（隔間成1至3個臥鋪及洗滌槽）

Coach containing berths with sheets, blankets, and pillows
有提供床單、毛毯及枕頭的臥鋪的車廂

First class 頭等車廂

Second class 二等車廂

One-way 單程車票

Round-trip 來回車票

Boat Service 乘船服務

Boat 小船

Cabin 客艙

Cruise 客輪

Crossing 渡口

Deck 甲板

Ferry 渡輪

Hydrofoil 水上飛機

Life Boat 救生艇

Port 港口

River Cruise 遊河客輪

Ship 船

Steamer 汽船

Words & Phrases

Time Square	n.	時代廣場
Central Park	n.	中央公園
Main Street Science World	n	緬街上的自然科學館
Coquitlam	n.	高貴林（大溫哥華某區）
ticket machine	ph.	自動售票機
cab	n.	計程車
fare	n.	車（船）費
international airport	ph.	國際機場
start the meter	ph.	開始計程車計價錶
keep the change	ph.	不用找（零錢）了
receipt	n.	收據
bus stop	ph.	公車站
booklet	n.	小冊子
Stanley Park	n.	溫哥華史丹利公園
Hollywood	n.	美國好萊塢
tram	n.	有軌電車（英國）
streetcar	n.	有軌電車（美國）
terminus	n.	終點站
Manhattan	n.	美國曼哈頓島
museum	n.	博物館
Seattle	n.	美國西雅圖
Whistler	n.	威士拿（加拿大滑雪勝地）

New York	n.	美國紐約
Philadelphia	n.	美國費城
get off	ph.	下車
next stop	ph.	下一站
railway station	ph.	火車站
round-trip	adj.	來回的
Boston	n.	美國波士頓
Cambridge	n.	英國劍橋
dinning car	ph.	餐車
sleeping car	ph.	臥車
platform	n.	月台
Bonn	n.	德國波昂
track	n.	鐵軌；軌道
timetable	n.	時刻表
a through train	ph.	直達火車
Hamburg	n.	德國漢堡
Bowen Island	n.	Bowen島（位於溫哥華附近）
cruise	n.	客輪
Alaska	n.	阿拉斯加
embarkation point	ph.	乘坐點
Roberson Street	n.	羅伯森街（位於溫哥華市區）
sixth	adj.	第六的
China Town	n.	中國城
don't mention it	ph.	不要客氣
pass	n.	通行證；車票；門票
North Vancouver	n.	北溫（大溫哥華某區）

zone	n.	地區；地帶
westbound	adj.	向西行的
waterfront	ph.	濱水區

1. Complete the sentences with a word from below.

round-trip change coach platform Central Park berth Cab dining car get off exit nearest cruise run a monthly pass ticket machine

(1) Excuse me. Could you tell me how to get to ____________?

(2) Excuse me. How do I get to the _________ subway station?

(3) Which _________ should I take for Time Square?

(4) Where's a ______________?

(5) Where can I get a_________?

(6) Keep the _________.

(7) How often does the bus ________ for Manhattan?

(8) I want to ____________ at the next stop.

(9) Two ____________ tickets to Boston, please.

(10) What ___________ does the train for Bonn leave from?

(11) When does the ____________ for Alaska leave?

(12) I'd like the lower _________.

(13) How much does ______________ cost?

(14) Can we get some snakes and drinks from the___________?

(15) When's the next _________ to London?

2. Name 10 public transportation services.

(1) ______________

(2) ______________

(3) ______________

(4) ______________

(5) ______________

(6) ______________

(7) ______________

(8) ______________

(9) ______________

(10) ______________

1. Complete the sentences with a word from below.

(1) Excuse me. Could you tell me how to get to **Central Park**?

(2) Excuse me. How do I get to the **nearest** subway station?

(3) Which **exit** should I take for Time Square?

(4) Where's a **ticket machine**?

(5) Where can I get a **cab**?

(6) Keep the **change**.

(7) How often does the bus **run** for Manhattan?

(8) I want to **get off** at the next stop.

(9) Two **round-trip** tickets to Boston, please.

(10) What **platform** does the train for Bonn leave from?

(11) When does the **cruise** for Alaska leave?

(12) I'd like the lower **berth**.

(13) How much does **a monthly pass** cost?

(14) Can we get some snakes and drinks from the **dining car**?

(15) When's the next **coach** to London?

2. Name 10 public transportation services.

(1) Bus 公車

(2) Cruise 客輪

(3) Ferry 渡輪

(4) Metro 地下鐵（法國巴黎）

(5) The MRT (the metro rapid transit) 捷運（台灣台北）

(6) Sea bus 渡輪（加拿大溫哥華）

(7) Sky train 架空列車（加拿大溫哥華）

(8) Subway 地下鐵（美國紐約）/ Underground 地下鐵（英國）

(9) Taxi (cab) 計程車

(10) Train 火車

Unit 6

Eating Around

Brian's baby brother Blaine bought big blue bunches of blueberries.

Tourists Speak Up

Give me 1 of these and 2 of those, please.

Give me the one to the **left / right**.

Give me the one **above / below**.

I'd like to order combo # 2 to go, please.

Can I have the meal # 6 for here, please?

I'd like a piece of cake.

A piece of that one, please.

I'd like a **regular / decaffeinated** coffee with cream.

I'd like a milkshake.

No thanks. That's all.

I'd like it to go, please.

For here, please.

May I have some more ketchup packets, please?

I'd like to try some fish and chips.

How much do you charge for three scoops of ice cream?

Can I try some of your ice cream?

Can I try the maple walnut?

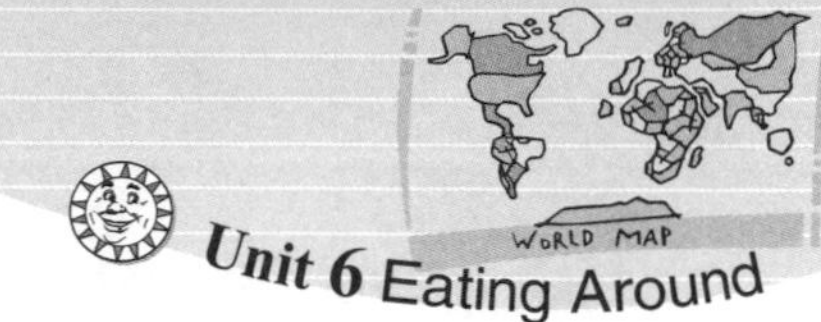

I would like the French vanilla with a waffle corn, please.

Practice asking and answering questions from the sentences above.

Order Takers Speak Up

May I help you, sir?

Hi there! How are you today?

Hi! How's it going?

Anything else?

Will you be eating here?

For here or to go?

Here you go.

There you go.

Here's your change. Thank you.

What flavor of ice cream would you like to try?

Practice asking and answering questions from the sentences above.

Teddy Bear Speak Up =_=;0_O

Freshly brewed coffee 現煮咖啡

Coffee Latte 那堤（拿鐵）咖啡

Teddy: Would you like a cup of freshly brewed coffee? ^O^

Bear: No, I prefer a cup of Coffee Latte. 0_O

Hot dog stand 路邊熱狗攤

Yummy 美味的

I'm starving 我快餓死了

Teddy: Let's go get some hot dogs at the hot dog stand. They look so yummy and smell so good. ^0^

Bear: Ok. I'm starving. ^o^

With ketchup and mustard 加番茄醬與芥末

Pickles 醃黃瓜

Not fair 不公平

Teddy: 3 hot dogs, with ketchup and mustard. No pickles, please. =_=

Bear: Why do you ask for 3? We've only got 2 people. 0_?

Teddy: 2 for me and 1 for you, dude. ^Q^

Bear: Hey... not fair! I want 2 hot dogs, too. @_@

1 slice of pizza 一片切片的比薩

A great deal (a good deal) 很划算

Bear: Wow, 1 slice of pizza costs only 99 cents. Let's go try one. ^.^

Teddy: Yeah. It's a great deal, isn't it? ^0^

Fish and chips shop 炸魚加炸薯條的店

Greasy 油膩的

Bear: There are many fish and chips shops near the beach. 0_O

Teddy: I'd like to try some, but eating too much greasy food isn't good for us. =_=

For here or to go 在這裡用或是外帶

Bear: May I have 2 slices of pizza, please? 0_O

Order Taker: Will that be for here or to go? n_n

Bear: To go (for here), please. 0_O

Yuck 討厭的東西

Tired of 厭煩

Hearty dishes 豐盛的菜餚

Fast food 速食

So do I 我也是

Bear: Yuck... I'm getting tired of eating those fast food. I really want to have some hearty dishes. ~"~

Teddy: So do I. ~"~

Find a partner for Teddy & Bear role playing game.

Conversations

At a burger shop

Order Taker: May I help you, sir?

Jimmy: Yes. I'd like a Big Mac, a Filet-O-Fish, a large fries, 2 medium cokes, 1 Oreo McFlurry, and a strawberry sundae.

Order Taker: Anything else?

Jimmy: No, thanks. That's all.

Order Taker: Will you be eating here?

Jimmy: No, I'd like it to go, please.

Order Taker: Sure. It comes to $19.75 after tax.

Jimmy: Here you go.

Order Taker: Here's your change. Thank you.

Jimmy: May I have some more ketchup packets, please?

Order Taker: Sure. There you go.

Jimmy: Thanks a lot.

Order Taker: No problem.

At an ice cream shop

Order Taker: Hi there! How's it going?

Amy: Pretty good. Thank you. How much do you charge for three scoops of ice cream?

Order Taker: It'll be $6.50 with a regular cone or cup and $7.00 with a waffle cone.

Amy: Can I try some of your ice creams?

Order Taker: Sure. What flavors would you like to try?

Amy: Can I try the old-fashioned French vanilla and the black raspberry cheesecake?

Order Taker: Here you go.

Amy: Mm... They tasted great. Please give me the old-fashioned French vanilla, the black raspberry cheesecake, and the chocolate chip mint with the waffle cone.

Order Taker: Anything else?

Amy: Yes. May I have 2 spoons? I'm going to share the ice cream with my husband in the park.

Order Taker: Here you go. Enjoy it.

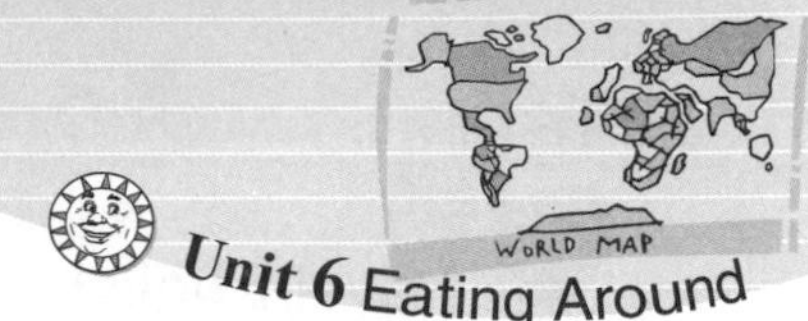

At a coffee shop

Julie: Let's go get a cup of coffee.

Linda: Good idea. I know there's a good coffee shop near this area.

Julie: Let's go there, then.

Linda: So many people are waiting. We've got to line up.

Julie: Wow, that's crazy! I've never seen such a busy coffee shop like this.

Order taker: Hi, there! May I take your order?

Linda: Yes, I'd like a large cup of regular coffee, please.

Order taker: Do you want cream and sugar?

Linda: Yes, double double, please.

Julie: Give me an iced capp (iced Cappuccino) and a donut, please.

Order taker: Here's your change and receipt. Please wait a second for your order.

Linda: Thanks.

1. Now is your turn to practice the dialogues with a partner.

2. Use the sentences from "Tourists Speak Up", "Order Takers Speak Up", or "Teddy Bear Speak Up" to create some new dialogues.

Useful Information

Burger Menu 漢堡菜單

Breakfast 早餐

Egg McMuffin蛋滿福堡（鬆餅）

Sausage McMuffin 香腸滿福堡（鬆餅）

English muffin 英式滿福堡（鬆餅）

Bacon, egg & cheese biscuit 培根、蛋、起司比司吉

Sausage biscuit with egg 香腸比司吉加蛋

Sausage biscuit 香腸比司吉

Bacon, egg & cheese McGriddles 培根、蛋、起司薄煎餅

Sausage, egg & cheese McGriddles 香腸、蛋、起司薄煎餅

Ham, egg & cheese bagel 火腿、蛋、起司培果

Spanish omelet bagel 西班牙式煎蛋捲培果

Steak, egg, cheese bagel 牛排、蛋、起司培果

Hotcakes and sausage 熱香餅加香腸

Scrambled eggs (2) 炒蛋（2顆蛋）

Hash browns 薯餅

Warm cinnamon roll 肉桂捲

Lunch & Dinner Sandwiches 午餐&晚餐三明治漢堡

Hamburger 漢堡

Cheeseburger 起司漢堡

Double cheeseburger 雙層起司漢堡

Big Mac 麥香堡

Filet-O-Fish 麥香魚

McChicken 麥香雞堡

Chicken McGrill 烤麥香雞堡

Crispy Chicken 麥脆雞堡

Hot'n Spicy McChicken 香辣麥脆雞堡

Chicken McNuggets (4, 6, 10, 20) 麥克雞塊（4塊，6塊，10塊，20塊）

McNuggets sauce (barbeque sauce, honey, hot mustard sauce, sweet-sour sauce) 麥克雞塊沾醬（烤肉醬，蜂蜜，辣芥末醬，酸甜醬）

French fries (small, medium, large) 炸薯條（小，中，大)

Ketchup packets 小包裝番茄醬

Salad 沙拉

Value Meals（加薯條與飲料的套餐）

1 Big Mac Meal

2 Cheeseburger Meal

3 Quarter Pounder Meal (with cheese)

4 Double Quarter Pounder Meal (with cheese)

5 10 Chicken McNuggets Meal

6 Big-Tasty Meal

7 Crispy Chicken Sandwich Meal

8 Chicken McGrill Meal

9 Filet-O-Fish Meal

10 McChicken Meal

Desserts 甜點

Baked apple pie 蘋果香酥派

Chocolate chip cookies 巧克力碎片餅乾

Oatmeal raisin cookies 葡萄乾燕麥餅乾

Ice Cream & Shakes 冰品

M&M McFlurry M&M巧克力冰炫風

Oreo McFlurry Ore 餅乾冰炫風

Triple thick shake (chocolate, strawberry, vanilla) 奶昔（巧克力，草莓，香草)

Hot caramel sundae 焦糖聖代冰淇淋

Hot fudge sundae 軟奶糖聖代冰淇淋

Strawberry sundae 草莓聖代冰淇淋

Fruit-yogurt parfait 優格冰淇淋水果凍

Vanilla reduced fat ice cream corn 低脂香草蛋捲冰淇淋

Beverages 飲料

1 % low fat milk 1%低脂牛奶

1 % low fat chocolate milk 1%低脂巧克力牛奶

Juice box (apple, orange) 盒裝果汁（蘋果，柳橙）

Coca-cola (child, small, medium, large) 可口可樂（兒童杯，小，中，大）

Diet coke (child, small, medium, large) 健怡可樂（兒童杯，小，中，大）

Sprite (child, small, medium, large) 雪碧（兒童杯，小，中，大）

Iced tea (child, small, medium, large) 冰紅茶（兒童杯，小，中，大）

Coffee (small, medium, large) 咖啡（小，中，大）

Combo 組合套餐

Combo 1 組合套餐 1

Combo 2 組合套餐 2

Combo 3 組合套餐 3

Combo 4 組合套餐 4

Combo 5 組合套餐 5

Drive through 得來速

Pasta Menu 義大利通心粉、麵條菜單

Rigatoni with meat sauce 肋狀通心粉加肉醬

Linguini with chicken 細扁長條義大利麵加雞肉

Spaghetti with Italian sausage 義大利麵條加義大利臘腸

Spaghetti with meat ball sauce 義大利麵條加肉丸加醬

Lasagna with meat sauce 義大利滷汁麵條（千層麵）加肉醬

Veggie pasta 義大利素食麵

Pasta 義大利麵條／通心粉

Rigatoni 肋狀義大利通心粉 / Spaghetti 義大利麵條 / Angel's Hair 義大利麵線 / Lasagna 義大利滷汁麵條（千層麵）/ Fettuccine 義大利寬扁平細麵條 / Linguini 細扁長條義大利麵 / Gnocchi 麵粉團 / Macaroni 義大利通心粉

Fried Chicken Menu 炸雞菜單

Great family deal 家庭餐

10 pieces of chicken (legs and thighs), large box of fries, 1 large salad (macaroni, coleslaw or potato), and med. gravy.

10塊雞塊（小腿和大腿）、大盒薯條、1盒大沙拉（通心粉、涼拌捲心菜或是馬鈴薯)，以及1盒中盒肉汁。

20 pieces deal 二十塊雞餐

20 pieces of chicken (legs and thighs) with 3 buttery corns.

20塊雞塊（小腿和大腿)，和3根奶油玉米。

2 pcs. with corn 兩塊雞餐

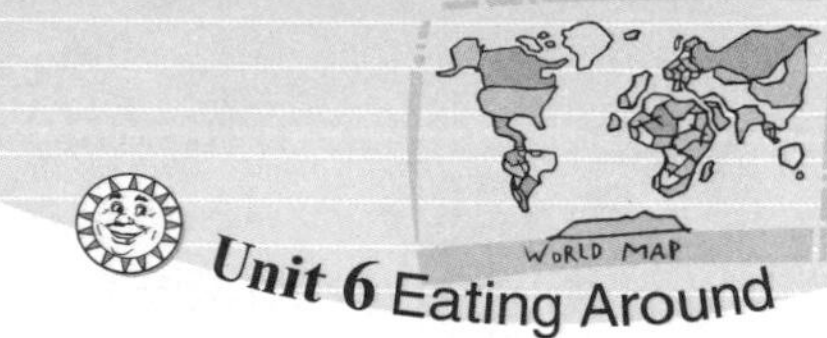

2 pieces of chicken (leg and thigh), with one hot buttery corn.
2塊雞塊（小腿和大腿），和1根熱騰騰的奶油玉米。

Chicken sandwich 雞肉三明治

Appetizer 開胃菜

Wings 辣雞翅

Zucchini 美洲南瓜

Pizza Menu 比薩菜單

	Small 10"（小10吋）	Medium 12"（中12吋）	Large 14"（大14吋）
Cheese 起司	$8.99	$10.99	$12.99
Add 1 topping 多加一種餡料	$9.99	$11.99	$13.99
Add 2 toppings 多加二種餡料	$10.99	$12.99	$14.99
Add 3 toppings 多加三種餡料	$11.99	$12.99	$14.99

Double-up your pizza! 2nd Small $4 2nd Medium $6 2nd Large $8
加倍你的比薩——買第二個小比薩加4元；買第二個中比薩加6元；買第二個大比薩加8元

Regular Toppings 一般的餡料

Shrimp蝦 / Crab meat蟹肉 / Anchovy 鯷魚 / Bacon 培根 / Ham 火腿 /

Beef topping 牛肉餡料 / Diced grilled chicken 烤雞小塊 / Italian sausage 義大利臘腸 / Mild sausage 淡味臘腸 / Pepperoni 義大利辣味香腸 / Salami 薩拉米義式蒜味香腸 / Cheddar cheese 切達乳酪 / Extra mozzarella cheese 特級義大利白乳酪 / Feta cheese 希臘白色軟乳酪 / Mushroom 蘑菇 / Red onion 紅洋蔥 / Spinach 菠菜 / Hot pepper 辣椒 / Green pepper 青椒 / Sun-dried tomato 太陽曬乾的番茄 / Diced tomato 番茄方塊 / Black olive 黑橄欖 / Pineapple 鳳梨

Appetizers 開胃小吃

Garlic Bread 大蒜麵包

Garlic Bread (with cheese) 大蒜麵包（加起司）

Caesar salad 凱撒沙拉

Breadsticks 麵包條

Buffalo Wings (BBQ, hot, or medium) 辣雞翅（烤肉口味、辣味或是中辣)

Dipping sauces 沾醬

Taco Menu 墨西哥玉米烙餅菜單

Hard shell corn tortilla taco 硬殼玉米粉薄烙餅

Seasoned ground beef, grated Cheddar cheeses, fresh lettuce and tomato stacked in a crisp corn tortilla.

調過味的絞牛肉、磨碎的切達起司、新鮮萵苣以及番茄，均勻地放在一個酥脆的玉米薄烙餅內。

Soft flour tortilla taco 軟皮玉米粉薄烙餅

Large soft tortilla loaded with seasoned ground beef, grated cheddar cheeses, crispy lettuce, and tomato, then wrapped.
大的軟皮玉米粉薄烙餅裝入調過味的絞牛肉、磨碎的切達起司、新鮮清脆的萵苣以及番茄，再包捲起來。

Burritos 墨西哥料理（以肉、乳酪、豆泥或是米飯做餡，包在軟皮玉米烙餅的麵餅捲）

Fajita 法士達

Chicken Fajita 雞肉法士達

Chicken strips, onions, and green pepper mixed with salsa, topped with grated Cheddar cheeses, crispy lettuce then wrapped in a large soft tortilla.
把雞肉條、洋蔥以及青椒用墨西哥式番茄洋蔥做的辣調味汁調味後，再把磨碎的切達起司、新鮮清脆的萵苣放於上頭，包捲在一張大的軟皮玉米粉薄烙餅內。

Seafood Fajita 海鮮法士達

Beef Fajita 牛肉法士達

Nachos 烤乾酪辣味玉米片

Coffee & Tea Menu 咖啡&茶

Coffee & espresso (hot) 咖啡&濃縮咖啡（熱飲）

Freshly brewed coffee 現煮咖啡

Freshly brewed decaf coffee 現煮無咖啡因咖啡

Cappuccino 卡布其諾（咖啡加肉桂粉、熱蒸奶，上頭覆蓋牛奶泡）

Coffee Latte 那堤（濃縮咖啡加熱蒸奶）

Vanilla Latte 香草那堤（濃縮咖啡加熱蒸奶與香草）

Caffe mocha 摩卡（濃縮咖啡加熱蒸奶、可可亞以及鮮奶油）

Mocha Valencia 摩卡瓦倫西亞（濃縮咖啡加瓦倫西亞柳橙、熱蒸奶、可可亞以及鮮奶油）

Caramel Macchiato 焦糖瑪奇朵（濃縮咖啡加牛奶泡、香草以及純焦糖）

Caffe Americano 美式咖啡（濃縮咖啡加熱水）

Espresso 濃縮咖啡

Espresso Macchiato 濃縮瑪奇朵（濃縮咖啡加牛奶泡）

Espresso con Panna 濃縮康保藍（濃縮咖啡上加鮮奶油）

Coffee on ice 咖啡冷飲

Iced coffee Latte 冰那堤（濃縮咖啡加牛奶加冰）

Iced vanilla Latte 冰香草那堤（濃縮咖啡加牛奶、香草加冰）

Iced caffe mocha 冰摩卡（濃縮咖啡加牛奶、可可亞以及鮮奶油加冰）

Iced caramel Macchiato 冰焦糖瑪奇朵（濃縮咖啡加牛奶泡、香草以及焦糖加冰）

Iced caffe Americano 冰美式咖啡（濃縮咖啡加水加冰）

Frappuccino blended beverages 星冰樂

Java chip 爪哇碎片星冰樂

Caffe vanilla 香草咖啡星冰樂

Coffee 咖啡星冰樂

Espresso 濃縮咖啡星冰樂

Mocha 摩卡星冰樂

Caramel 焦糖星冰樂

Blended cream 奶霜星冰樂

Double chocolate chip cream 雙份巧克力碎片奶霜星冰樂

Strawberry cream 草莓奶霜星冰樂

Tazo chai cream 泰舒茶奶霜星冰樂

Tea 茶

Tazo chai tea Latte 泰舒那堤茶

Tazo hot tea 泰舒熱茶

Tazo iced chai tea Latte冰泰舒那堤茶

Iced tea 冰茶

Passion herbal tea lemonade 檸檬水花草茶

Black tea lemonade 檸檬水紅茶

Others 其他飲料

Hot chocolate 熱巧克力

Caramel apple cider 焦糖蘋果醋

Size of coffee cups 咖啡杯大小的講法

Tall (small) 小杯

Grande (medium) 中杯

Venti (large) 大杯

Extra large 特大杯

Cream & sugar 奶球&糖包

Single-single (one and one) 一個奶球，一個糖包

Double-double (two and two) 兩個奶球，兩個糖包

Triple-triple (three and three) 三個奶球，三個糖包

Black coffee 不加奶精不加糖的咖啡

Ice Cream Menu 冰淇淋口味

Ice cream 冰淇淋

Strawberry 草莓 / French vanilla 法國香草 / Chocolate 巧克力 / Caribbean mango raspberry 加勒比海芒果覆盆子 / Praline caramel crunch 胡桃焦糖脆片 / Butterscotch ripple 奶油糖果漣漪 / Espresso flake 濃縮咖啡薄片 / Mocha almond fudge 摩卡咖啡杏仁奶脂軟糖 / Butter pecan 奶油胡桃 / Rocky road 岩石路 / Blueberry crumble 碎藍莓 / Chocolate chip 巧克力碎片 / Cookie dough 餅乾麵糰 / Cotton candy 棉花糖 / Black licorice 黑甘草 / Blue bubblegum 藍色泡泡糖 / Mango marble 芒果大理石 / Chocolate chip mint 薄荷巧克力碎片 / Cookies and cream 餅乾奶油 / Black raspberry cheesecake 黑覆盆子起司蛋糕 / Cheesecake 起司蛋糕 / Birthday cake 生日蛋糕 / Peanut butter chocolate花生巧克力 / Maple walnut 楓糖胡桃 / Candy bar whirl 旋轉糖果條 / Chocolate mousse 巧克力慕司 / Peaches & cream 奶油水蜜桃

Yogurt 優格

Frozen yogurt 冷凍優格 / Raspberry frozen yogurt 覆盆子冷凍優格 / French vanilla frozen yogurt 法國香草冷凍優格

Sherbet 果汁牛奶凍

Rainbow sherbet 彩虹果汁牛奶凍 / Orange sherbet 柳橙果汁牛奶凍 / Strawberry sherbet 草莓果汁牛奶凍 / Cranberry sherbet 蔓越莓果汁牛奶凍

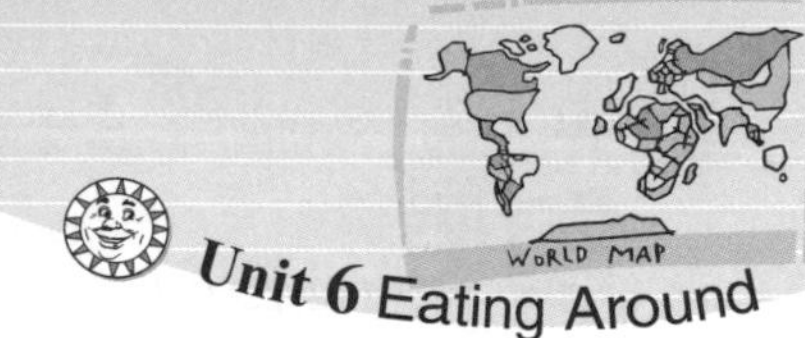

Regular cone & cup 一般甜筒&紙杯

1 scoop 一球 $3.20

2 scoops 二球 $5.20

3 scoops 三球 $6.50

Waffle cone 奶蛋格子餅（華夫餅）甜筒

1 scoop 一球 $3.70

2 scoops 二球 $5.70

3 scoops 三球 $7.00

Sundae 聖代

Banana split 香蕉船

Words & Phrases

above	prep.	在…之上
below	prep.	在下方
combo	n.	組合餐
regular coffee	ph.	一般咖啡
decaffeinated coffee	ph.	無咖啡因咖啡
cream	n.	奶油
ketchup packet	ph.	番茄醬包
scoop	n.	一勺；一鏟；一球（冰淇淋）
old-fashioned	adj.	古早味的
hi there		嗨！你好

for here	ph.	在這裡用
to go	ph.	外帶
here you go	ph.	拿去吧
there you go	ph.	拿去吧
flavor	n.	口味
come to	ph.	共計
plus	prep.	外加
have a good one	ph.	玩得愉快

1. Choose the correct answers.

(1) May I help you?

(a) Yes. I'd like a Big Mac, please.

(b) No, you are not.

(2) Anything else?

(a) No, I don't.

(b) No, thanks. That's all.

(3) Will you be eating here?

(a) Here you go.

(b) No, I'd like it to go, please.

(4) May I have some more ketchup packets, please?

(a) Sure. There you go.

(b) Thanks a lot.

(5) Hi there! How's it going?

(a) I'm going to downtown.

(b) Pretty good. Thank you.

(6) Let's go get a cup of coffee.

(a) Great.

(b) Here you go.

(7) Do you want cream and sugar?

(a) Yes, double double, please.

(b) No, I am not.

(8) Can I try some of your ice cream?

(a) May I take your order?

(b) Sure.

(9) What would you like to order?

(a) I'd like a milkshake.

(b) Yes, I'm ready to order.

(10) For here or to go?

(a) I won't be here too long.

(b) For here, please.

2. Name 10 famous fast food restaurants and coffee shops.

(1) __________

(2) __________

(3) __________

(4) __________

(5) __________

(6) __________

(7) __________

(8) __________

(9) __________

(10) __________

1. Choose the correct answers.

(1) May I help you?

(a) Yes. I'd like a Big Mac, please.

(2) Anything else?

(b) No, thanks. That's all.

(3) Will you be eating here?

(b) No, I'd like it to go, please.

(4) May I have some more ketchup packets, please?

(a) Sure. There you go.

(5) Hi there! How's it going?

(b) Pretty good. Thank you.

(6) Let's go get a cup of coffee.

(a) Great.

(7) Do you want cream and sugar?

(a) Yes, double double, please.

(8) Can I try some of your ice cream?

(b) Sure.

(9) What would you like to order?

(a) I'd like a milkshake.

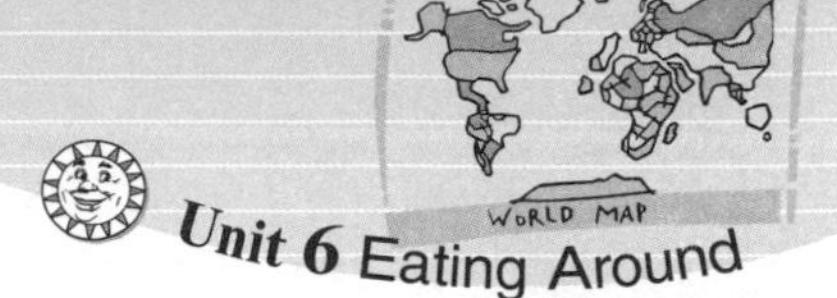

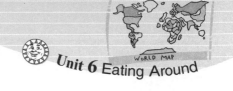

(10) For here or to go?

(b) For here, please.

2. Name 10 famous fast food restaurants and coffee shops.

(1) McDonald

(2) Taco Bell

(3) Wendy's

(4) Burger King

(5) Church's

(6) Kentucky

(7) Sub

(8) Starbucks

(9) Seattle's best coffee

(10) Second cup

Unit 7

Sightseeing And Relaxing

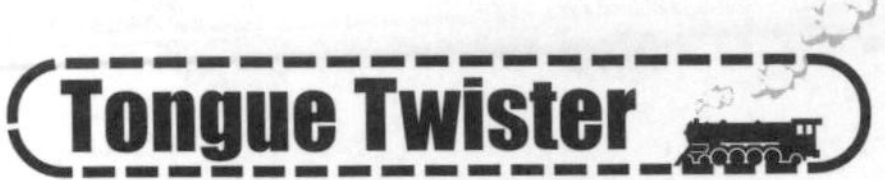

Betty's big bunny bobbled by the blueberry bush.

Tourists Speak Up

Where is the tourist information **office / center**?

May I have a city map?

May I have a free city map?

Do you have any tour guidebook?

Do you have a bus route map?

Could you recommend some tourist attractions?

What are the interesting spots near by?

What are the points of interest?

I'm interested in **fine arts / architecture / music / ceramics / history / painting**.

Thank you for all the information.

Can you recommend a sightseeing tour?

Can you recommend an excursion?

Can you recommend some popular sightseeing tours?

Do you have any guided tours?

What kind of tours is available?

Do you have any **package tours / sightseeing tours** of the city?

Could I have some sightseeing brochures?

How much does the tour cost?

What time does the tour start?

What time do we go back?

Does the charge include meals?

Does the tour include meals?

Do we have free time in Las Vegas?

Do we have any free time during the tour?

Where is the point of departure?

Where should we wait?

Is there an English-speaking guide?

During the tour

How much is the entrance fee?

Is there any reduction for **children / disabled / groups / pensioners / students**?

Do you have a guidebook in English?

Where is the entrance?

Where is the exit?

What's that building over there?

How old is the building?

Who was the architect?

Where is the museum?

Who painted that pictures?

Who built it?

Is it all right to take pictures here?

Can I take pictures here?

Could you take a picture for me?

Would you mind taking a picture for us?

Just press this button.

One more, please.

Excuse me. May I take a picture with you?

Would you mind posing with me?

Say "cheese".

I'd like to visit the church.

Is there a scenic route along the coast?

How far is it to the lake?

How high is the mountain?

What kind of **animal** / **bird** / **flower** / **tree** is that?

I'm interested in **painting** / **fine arts** / **history** / **music**.

It's **amazing** / **beautiful** / **impressive** / **lovely** / **romantic** / **interesting** / **pretty**.

It's **awful** / **gloomy** / **strange** / **terrible** / **ugly**.

Where is the washroom (rest room)?

What time should we meet?

What time should we be back?

At the beach

Is there a sandy beach?

How far is the beach?

Is it safe to swim at the beach?

Is there a lifeguard?

What time is the high tide?

What time is the low tide?

Entertainment

Could you recommend a **ballet** / **concert** / **opera** / **good film** / **musical** / **play**?

Where is the **opera house** / **cinema (movies)** / **concert hall** / **theater**?

Excuse me. How much is the ticket?

Do you have any tickets for the matinee on Saturday?

Are there any tickets for tonight?

I want a seat **in the stalls** / **in the orchestra** / **in the middle** / **in the circle** / **in the balcony**.

How much is the seat in the circle?

Where is the cloakroom?

What's on at the opera tonight?

What's the most popular musical on tonight?

How late is the theater open?

What time does the show begin?

What time does the performance end?

Who's singing?

Who's dancing?

Who's the conductor?

The next screening will begin in 30 minutes.

Amusement park

What time does the park **open / close**?

How much is an all-day pass?

I'd like to get an all-day pass.

I want to go on all the rides.

Let's get in line.

We have to line up.

Where do you want to start?

I want to go on the roller coaster.

Free fall is too scary for me.

Sports

Is there a football (soccer) game anywhere this weekend?

Which teams are playing?

Where are the tennis courts?

I want to rent some rackets.

Is there a heated swimming pool?

Can people swim in the **lake / river**?

I want to rent a motorboat.

I want to rent some skin-diving equipments.

Golf

Where is the nearest golf course?

How much are the green fees?

Would you like to play through?

May I play through?

Who's up?

Who's away?

Who's next?

Good shot!

Great putt!

I'm teeing off.

I'm hitting the ball.

I'm putting.

Practice asking and answering questions from the sentences above.

Teddy Bear Speak Up =_=;0_O

Backpack traveling 背負簡便行李旅行

Mainland China 中國大陸

No way 絕不

Bear: The American guy is backpacking across Europe. Isn't it cool? 0_O

Teddy: Hey..hey... How about let's go backpack traveling across Mainland China? ^Q^

Bear: No way. X_X

Cruise 客輪；郵輪

Virtually 簡直是；實際上

Bet 打賭

Out of shape 身材變型；健康不佳

Teddy: Wow, this cruise ship offers plenty of delicious food. And there's virtually no limit on what or how much we can order. =_=

Bear: Yeah.., You know what? The best of all is no price on the menu. I bet we'll come home out of shape. 0_O

Workout 運動；鍛鍊

Fitness center 健身中心

In shape 身材健美；身體健康

Come along 一起來

My goodness 我的天啊

Too full to move 飽到不能動

Bear: I'm going to do some workout at the fitness center to help me keep in shape. Want to come along? 0_O

Teddy: Oh! My goodness. I'm too full to move. @_@

Tee-off 發球（高爾夫球）

Next hole 下一場

The lowest score 最低分（The lowest score wins. 最低分者贏）

Previous hole 前一場

Teddy: Who's going to tee-off first on the next hole? =_?

Bear: The person who got the lowest score on the previous hole tees-off first. 0_O

Four 打高爾夫球時告訴其他人小心被球打到的用語

Get it 懂了；了解

Golf Players: "Fore...", "Fore..." n_n

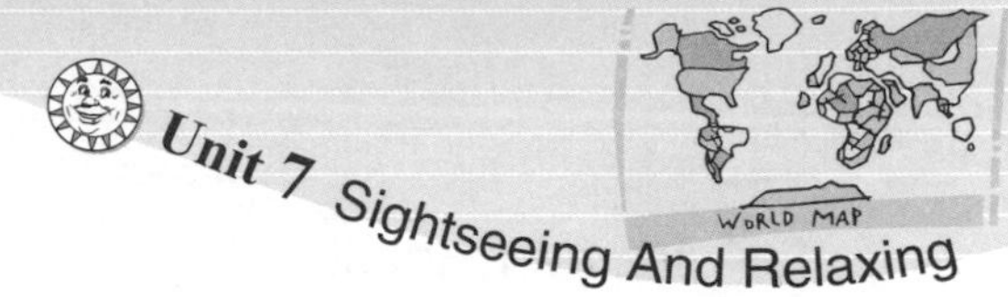

Bear: How come people yell "Four..." in the golf course all the time? 0_?

Teddy: Because they think their balls are going to hit another player. =_=

Bear: Oh! I get it! It's a warning. 0_O

Teddy & Bear: "Fore...", "Fore..." =_= , 0_O

Let someone play through 讓別人先打

Bear: Hey, our group is playing too slowly. Why don't you stop and let the group behind us play through? 0_O

Teddy: Okay! Excuse me, would you like to play through? =_=

Cartoon character 卡通人物

I like... the best 我最喜歡…

Mickey Mouse 米老鼠

Hug 擁抱

Autograph 簽名

Minnie's ears 米妮（米老鼠女友）的耳朵，可戴在頭上

Teddy: Which is your favorite Cartoon character? =_?

Bear: I like Mickey Mouse the best. ^O^

Teddy: Hey! There's Mickey. ^.^

Bear: Hurry! Let's go give him a big hug and get his autograph. 0_^
Oh! I can't believe Mickey is kissing that girl who has Minnie's ears on. X X

Teddy: Are you jealous? @_@

The Phantom of the Opera 歌劇魅影

Musicals 歌劇

Matinees 早場

Evenings 晚場

Imply 暗示

Teddy: The Phantom of the Opera is one of the most famous musicals in New York. =_=

Bear: Yeah.... I'd like to see one while I am here. 0_O

Teddy: The matinees are cheaper than the evenings. =_=

Bear: The performers during the day time and in the evening are not always the same. 0_O

Teddy: What do you imply? =_?

Find a partner for Teddy & Bear role playing game.

Reservation: May I help you, sir?

Johnson: Yes, can you recommend a sightseeing tour for me to see the French capital?

Reservation: Certainly, sir. I'll recommend the Paris city bus tour. It's by far the best way to see the French capital.

Johnson: Could you tell me about the Paris city bus tour in detail?

Reservation: It's a guided 3-hour tour in 4 languages, English, Spanish,

German, or Japanese, it will guide you through the streets aboard one of Europe's open top double-decker bus.

Johnson: Where does the tour go?

Reservation: The sights include the Eiffel Tower, Nortre Dame, Musee du Louvre, and Champs Elysees.

Johnson: How much does the tour cost?

Reservation: It costs 150 Francs per person.

Johnson: Will the bus pick us up at the hotel?

Reservation: A tour guide will pick you up at the hotel.

Johnson: What time does the tour start?

Reservation: It starts at 9:00 in the morning.

Johnson: It sounds fabulous. Please book me the tour for tomorrow.

A shore excursion

Reservation: May I help you, ma'am?

Vivian: Yes, could you tell me what does a shore excursion mean?

Reservation: Sure. A shore excursion means that anything you do off the ship, in port.

Vivian: I'm sorry. I still don't understand.

Reservation: Okay. In this way, it might help you understand easily. At every stop of the cruise, you'll have the option of visiting the area on your own or take a group sightseeing tour. Here are some brochures for your reference.

Vivian: Oh... I see, it's a shore trip in other words. Thank you so much.

Reservation: You're welcome.

Vivian: The evening whale watching in Juneau excursion sounds great. I'd like to sign up for this one.

Reservation: Good choice! That one is the hit. May I have your cabin number, please?

Vivian: Yes, it's 519-1.

At the beach

Dina: Excuse me. Could you tell me where is the beach?

Concierge: Certainly, ma'am. Just go outside of the hotel, turn right, go straight along the trail and you will see the white sand beach on your left.

Dina: How far is the beach from here?

Concierge: It'll take you about 10 minutes on foot.

Dina: Is it very crowded on the beach now?

Concierge: Oh... yeah..., it's always crowded in the summer time.

Dina: Is it safe to swim?

Concierge: Yes, it's safe to swim. Besides, there's a lifeguard on duty all the time.

Dina: Thanks a lot.

Concierge: You're welcome. Watch out for your belongings while on the beach!

1. Now is your turn to practice the dialogues with a partner.

2. Use the sentences from "Tourists Speak Up" or "Teddy Bear Speak Up" to create some new dialogues.

Useful Information

To Describe What Kind of Traveler Are You
描述自己是個什麼樣的旅客

I like to go shopping. 我喜歡逛街購物。

I like outdoor activities. 我喜歡戶外運動。

I like spending time indoors. 我喜歡待在室內。

I am an active person. 我是個活躍的人。

I like eating out. 我喜歡上館子吃飯。

I like to be in the sun. 我喜歡待在陽光下。

I don't like to be in the sun. 我不喜歡待在陽光下。

I like to be on the beach. 我喜歡待在海邊。

I like adventure. 我喜歡冒險。

I like nightlife. 我喜歡夜生活。

I like amusement parks. 我喜歡遊樂園。

I like national parks. 我喜歡國家公園。

I like hiking. 我喜歡徒步旅行。

I like cycling. 我喜歡騎腳踏車兜風。

I like swimming. 我喜歡游泳。

I like skiing. 我喜歡滑雪。

I like mountain climbing. 我喜歡登山。

I like casino. 我喜歡賭場。

I like cities. 我喜歡城市。

I like countryside. 我喜歡鄉村。

I like water sports. 我喜歡水上運動。

I like wind surfing. 我喜歡玩風帆。

I like motorboat. 我喜歡玩汽艇。

I like animals. 我喜歡動物。

I like botanical gardens. 我喜歡植物園。

I like exploring the country I visit. 我喜歡探索我拜訪的國家。

I like learning about the culture, history or art of the country I visit.
我喜歡學習我拜訪的國家的文化、歷史或是藝術。

I like breathing the fresh air in the woods. (I like wood breathing.)
我喜歡在森林裡呼吸新鮮的空氣。（我喜歡森林浴。）

All about Tourist Attractions 觀光勝地

Amusement parks 遊樂場

Disney Land (Los Angeles) / Disney World (Orlando)

Beaches 海邊

Miami South Beach (Miami) / Waikiki Beach (Hawaii)

Canals 運河

Casinos 賭場

Atlantic City (New Jersey) / Las Vegas (Nevada)

Cruise 客輪

Dog sleighs 由狗拉的雪橇

Hot springs 溫泉

Ice fields 冰原

Columbia Ice Field (Canada)

Lakes 湖泊

Buntzen Lake (Vancouver) / Lake Louise (Canadian Rockies)

Limestone caves 石灰岩洞

Stalactitle 鐘乳石

Monorails **單軌鐵路**

Seattle Monorail (Seattle)

Museums 博物館

National parks 國家公園

Canadian Rockies (Canada) / Yellow Stone National Park (USA)

Gondolas 纜車

Outlet 工廠直營的名牌商店區

Parks 公園

Queen Elizabeth Park (Vancouver) / Stanley Park (Vancouver)

Public markets 公衆市場

Pike Place Market (Seattle)

Pyramids 金字塔

Snow mobil 雪車

Square 方形廣場

Pioneer Square (Seattle) / Time Square (New York)

Suspension bridges 吊橋

Capilano Suspension Bridge (Vancouver) / Lynn Canyon Suspension Bridge (Vancouver)

Towers 塔

CNN Tower (Toronto) / Space Needle (Seattle)

Trolley 有軌電車

Places to See

Abbey 修道院 / Amusement park 遊樂園 / Art gallery 美術館 / Beach 海灘 /Botanical gardens 植物園 / Business district 商業中心 / Casino hotel 賭場飯店 / Cathedral 大教堂 / Cave 洞穴 / Chapel 小禮拜堂 / City hall 市政府 / Concert hall 音樂廳 / Convention center 會議中心 / Down town 市中心 / Gardens 花園 / Harbor 港灣 / Hill 小山 / Lake 湖泊 / Public market 公眾市場 / Monument 紀念碑 / Mountain 高山 / Museum 博物館 / Old town老城 / Opera house 歌劇院 / Palace 宮殿 / Park公園 / River 河川 / Shopping mall 購物中心 / Hot spring 溫泉區 / Square 廣場 / Stadium 體育場 / Theater 劇院 / Tower 塔/ Valley 溪谷 / Village 村莊 / University 大學 / Waterfall 瀑布 / Zoo 動物園

Where is the ...?

Where are the ...?

Walt Disney World (Orlando Florida)
迪士尼世界（佛羅里達州的奧蘭多）

Walt Disney World's 4 theme parks 迪士尼世界的4個主題樂園

Magic Kingdom

Epcot

Disney-MGM Studios

Disney's Animal Kingdom Theme Park

Disney Water Parks 迪士尼世界的水上樂園

Disney's Blizzard Beach Water Park 迪士尼的暴風雪海灘水上樂園

Disney's Typhoon Lagoon Water Park 迪士尼的颱風瀉湖水上樂園

Downtown Disney Pleasure Island 迪士尼市區快樂島

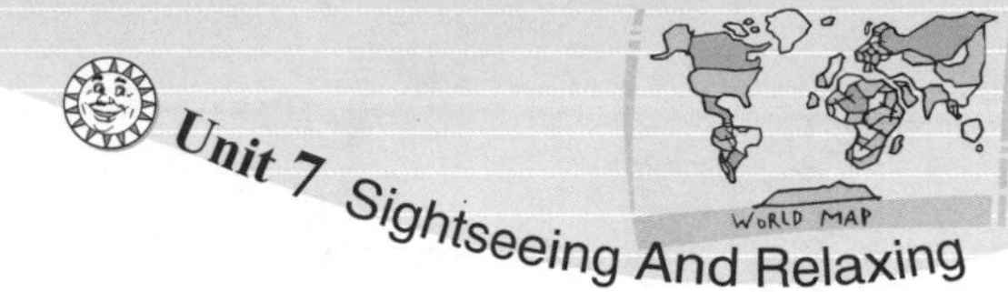

Disney's Wide World of Sports Complex 迪士尼綜合運動的大千世界

Walt Disney World Transportation System 迪士尼世界的公共運輸系統

Monorails 單軌鐵路

Water launches 遊艇

Motor coaches 公共汽車

迪士尼世界位於佛羅里達州的奧蘭多，它的每一個主題樂園大到至少都要花上一天的時間，都還不見得可以玩得完喔！

玩完Disney World還不過癮的話可以再參觀：

Universal Studios 環球影城

Universal's Islands of Adventure 環球的探險之島

Sea World 海洋世界

Casino Hotels In Las Vegas 賭城拉斯維加斯的飯店

Aladdin / Bally's / Bellagio / Circus Circus / Excalibur / Flamingo / Golden Nugget / Imperial Place / Las Vegas Hilton / Luxor / Mandalay Bay / Mgm Grand / Monte Carlo / Paris / Primm Valley / Stardust / Stratosphere / The Mirage / The Venetian / Treasure Island

別忘了！拉斯維加斯的飯店可是這兒的重要觀光景點喔！

Cruise Ship 客輪（遊輪）

Cruise lines客輪公司（遊輪公司）

Carnival / Celebrity / Clipper / Costa Cruises / Cruise West / Crystal /

Cunard / Delta Queen / Disney / Holland America / MSC Italian Cruises / Norwegian / Oceania Cruises / Orient Lines / Peter Deilmann / Princess / Radisson / Royal Caribbean / Seabourn / SeaDream Yacht Club / Silverswa / Star Clippers / Uniworld / Viking River Cruises / Windjammer / Windstar

Cruise destination 客輪（遊輪）航行路線

Africa 非洲 / Alaska 阿拉斯加 / Alaska cruise tours 阿拉斯加客輪（遊輪）團 / Antarctica 南極洲 / Asia 亞洲 / Far East 遠東 / Australia & New Zealand 澳洲以及紐西蘭 / Bahamas 巴哈馬 / Bermuda 百慕達 / Canada & New England 加拿大以及新英格蘭 / Caribbean 加勒比海 / Disney World & Bahamas 迪士尼以及巴哈馬 / Europe cruise tours 歐洲客輪（遊輪）團 / Creek Isles 克里克小島 / Hawaii & South Pacific 夏威夷以及南太平洋 / Indonesia 印尼 / Mediterranean 地中海 /

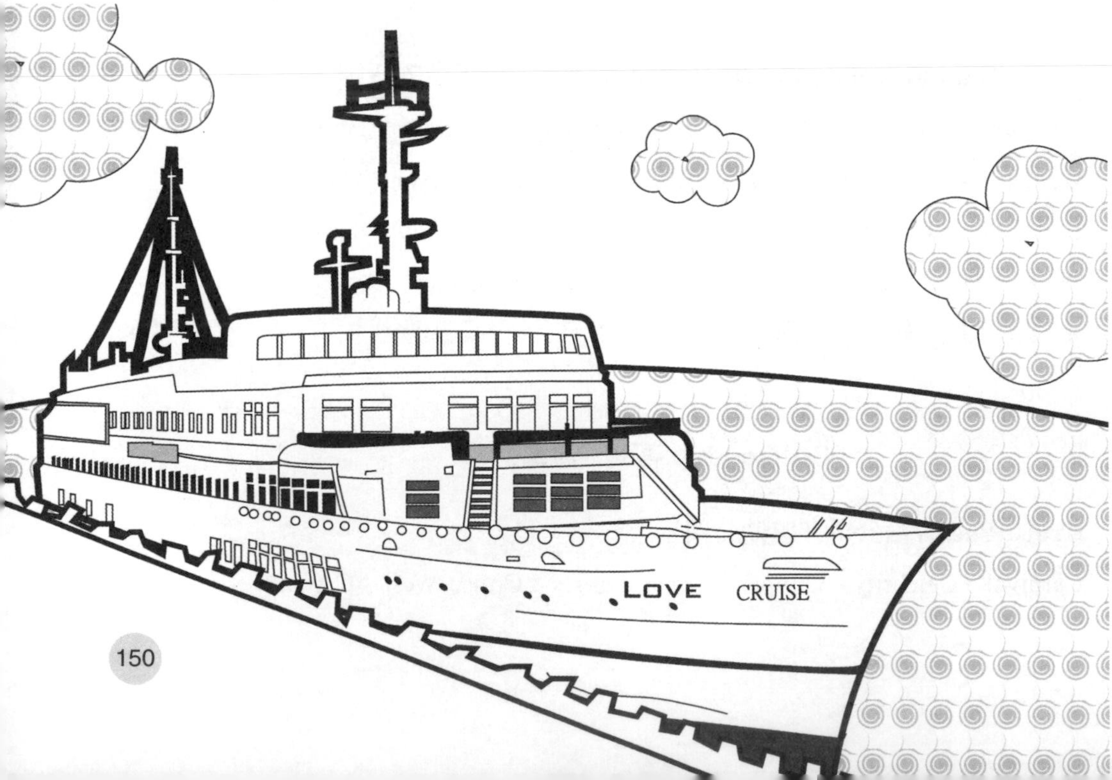

Mexico & Central America 墨西哥以及中美洲 / Middle East 中東 / Northern Europe 北歐 / Pacific Northwest太平洋西北部 / Panama Canal 巴拿馬運河 / River cruises (America) 美國遊河客輪（遊輪）/ River cruises (international) 國際遊河客輪（遊輪）/ South America 南美 / Trans-Atlantic 穿越大西洋

Onboard activities 船上活動

Barber shop 理髮店

Card room 玩牌室

Casino 賭場

Children's playroom 兒童遊戲室

Cruise cuisine 客輪（遊輪）上的各式各樣的佳餚（包括早餐、午餐、晚餐、自助餐、簡餐、宵夜、點心，除了酒精類飲料要收費外，其餘皆免費供應）

Disco 舞廳

Duty-free shops 免稅商店

Fitness facilities 健身設備

Libraries圖書館

Live entertainment 現場秀表演

Mini golf course 迷你高爾夫球場

Movie theater 電影院

Night club & lounges 夜總會

Rock climbing wall 攀岩牆

Room service 客房送餐服務

Spas and beauty salons 三溫暖spa區以及美容沙龍

Swimming pool 游泳池

Tennis court 網球場

Water sports platform 水上運動台

24-hour television programming 24小時電視節目

Live entertainment 現場秀表演

Broadway-style musicals 百老匯風格的歌舞劇

Las Vegas-style revues 拉斯維加斯風格的諷刺實事滑稽劇

Shore excursions (shore trips) 岸邊的各種短程旅行

Entertainments and Relaxing 消遣；娛樂

Entertainments 消遣

Ballet 芭蕾

Broadway-style musicals 百老匯風格的歌舞劇

Cinemas (movies) 電影

Concert 音樂會

Las Vegas-style revues 拉斯維加斯風格的諷刺實事滑稽劇

Night clubs 夜總會

Opera 歌劇

Sports 運動

Badminton 羽毛球 / Basketball 籃球運動 / Boxing 拳擊 / Football (soccer) 足球 / Golf 高爾夫球 / Horse racing 賽馬 / Horseback riding 騎馬 / Ice hockey 冰上曲棍球 / Skating 溜冰 / Skiing 滑雪運動 / Swimming 游泳 / Table-tennis 桌球 / Tennis 網球 / Volleyball 排球

Outdoor activities 戶外活動

Bar-B-Q 野外烤肉 / Biking 騎腳踏車 / Camp 露營 / Canoeing 划獨木舟 / Cycling 騎腳踏車兜風 / Fishing 釣魚 / Hiking 徒步旅行 / Kayaking 划船 / Mountaineering 登山運動 / Rafting 泛舟 / Skin diving 潛水 / Snowboarding 滑雪板滑雪 / Windsurfing 風帆衝浪運動

Amusement Park 遊樂園

Bumper cars 碰碰車 / Climbing wall 攀牆 / Corkscrew 螺旋列車 / Ferris wheel 摩天輪 / Free fall 自由落體 / Glass house 玻璃屋 / Haunted house 鬼屋 / Hellevator 快速升降電梯 / Merry-go-round 旋轉木馬 / Music express 旋轉音樂快車 / Octopus 旋轉章魚 / Pirate ship 海盜船 / Roller coaster 雲霄飛車 / Wave swinger 旋轉鞦韆

All about W.C. 廁所的說法

Bathroom

Gentlemen's room

John

Ladies' room

Lavatory

Men's room

Rest room

Toilet

Washroom

W.C. (Water closet)

Women's Room

Words & Phrases

tourist information center	ph.	旅客資訊中心
guidebook	n.	旅遊手冊
bus route map	ph.	公車路線圖
tourist attraction	ph.	觀光勝地
interesting spot	ph.	令人感興趣的旅遊景點
near by	ph.	附近
point of interest	ph.	令人感興趣的旅遊景點
fine art	ph.	藝術
architecture	n.	建築學
ceramics	n.	陶藝
sightseeing tour	ph.	觀光旅遊
excursion	n.	短途旅行
popular	adj.	流行的；受歡迎的
guided tour	ph.	有導遊的旅遊
package tour	ph.	由旅行社包辦的旅行
brochure	n.	小冊子
point of departure	ph.	出發地點
entrance fee	ph.	入場費
reduction	n.	減少
disabled	adj.	殘障的
pensioner	n.	領養老金的人
exit	n.	出口

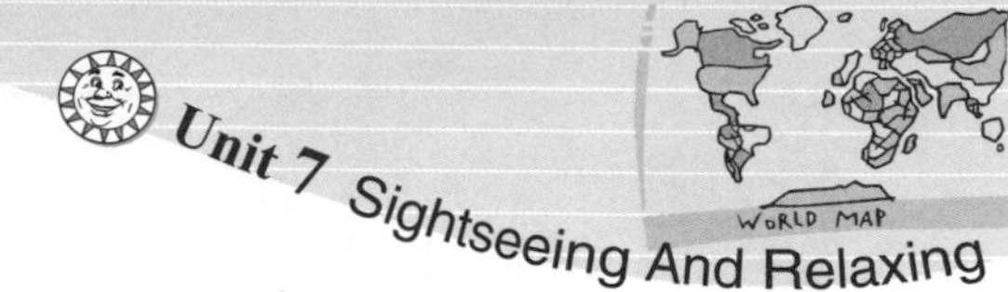

architect	n.	建築師
say "cheese"		照相時說cheese（笑一個之意）
I'd like (I would like)	ph.	我想要
scenic route	ph.	風景秀麗的路線
amazing	adj.	驚人的
impressive	adj.	令人印象深刻的
awful	adj.	嚇人的
gloomy	adj.	陰沉的
ugly	adj.	醜的
sandy beach	ph.	多沙的海邊
lifeguard	n.	救生員
high tide	ph.	漲潮
low tide	ph.	退潮
opera house	ph.	歌劇院
cinema (movies)	n.	電影院
concert hall	ph.	音樂廳
matinee	n.	日場
in the stall	ph.	劇場的正廳前座區
in the orchestra	ph.	劇場的一樓前方頭等座區
in the middle	ph.	中間的位子
in the circle	ph.	劇場成弧形的梯級座位；包廂
in the balcony	ph.	劇場的包廂；樓座
cloakroom	n	寄物處
musical	n.	歌舞劇
conductor	n.	指揮
next screening	ph.	下一場

an all-day pass	ph.	一天的票
get in line	ph.	排隊
scary	adj.	引起驚慌的
football	n.	足球（或是美國的橄欖球）
soccer	n.	足球（美式說法）
tennis court	ph.	網球場
racket	n.	網球拍；羽毛球拍
heated swimming pool	ph.	溫水游泳池
skin diving	ph.	潛水
golf course	ph.	高爾夫球場
shoot	v.	擊球
putt	v.	高爾夫的推球入洞
open top	ph.	無車頂的
double-decker	ph.	雙層
Eiffel Tower	ph.	艾菲爾鐵塔
Nortre Dame	ph.	聖母院
Musee du Louvre	ph.	羅浮宮
Champs Elysees	ph.	香榭大道
Franc	n.	法郎
off the ship	ph.	下船
in port	ph.	在港口內
in other words	ph.	換言之
whale watching	ph.	賞鯨
Juneau	n.	朱諾（阿拉斯加首府）
sign up	ph.	登記
cabin number	ph.	船艙號碼

crowded	adj.	擁擠的
concierge	n.	旅館服務台人員；門房

1. Complete the sentences.

(1) __________ is the tourist information **office / center**?

(2) __________ I have a city map?

(3) __________ you have any tour guidebook?

(4) __________ you recommend some tourist attractions?

(5) __________ are the interesting spots near by?

(6) __________ you recommend a sightseeing tour?

(7) __________ you have any guided tours?

(8) __________ much does the tour cost?

(9) __________ the charge include meals?

(10) __________ is the point of departure?

(11) __________ there an English-speaking guide?

(12) __________ was the architect?

(13) __________ you mind taking a picture for us?

(14) __________ there any tickets for tonight?

(15) __________ teams are playing?

2. Name 10 of the casino hotels in Las Vegas.

(1) ________________

(2) ________________

(3) ____________________

(4) ____________________

(5) ____________________

(6) ____________________

(7) ____________________

(8) ____________________

(9) ____________________

(10) ____________________

Name 5 sports.

(1) ____________________

(2) ____________________

(3) ____________________

(4) ____________________

(5) ____________________

Name 5 outdoor activities.

(1) ____________________

(2) ____________________

(3) ____________________

(4) ____________________

(5) ____________________

1. Complete the sentences.

(1) **Where** is the tourist information **office / center**?

(2) **May** I have a city map?

(3) **Do** you have any tour guidebook?

(4) **Could** you recommend some tourist attractions?

(5) **What** are the interesting spots near by?

(6) **Can** you recommend a sightseeing tour?

(7) **Do** you have any guided tours?

(8) **How** much does the tour cost?

(9) **Does** the charge include meals?

(10) **Where** is the point of departure?

(11) **Is** there an English-speaking guide?

(12) **Who** was the architect?

(13) **Would** you mind taking a picture for us?

(14) **Are** there any tickets for tonight?

(15) **Which** teams are playing?

2. Name 10 of the casino hotels in Las Vegas.

(1) Aladdin

(2) Bally's

(3) Bellagio

(4) Circus Circus

(5) Excalibur

(6) Flamingo

(7) Golden Nugget

(8) Imperial Place

(9) Las Vegas Hilton

(10) Luxor

Name 5 sports.

(1) Badminton

(2) Basketball

(3) Football (Soccer)

(4) Golf

(5) Horse Racing

Name 5 outdoor activities.

(1) Bar-B-Q

(2) Biking

(3) Fishing

(4) Hiking

(5) Kayaking

Unit 8

Shopping Around

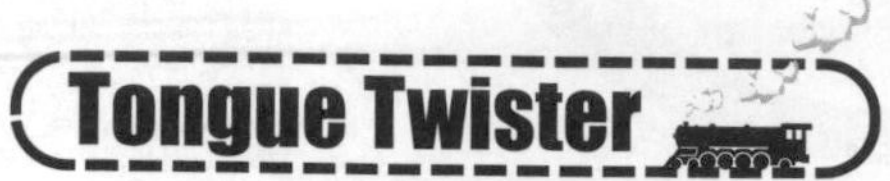

Paul's small ball falls off the tall wall.

Tourists Speak Up

Where is the **shopping mall** / **flea market** / **art craft shop** / **souvenir shop** / **factory outlet**?

When does the mall open?

What time does the store open?

Where is the shoe department?

I'm just looking.

Can you show me some...?

Do you have anything good for souvenirs?

I'm looking for a handbag.

Do you carry any handmade art crafts?

Are they made by hand?

Which one is popular?

Is there anything for about 10 dollars?

How much does this cost?

What is the price of this?

That's very expensive.

Would you give me a discount?

Can you make it cheaper?

Can you wrap it as a gift?

Could you wrap these separately?

Can I return this?

Would you refund the money?

Can I have a refund?

I'd like to get a refund.

I'd like my money back, please.

Clothing

I want something in pink.

I want a **darker / lighter** shade.

I want something to match this.

I don't like the color.

I want a dress for a 8-year-old girl.

I want some shorts for a 6-year-old boy.

Do you have anything better quality?

What's the material of this coat?

Is that pure cotton?

Is it hand washable?

Is it machine washable?

Will it shrink?

Could you measure me?

I take size 40.

I wear size 38.

I don't know the America sizes.

Can I try it on?

Where is the fitting room (dressing room)?

It fits very well.

It doesn't fit.

It's too **long** / **short** / **tight** / **loose**.

Shoes

I'd like a pair of boots.

These are too **narrow** / **wide** / **large** / **small**.

Do you have a **larger / smaller** size?

Do you have the same in black?

I take size 6.

Are these genuine leather?

Jeweler's

I'd like a present for my mother.

I'd like a necklace for my wife.

I'd like some earrings.

Could I please see that?

Is this real gold?

Is this real silver?

Do you have anything in gold?

Is the necklace made of natural pearls?

Do you have any amber necklaces?

Do you have any diamond rings?

Drugstore

I want something for **a cold** / **a cough** / **a hangover** / **hay fever** / **insect bites** / **sunburn** / **travel sickness** / **an upset stomach.**

CDs shop

Do you have any songs by Michael Jackson?

I'd like a **light music** / **jazz** / **classical music** / **pop music** / **instrumental music.**

Practice asking and answering questions from the sentences above.

Shopkeepers Speak Up

Can I help you?

Hi! There. How's it going?

How are you today?

If you need any help just let me know.

These are on sale.

Are you doing okay here?

What color are you looking for?

What size do you wear?

How does it fit?

Fitting room (dressing room) is over there.

They look great together.

Please tell the sales person what you want and they will check it for you.

What's the price range do you have in mind to pay for a gift?

Those are new arrival.

This is a discount price.

Cash or charge?

Is there anything wrong?

Do you have your receipt with you?

Do you have a receipt?

Practice asking and answering questions from the sentences above.

Teddy Bear Speak Up =_=;0_O

No longer valid 無效的

Window-shopping 只逛街不買東西

Teddy: Gee, the clerk of the shop said that my credit card has no longer valid. ~"~

Bear: Don't worry, man! Let's go window-shopping, then. 0_O

Just looking 只是看看而已

Just kidding 開玩笑

Clerk: May I help you, sir? n_n

Teddy: No, we're just looking. My credit card is dead. ~"~

Clerk: Excuse me, sir. ?_?

Bear: Oh... my friend is just kidding. X_X

Flashy 花俏的

Plain 樸素的

Teddy: I'd like to get a skirt for my mom. Which one do you think is better? =_=

Bear: This one is too flashy and that one is too plain. 0_O

Refund 退錢

Weird 奇怪的

Bear: Excuse me. Can I return this shirt and get a refund? O_?

Clerk: Is there anything wrong? n_n

Bear: Yes, this ugly purple and yellow shirt looks weird. ~"~

Find a partner for Teddy & Bear role playing game.

Conversations

Buying a blue T-Shirt

Clerk: May I help you?

Amy: Yes, I'm looking for a blue short-sleeved T-Shirt to match these jeans. Do you carry any short-sleeved T-Shirts?

Clerk: Yes, our short-sleeved T-Shirts are in this section and they are on sale now.

Amy: That'll be great. Here... this one looks good. May I try it on?

Clerk: Yes, our fitting room is over there.

Amy: Thanks.

Clerk: Are you doing OK, ma'am? How did it fit?

Amy: It's too big. Do you have a smaller size?

Clerk: How about this one?

Amy: Okay, this one fits very well. But will it shrink in the wash?

Clerk: No, it won't. Don't worry about that.

Amy: Okay. I'll take it.

Clerk: Great. That's 15 dollars. Cash or charge?

Amy: Charge, please.

 Buying shoes

Clerk: May I help you?

Jennifer: Yes. I'd like a pair of boots.

Clerk: How about these?

Jennifer: No, thanks. I like those in the window.

Clerk: What's your size?

Jennifer: I take size 7.

Clerk: Try these on. How do they fit?

Jennifer: They fit perfectly. But I don't like the color. Do you have the same in black?

Clerk: Let me check. Yup... here you go.

Jennifer: Are these genuine leather?

Clerk: Yes, they are handmade genuine leather boots.

Jennifer: Okay, give me two pairs of these.

 At a souvenir shop

Jimmy: Hi, there. I bought this picture frame here this morning.

Clerk: Yes.

Jimmy: But I found there is a crack in the glass of it when I opened the box. I guess I didn't notice when I bought it.

Clerk: Oh, is it?

Jimmy: Would you change it to a new one?

Clerk: Certainly, sir. Do you have the receipt?

Jimmy: Yes, I have it right here.

Clerk: Just wait for one second, please. Let me get a new one for you.

Jimmy: Thank you.

At a florist's

Colin: Could you tell me what kind of flowers are these?

Clerk: They are tulips.

Colin: How much do they cost?

Clerk: One bunch of tulips costs $3.99, and 3 bunches cost only $10.00.

Colin: How many stems are there in one bunch?

Clerk: There are 5 stems in one bunch.

Colin: Okay. I'd like one bunch of white tulips and two bunches of pink tulips, please. Could you put them all together and wrap as a gift?

Clerk: Sure, I'm going to put some bear grass with the tulips and wrap them in cellophane and some raffia to make a bouquet for you.

Colin: Sounds great.

Clerk: Here you go.

Colin: Wonderful. Do you think these will make a girl happy?

Clerk: Definitely.

At customer service

Clerk: May I help you, ma'am?

Victoria: Yes. Can I return these jeans?

Clerk: Is there anything wrong?

Victoria: They are too tight and I can hardly wear them. Can I ask for a refund?

Clerk: Sure you can. Did you bring the receipt with you?

Victoria: Yes, here you go.

Clerk: That's 30 dollars.

Victoria: Thank you.

Clerk: Sorry for the inconvenience.

1. Now is your turn to practice the dialogues with a partner.

2. Use the sentences from "Tourists Speak Up", "Shopkeepers Speak Up", or "Teddy Bear Speak Up" to create some new dialogues.

Shops 各式商店

Art crafts shop 手工藝品店

Book shop 書店

Department stores 百貨公司

Dollar store (Looney store) 一元商店（加拿大的一元商店）

Drug store 藥房

Duty-free shop 免稅店

Flea market 跳蚤市場

Florist's 花店

Factory outlet 工廠直營商品

Grocery 食品雜貨店

Health food shop 健康食品店

Jeweler's 珠寶店

Market 市場

Shopping center 購物中心

Shopping mall 大型購物中心

Souvenir shop 紀念品店

Sporting goods shop 運動商品店

Supermarket 超級市場

Women's Wear 女裝

Bathing suit 泳裝 / Bikini 比基尼泳裝 / Blouse 短衫 / Bra 胸罩 / Coat 外套；大衣 / Dress 連身女裝 / Evening dress 晚禮服 / Fur coat 毛皮大衣 / Jacket 夾克 / Jeans 牛仔褲 / Nightgown 女睡袍 / Pants 褲子 / Panty hose 褲襪 / Pullover 套頭毛衣 / Robe 長袍；浴袍 / Shawl 方型披巾 / Shorts 短褲 / Skirt 裙子 / Slacks 寬鬆的長褲 / Slip 有肩帶的連身襯裙 / Stockings 長襪 / Suit 套裝 / Swimming suit 游泳衣

Shoes 鞋類

Boots 靴子 / High heels 高跟鞋 / Platform shoes 厚底鞋；木屐鞋；麵包鞋 / Pumps 無帶淺口有跟女鞋 / Sandals 涼鞋

Accessories 配件

Bracelet 手鐲 / Gloves 手套 / Handbag 手提包 / Handkerchief 手帕 / Hat 帽子 / Mittens 連指手套 / Necklace 項鍊 / Purse 錢包 / Scarf 圍巾

Men's Wear 男裝

Boxers 有鬆緊帶之男用短內褲 / Briefs 短內褲 / Coat 外套；大衣 / Jacket 夾克 / Jeans 牛仔褲 / Cardigan 胸前開釦羊毛衫 / Pajamas 睡衣褲 / Pullover 套頭毛衣 / Shirt 襯衫 / Shorts 短褲 / Suit 套裝 / Suspenders 吊褲帶 / Turtle neck sweater 高領毛線衣 / T-shirt 圓領汗衫 / Vest 背心 / V-neck sweater V型領毛線衣

Other accessories 其他配件

Belt 皮帶 / Socks 襪子 / Tie 領帶 / Wallet 皮夾子 / Watch 手錶

Shoes 鞋類

Running shoes 球鞋 / Sneakers 運動鞋

Size 尺寸

Extra extra large (XXL) / Extra large (XL) / Large (L) / Medium (M) / Small (S) / Extra small (XS)

Material 質料

Cashmere 喀什米爾 / Cotton 棉 / Polyester 人造纖維 / Rayon 人造絲 / Silk 絲 / Wool 羊毛

Material for shoes 鞋類質料

Cloth 布料 / Leather 皮革 / Rubber 橡膠 / Suede 絨面革 / Genuine Leather 眞皮

American English 美語 **British English 英語**

Bathing Suit 游泳裝	Swimming Costume 游泳衣
Cardigan 胸前開鈕羊毛衫	Cardie 胸前開鈕羊毛衫
Dress 連身女裝	Frock 連身女裝
Robe 罩袍	Dressing gown 晨袍
Pants 寬鬆的長褲	Trousers 長褲
Scarf 圍巾	Muffler 圍巾
Sweater 毛線衣	Jersey 毛線衣

所有的長褲、短褲以及鞋類都是成雙成對的複數，要記得加 s。

Colors 顏色

Beige 米色 / Black 黑色 / Blue 藍色 / Brown 棕色 / Fawn 淡黃褐色 / Golden 金色 / Green 綠色 / Grey 灰色 / Orange 橘色 / Pink 粉紅色 / Purple 紫色 / Red 紅色 / Scarlet 鮮紅色 / Silver 銀色 / Turquoise 藍綠色 / White 白色 / Yellow 黃色

Light 淺色

Dark 深色

Prints (patterns) 花色

Check 格子布 / Dot 小圓點 / Stripe 條紋布

Size for Women 女士的尺寸

Dresses & suits

America	8	10	12	14	16	18
British	10	12	14	16	18	20

Continental	36	38	40	42	44	46

Stockings

America	8	8.5	9	9.5	10	10.5
British	8	8.5	9	9.5	10	10.5
Continental	0	1	2	3	4	5

Shoes

America	6	7	8	9
British	4.5	5.5	5.5	6.5
Continental	37	38	40	41

Size for men 男士的尺寸

Overcoats & suits

America	36	38	40	42	44	46
British	36	38	40	42	44	46
Continental	46	48	50	52	54	56

Shirts

America	15	16	17	18
British	15	16	17	18
Continental	38	41	43	45

Shoes

America	5	6	7	8	8.5	9	9.5	10	11
British	5	6	7	8	8.5	9	9.5	10	11
Continental	38	39	41	42	43	43	44	44	45

Size can be vary somewhat from one manufacturer to another, so be sure to try on shoes and clothing before you buy.

Souvenir Shop 紀念品店

Art crafts 手工藝品 / CDs 唱片 / Glasses 玻璃杯 / Hats 帽子 / Key chains 鑰匙圈 / Mugs 馬克杯 / Overcoat 大衣 / Picture frame 相框 / Porcelain 瓷器 / Postcards 明信片 / Swiss army knife 瑞士軍隊刀具 / T-shirts T恤 / Watch 錶 / Wood carving 木雕

Jeweler's 珠寶店

Amber 琥珀 / Amethyst 紫水晶 / Copper 銅 / Coral 珊瑚 / Crystal 水晶 / Diamond 鑽石 / Gold 金 / Ivory 象牙 / Jade 玉 / Onyx 瑪瑙 / Pearl 珍珠 / Platinum 白金 / Ruby 紅寶石 / Sapphire 藍寶石 / Silver 銀

CDs shop 唱片店

Blues 藍調 / Classical 古典樂 / Country 鄉村 / Folk 民謠 / Jazz 爵士樂 / Latin 拉丁樂 / Light music 輕音樂 / Love songs 情歌 / Opera 歌劇 / Pop 流行音樂 / Rock 搖滾樂 / Vocal 聲樂

Words & Phrases

just looking	ph.	只是看看而已
carry	v.	販售
made by hand	ph.	手工製造

expensive	adj.	高價的；昂貴的
discount	n.	折扣
cheaper	adj.	便宜點的
wrap it as a gift	ph.	像禮物般包裝
wrap separately	ph.	分開包
refund	v.	退錢
match	v.	相配
better quality	ph.	好一點的品質
material	n.	材料
pure cotton	ph.	純棉
hand washable	ph.	可手洗的
shrink	v.	縮水

fitting room (dressing room)	ph.	試衣間
tight	adj.	緊的
loose	adj.	鬆的
a pair of boots	ph.	一雙靴子
genuine leather	ph.	眞皮
necklace	n.	項鍊
earring	n.	耳環
silver	n.	銀
natural pearl	ph.	天然珍珠
amber	n.	琥珀
diamond ring	ph.	鑽戒
a hangover	ph.	宿醉
hay fever	ph.	花粉症
insect bite	ph.	昆蟲咬
sunburn	n.	曬傷
travel sickness	ph.	暈車（機）
light music	ph.	輕音樂
jazz	n.	爵士音樂
classical music	ph.	古典音樂
pop music	ph.	流行音樂
instrumental music	ph.	樂器演奏音樂
on sale	ph.	拍賣
cash or charge	ph.	付現或是刷卡
jeans	n.	牛仔褲
short-sleeved	adj.	短袖的
picture frame	ph.	相框

crack	n.	裂痕
florist	n.	花店
shopkeeper	n.	店主
tulip	n.	鬱金香
bunch	n.	束
stem	n.	莖
bear grass	ph.	熊草
cellophane	n.	玻璃紙
raffia	n.	拉菲亞樹葉之纖維
bouquet	n.	花束
sounds great	ph.	聽起來太棒了
definitely	adv.	肯定地
hardly	ph.	幾乎不
inconvenience	n.	不方便

1. Match the customers and the shopkeepers' dialogues.

(1) When does the mall open?

(2) Where is the shoe department?

(3) Do you carry any handmade art crafts?

(4) Would you refund the money?

(5) What's the material of this shirt?

(6) I wear size 38.

(7) Where is the fitting room (dressing room)?

(8) Are these genuine leather?

(9) I'd like a necklace for my wife.

(10) I'm just looking.

(11) Would you give me a discount?

(12) I'd like to pay cash.

(13) It fits very well.

(14) What time does the store open till?

(15) Could you tell me what kind of flowers are these?

(a) Can I help you?

(b) If you need any help just let me know.

(c) What size do you wear?

(d) It's open from 9:00 in the morning.

(e) Yes, we do.

(f) Fitting room (dressing room) is over there.

(g) Is there anything wrong?

(h) Cash or charge?

(i) This is a discount price.

(j) It's pure cotton.

(k) It's open till 10:00 at night.

(l) How does it fit?

(m) It's at the second floor.

(n) No, they aren't.

(o) They are tulips.

2. Name 10 places where you can shop.

(1) ____________________

(2) ______________________

(3) ______________________

(4) ______________________

(5) ______________________

(6) ______________________

(7) ______________________

(8) ______________________

(9) ______________________

(10) ______________________

Write the items below in British English.

(1) Bathing Suit

____

(2) Cardigan

____

(3) Dress

____

(4) Robe

____

(5) Pants

____

(6) Scarf

____

(7) Sweater

____

1. Match the customers and the shopkeepers' dialogues.

(1) (d) It's open from 9:00 in the morning.

(2) (m) It's at the second floor.

(3) (e) Yes, we do.

(4) (g) Is there anything wrong?

(5) (j) It's pure cotton.

(6) (c) What size do you wear?

(7) (f) Fitting room (dressing room) is over there.

(8) (n) No, they aren't.

(9) (a) Can I help you?

(10) (b) If you need any help just let me know.

(11) (i) This is a discount price.

(12) (h) Cash or charge?

(13) (l) How does it fit?

(14) (k) It's open till 10:00 at night.

(15) (o) They are tulips.

2. Name 10 places where you can shop.

(1) Duty-free shop 免稅店

(2) Flea market 跳蚤市場

(3) Factory outlet 工廠直營商品

(4) Grocery 食品雜貨店

(5) Jeweler's 珠寶店

(6) Market 市場

(7) Shopping center 購物中心

(8) Shopping mall 大型購物中心

(9) Souvenir shop 紀念品店

(10) Sporting goods shop 運動商品店

Write the items below in British English.

(1) Swimming costume

(2) Cardie

(3) Frock

(4) Dressing gown

(5) Trousers

(6) Muffler

(7) Jersey

Unit 9

Making Friends

Tongue Twister

Silly Sally sings songs sweetly while sitting on the streaming sidewalk when the sizzling summer sun was shining.

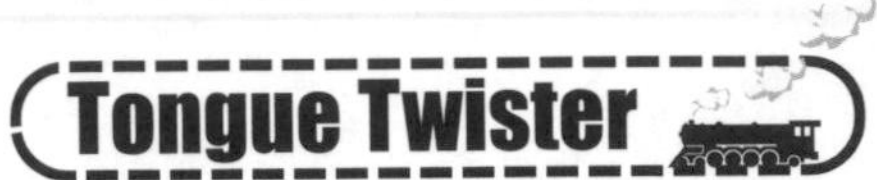

First time meeting people

It's nice to meet you. (Nice to meet you, too.) (Pleased to meet you, too.)

How do you do? (How do you do?) (It's nice to meet you, too.)

I'm glad to meet you.

It's my pleasure to meet you.

It's great meeting you.

Greetings

Hi!

Hello.

Good morning. (Good morning.)

Good afternoon. (Good afternoon.)

Good evening. (Good evening.)

Good night. (Good night.)

How are you? (I'm fine, thank you. And you?) (Pretty good.)

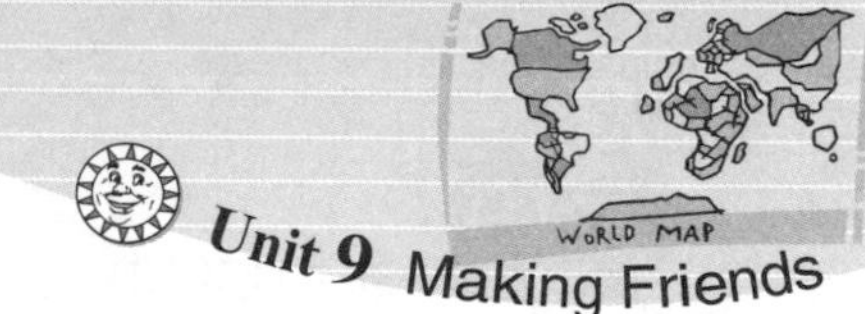

How are you doing?	(I'm fine, thank you. And you?) (I'm fine, thank you.) (Not too bad.) (Not so good.) (So far so good.)
How's it going?	(Pretty good.) (Pretty well.)
What's up?	(Nothing much.)
What's new?	(Not much.)
How's everything?	(Can't complain.) (It's going pretty well.) (Same as always.)
How's everything going?	
How's your family?	(Everyone is fine, thank you.)

Introductions

（先把晚輩介紹給長輩，再介紹長輩給晚輩）（先把下屬介紹給上司，再介紹上司給下屬）（先把男士介紹給女士，再介紹女士給男士，如果男士階級較高，則反之）

Miss Liu, this is Mr. Lee.

Mr. Lee, I want you to meet Miss Liu.

May I introduce Ms. Chu.

What's your name?

How do you spell your name?

Where are you from?

Where do you come from?

What's your occupation?

I'm Zoe.

My name is Bear.

Hi! I'm Teddy.

I'm from **Taiwan** / **Japan** / **Korea** / **Hong Kong** / **Singapore**.

I'm **American** / **Canadian** / **British** / **English** / **Irish** / **Chinese** / **Japanese** / **Korean**.

I'm **a teacher** / **a student** / **a purchasing director** / **a sales manager** / **a marketing director** / **a secretary** / **a stockbroker** / **a doctor** / **a nurse** / **a movie star** / **a singer**.

I'm **an engineer** / **an actor** / **an actress** / **an attorney**.

 Getting to know someone

Do you travel a lot?

Are you a student?

How long have you been here?

Is this your first visit to England?

Are you enjoying your stay?

What do you think of the country?

How do you like the city?

How do you like it so far?

What are your hobbies?

Have you ever traveled to other **countries** / **cities**?

Do you mind if I smoke?

Would you like a cigarette?

 Invitations

Would you like to have dinner with us on this coming Friday?

Would you come over for dinner this evening?

May I invite you for **a cup of coffee** / **a cup of tea** / **a drink**?

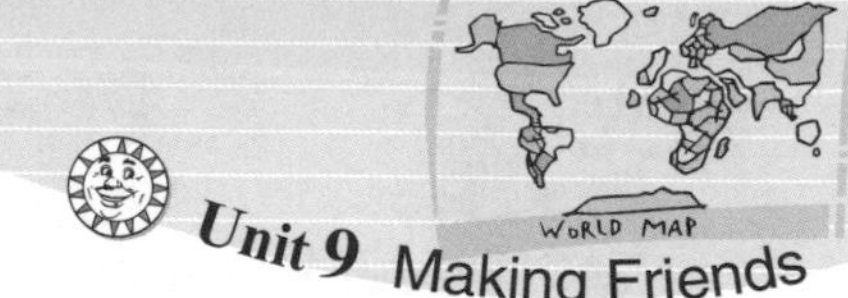

There's a party tonight. Are you coming?

Can I buy you a drink?

Would you like to go out with me tonight?

Would you like to go dancing?

Shall we go to the movies tonight?

Answers for invitations

That's very kind of you.

Great. I'd like to come. Thank you.

What time shall I come?

May I bring **a friend** / **a girlfriend** / **a boyfriend**?

I'd love to, thank you very much.

Thank you, but I am busy.

I'd love to, but I have another party. Maybe next time.

Leave me alone, please.

On leaving

Thank you so much. It's been a wonderful evening.

Thank you so much. It was so kind of you to invite me.

Thank you so much for a lovely evening.

I've had a delightful evening.

I've enjoyed myself.

I'm afraid I've got to leave now.

I'm afraid it is time for us to go.

I've got to go.

Practice asking and answering questions from the sentences above.

Teddy Bear Speak Up =_=;0_O

Greet 打招呼

Western countries 西方國家

Get used to 習慣於

Have you had your dinner? 你吃過飯了嗎？

At home 在國內時

Teddy: How do we greet people in western countries? =_?

Bear: Just say "good morning, good afternoon, good evening and how are you?" 0_O

Teddy: But I get used to saying "Have you had your dinner?" at home. =_?

Bear: You can say that if you want, but people here might think you are going to invite him to dinner with you. @_@

I could be better 不是很好

Couldn't be better 好的不得了

Somebody: How are you doing? n_n

Teddy: I could be better. X_X

Bear: Couldn't be better. ^0^

Mind your own business 管自己的事

Gay 同性戀

Get out of my face 在我面前消失

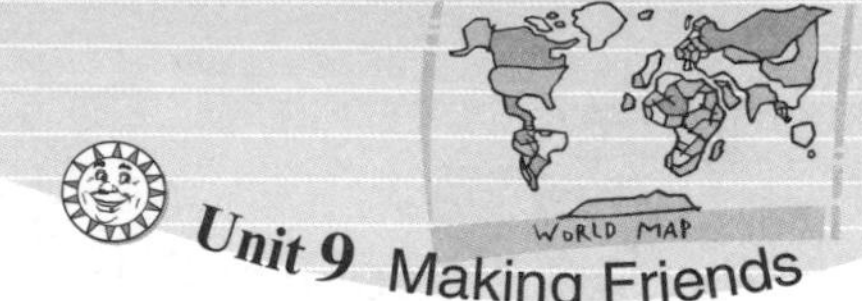

Get out of here 離開這裡

Freak 怪人

Swear 發誓

Serious 嚴肅

The stranger: Are you tourists? *_^

Teddy: Yes, we are. =_?

The stranger: How old are you? *_^

Teddy: Sorry, I don't want to answer too personal questions. ~"~

The stranger: Are you gay? *_^?

Teddy: Hey! Mind your own business, man. Get out of my face. ~"~

Bear: Let's get out of here. He is such a freak. 0_?

Teddy: Ew..., I'm interested in women, I swear. ~"~

Bear: Take it easy. Don't be so serious. 0_O

It's my pleasure to meet you 認識你是我的榮幸

Quite 完全地

Catch the name 聽清楚名字

The pleasure is mine 認識你才是我的榮幸

Somebody: Hi! I'm Kevin Chen. It's my pleasure to meet you. n_n

Teddy: I'm sorry. I did not quite catch your name. =_?

Somebody: My name is Kevin Chen. n_?

Teddy: The pleasure is mine, Mr. Chen. ^.^

Find a partner for Teddy & Bear role playing game.

Introduction

Jessica: Gina, this is Paul, my colleague in the computer company. Paul, this is Gina, she is a close friend of mine.

Paul: Pleased to meet you, Gina.

Gina: Nice to meet you, too, Paul.

Jessica: Gina is from Japan and she is on her vacation now.

Paul: Wow, what a great life! Sushi is one of my favorite Japanese foods. Do you know how to make yummy yummy sushi, Gina?

Gina: My mom is good at making sushi, but I'm only good at eating sushi though.

Paul: Really? Then I'd like to meet your mom someday.

Gina: Sure.

Jessica: We're going to have some beers in the downtown area. Would you like to join us?

Paul: Sure, why not? Let's go!

Meeting a friend

Christine: Hi! I'm Christine. How do you do?

Rebecca: Hi! My name is Rebecca. Nice to meet you, too.

Christine: Is this your first visit to Spain?

Rebecca: No, I come here with my family once a year from Mexico. My

uncle is living in Madrid. How about you?

Christine: Yes, it's my first trip here.

Rebecca: Are you enjoying your stay?

Christine: Yes, I like it very much.

Rebecca: How long have you been here?

Christine: I've been here for 3 days. I'm going to stay 2 more days here and I'll be leaving for England next. I'm on a business trip now.

Rebecca: How do you like it so far?

Christine: Great. I like the landscape a lot.

Rebecca: Do you? Where are you from?

Christine: I'm from Taiwan. Have you ever heard of it?

Rebecca: Yeah... actually, I've met some friends from Taiwan while I was studying in the States. They took me to some good Chinese restaurants sometimes. I like Chinese food very much, because they are so delicious.

Christine Okay!... If you've got a chance, welcome to Taiwan. I'll recommend you some good restaurants to dine in.

Rebecca: That'll be great. Maybe I should plan a trip to visit your country next year.

Talking about hobbies

Stephanie: Do you travel a lot?

Kate: Yeah. I like traveling. I'm planning to travel around the world before my sixtieth birthday.

Stephanie: It sounds cool. What are your hobbies other than traveling?

Kate: I am also interested in shopping, seeing movies, jogging, hiking, outing, and eating out.

Stephanie: You're a really outgoing person.

Kate: Yes, I am. How about you?

Stephanie: I enjoy reading, cooking, collecting stamps, gardening, and raising pets a lot. I'm also good at painting.

Kate: What a family woman. I bet you must be interested in watching TV, then.

Stephanie: You bet.

Kate: What's on now?

Stephanie: There's a movie on channel 8.

Kate: Okay. Let's turn the TV on.

1. Now is your turn to practice the dialogues with a partner.

2. Use the sentences from "Tourists Speak Up" or "Teddy Bear Speak Up" to create some new dialogues.

Useful Information

Useful Information

All about Personality 有關人的個性

Brave 勇敢的 / Carefree 無憂無慮的 / Clumsy 笨拙的 / Crazy 瘋狂的 / Energetic 充滿活動力的 / Friendly 友善的 / Geek 古怪的 / Independent 獨立的 / Modest 謙虛的 / Moron 低能的 / Outgoing 外向的 / Selfish 自私的 / Shy 害羞的 / Sissy 娘娘腔的 / Sloppy 邋遢的 / Smart 聰明的 / Stingy 吝嗇的；小氣的 / Stubborn 固執的 / Stuck up 傲慢的

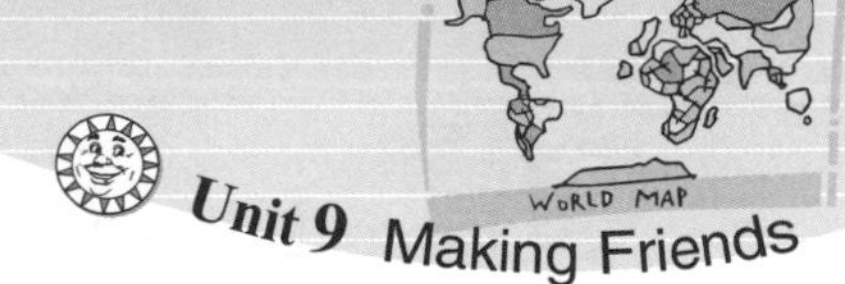

I'm energetic.

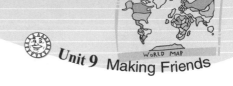

You're friendly.

She is shy.

He is crazy.

Hobbies 嗜好

Collecting things 收集物品 / Cooking 烹飪 / Dancing 跳舞 / D.I.Y.-Do It Yourself 自己動手作 / Drawing 畫畫 / Eating out 上館子 / Fishing 釣魚 / Gardening 園藝 / Going to concerts 聽音樂會 / Going to the parks 到公園 / Hiking 走路旅行 / Jogging 慢跑 / Learning foreign languages 學習外國語言 / Listening to music 聽音樂 / Making friends 交朋友 / Outing 遠足；郊遊 / Playing musical instruments 玩樂器 / Photographing照相 / Playing chesses 下西洋棋 / Playing sports 運動 / Raising pets 養寵物 / Reading 閱讀 / Seeing movies 看電影 / Shopping 逛街 / Singing songs 唱歌 / Skiing 滑雪 / Surfing the web 上網 / Swimming 游泳 / Traveling 旅行 / Watching television看電視

I like cooking.

I enjoy traveling very much.

I'm interested in learning foreign languages and surfing the web.

Religions 宗教信仰

Christianity 基督教	（Christian 基督教徒）
Catholicism 天主教	（Catholic 天主教徒）
Mormonism 摩門教	（Mormon 摩門教徒）

Islam (Muslim) 伊斯蘭教（回教）　（Islamite 伊斯蘭教徒；Muslim 回教徒）

Buddhism 佛教　（Buddhist 佛教徒）

Judaism 猶太教　（Judaist 猶太教徒）

Nonreligious (Atheism) 無神論　（Atheist 無神論者）

Chinese Religions 中國信仰（Combine Mahayana Buddhists, Confucianism, and Taoism 結合大乘佛教、儒家思想，以及道家思想）

Avoiding Personally or Culturally Embarrassing Questions When You First Time Meet Someone
初次見面時，應避免問到私人以及文化上會令人尷尬的問題

Common questions 一般常問的問題

What's your name?

你叫什麼名字？

Can you speak **English** / **Japanese** / **Chinese** / **French** / **Italian** / **Spanish**?

你會說英語 / 日語 / 華語 / 法語 / 義大利語 / 西班牙語嗎？

Where are you from?

你從哪裡來的？

Where do you come from?

你從哪裡來的？

What do you do?

你是做什麼的？

What kind of food do you like?

你喜歡吃哪種食物？

Do you like **Chinese food** / **Japanese food** / **Thai food** / **Italian food**?

你喜歡中國菜 / 日本菜 / 泰國菜 / 義大利菜嗎？

What are your hobbies?

你的嗜好是什麼？

What's your telephone number?

你的電話號碼幾號？

Who is your idol?

誰是你的偶像？

What do you think about **America** / **Canada** / **Taiwan** / **China** / **Australia** / **England**?

你覺得美國 / 加拿大 / 台灣 / 中國 / 澳洲 / 英國怎麼樣？

Have you been to **America** / **Canada** / **Taiwan** / **China** / **Africa** / **Europe**?

你曾經去過美國 / 加拿大 / 台灣 / 中國 / 非洲 / 歐洲嗎？

What's that on your **face** / **nose** / **hair**?

那是什麼東西在你的臉上 / 鼻子上 / 頭髮上？

Do you have any brothers or sisters?

你有兄弟姐妹嗎？

How many brothers and sister do you have?

你有幾個兄弟姐妹？

What's your religion?

你的宗教信仰是什麼？

What's your e-mail address?

你有e-mail嗎？

Where do you live?

你住哪裡？

Taboo questions 禁忌的問題

How old are you?

你幾歲？

How much do you make per month?

你一個月賺多少錢？

Are you married or single?

你結婚了還是單身？

How much do you weigh?

你多重？

Are you pregnant?

妳是否懷孕了？

Are you gay?

你是男同志嗎？

Are you lesbian?

妳是女同志嗎？

Are you bisexual?

你是雙性戀嗎？

What do you wear at home?

你在家都穿什麼？

Do you wear underwear to bed?

你上床睡覺時有穿內衣嗎？

What kind of birth control do you use?

你都如何避孕的？

Do you take drugs?

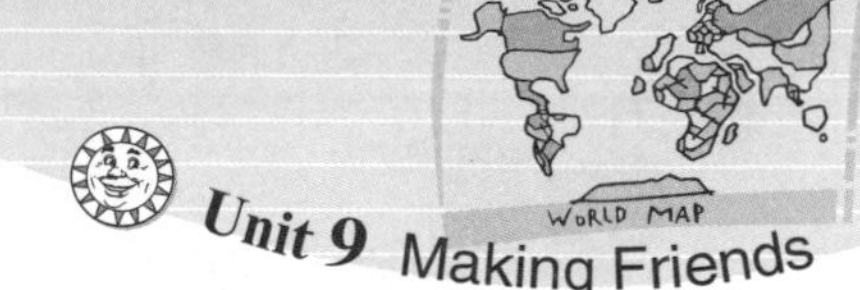

你嗑藥嗎？

What's wrong with your **face** / **nose** / **hair**?

你的臉 / 鼻子 / 頭髮是否不對勁？（嫌人長得奇怪）

Do you brush your teeth? (You smell bad.)

你刷牙了嗎？（嫌人臭）

Where are you going?

你要去哪裡？（似乎在調查別人隱私，老外是很注重個人隱私的）

Where have you been?

你剛剛去哪裡了？（似乎在調查別人隱私，老外是很注重個人隱私的）

Words & Phrases

appointment	n.	正式約會
meet	v.	認識
pleasure	n.	榮幸
greeting	n.	問候
what's up	ph.	怎麼了
nothing much	ph.	不怎樣
what's new	ph.	有什麼新鮮事
not much	ph.	沒什麼
introduce	v.	介紹
spell	v.	拼字
occupation	n.	職業
purchasing director	ph.	採購協理
sales manager	ph.	業務經理
marketing director	ph.	行銷協理
stockbroker	n.	股票經理人
engineer	n	工程師
actor	n.	男演員
actress	n.	女演員
attorney	n.	律師
hobby	n.	嗜好
invitation	n.	邀請
leave me alone	ph.	不要打擾我

delightful	adj.	令人愉快的
colleague	n.	同事
sushi	n.	壽司
yummy	adj.	美味的
good at	ph.	擅長
Madrid	n.	馬德里（西班牙首都）
so far	ph.	到目前爲止
landscape	n.	風景
dine	v.	用餐
collecting stamps	ph.	集郵
you bet	ph.	那還用說

Quizzes

1. Respond the greetings.

(1) It's nice to meet you.

____

(2) How do you do?

____

(3) It's my pleasure to meet you.

____

(4) How are you?

____

(5) How's it going?

____

(6) What's up?

____

(7) What's new?

____

(8) How's everything?

____

(9) How's your family?

____

(10) How's business?

____

2. Write 5 taboo questions to ask a partner (have fun!)

(1) ______________________________________?

(2) ______________________________________?

(3) ______________________________________?

(4) ______________________________________?

(5) ______________________________________?

1. Respond the greetings.

(1) Nice to meet you, too.

Pleased to meet you, too.

(2) How do you do?

It's nice to meet you, too.

(3) The pleasure is mine.

(4) I'm fine, thank you. And you?

Pretty good.

(5) Pretty good.

Pretty well.

(6) Nothing much.

(7) Not much.

(8) Can't complain.

It's going pretty well.

Same as always.

(9) Everyone is fine, thank you.

(10) Not bad.

2. Write 5 taboo questions to ask a partner (have fun!)

Answers will vary.

Unit 10

Other Activities

She sells seashells by the seashore.

Tourists Speak Up

Where is the nearest **bank** / **post office** / **telephone booth**?

What time does the **bank** / **post office** open?

What time does the **bank** / **post office** close?

Where can I make photocopies?

At the bank

I want to change some dollars.

I'd like to exchange this for dollars, please.

May I cash a traveler's check (cheque) here?

What's the exchange rate?

At the post office

Which window is for mail service?

At which window can I mail a registered mail?

I want to have this letter registered.

I want to send this as printed matter.

What's the postage for a postcard to **Asia** / **America** / **Europe** / **Africa** /

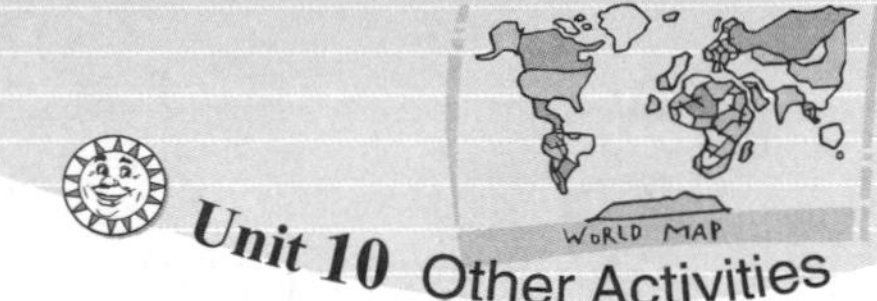

Australia?

What's the postage for **a postcard** / **a letter** to Taiwan?

How much is the postage on this?

I want to send this **letter** / **parcel** to Taiwan.

I'd like to mail this **letter** / **parcel** to Taiwan.

I want to post this **letter** / **parcel** to Taiwan.

What's the cheapest way to mail this?

How long will it take by airmail?

Will it get there by next Friday?

Where's the mailbox?

I want to send this by **airmail** / **sea mail** / **express** / **special delivery** / **registered mail**.

 Telephoning

Is there a pay phone near by?

Where is the telephone booth?

Do you mind if I use your phone?

May I use your phone?

Do you have a telephone dircctory?

What's the dialing code for London?

What's the area code for Vancouver?

Hello, may I speak to Erin, please?

May I speak with Erin, please?

I'd like to speak to Erin, please.

Extension 222, please.

May I have extension 102, please?

I'm sorry for calling you this **late** / **early**.

What time do you expect **her** / **him** back?

When will **she** / **he** be back?

Can I leave a message?

Would you please take a message?

Would you tell **her** / **him** I called?

Who's calling, please?

Who's speaking, please?

May I ask who's calling?

Hold on, please.

Just a **moment** / **second**, please?

I'll transfer your call.

Sorry, he's not in right now.

He's out.

He should be back in half hour.

Would you please call back later?

May I take a message?

Thanks for calling.

I'd like to place a station-to-station call, please.

I'd like to place a person-to-person call, please.

I'd like to make an international call.

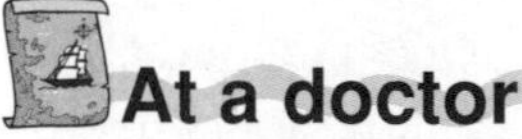

At a doctor

I have **a headache** / **a sore throat** / **a stomachache** / **a fever** / **a cold** / **a cough** / **a toothache**.

I feel like **vomiting** / **throwing up**.

I feel dizzy.

I can hardly sleep.

I can't stop coughing.

I can't stop sneezing.

I have a running nose.

I have a stuffed nose.

I have a pounding headache.

I have heartburn.

I have diarrhea.

I twisted my ankle.

I hurt my **leg** / **arm** / **finger**.

I'm allergic to **penicillin** / **antibiotics**.

Can you give me a prescription for this?

Are you going to give me a prescription?

When will I fell better?

When will the results come?

At the pharmacy

I have **a headache** / **a sore throat** / **a stomachache** / **a fever** / **a cold** / **a cough** / **a toothache**.

Do you have something for **a headache** / **a sore throat** / **a stomachache** / **a fever** / **a cold** / **a cough**?

How often do I take this medicine?

How many times a day should I take it?

Is there anything I can buy without a prescription from a doctor?

Could you please make up this prescription?

Practice asking and answering questions from the sentences above.

Doctors Speak Up

What's wrong with you?

Where does it hurt?

What kind of pain do you have?

What kind of pain is it?

Dull pain or sharp pain?

How long have you had this pain?

How long have you feeling like this?

Have you been sleeping well?

Let me take your temperature.

I'll take your blood pressure.

Roll up your sleeve, please.

Lie down over here, please.

Open your mouth.

Take a deep breath.

Breathe deeply.

Cough, please.

You've got **a flu** / **food poisoning**.

Do you have any allergies?

I want you to have an X-ray taken.

I'll write you a prescription.

I'd like you to come back in 3 days.

You must stay in bed for 2 days.

Drink lots of water and rest.

You should stay home and drink more water.

You should feel better in a few days.

You take it easy now.

Practice asking and answering questions from the sentences above.

Teddy Bear Speak Up =_=;0_O

Break 兌開大額鈔票

How would you like it 要多大面額的鈔票

Teddy: Would you please break this fifty for me? =_?

Clark: Surely, sir. How would you like it? n_n

Teddy: May I have two twenties, two tens, two fives and... ? =_=

Bear: Hey, stop! It's over fifty, man. 0_?

Postcard 明信片

Printed matter 印刷品

By express 快遞的

Teddy: Hi! I'd like to mail this postcard to Taiwan. When will it get to Taiwan? =_?

Clerk: It'll take about one week to get to Taiwan. n_n

Bear: How about printed matter? 0_?

Clerk: It'll be the same as sending a postcard unless you send it by express. n_?

Carry 出售

Calling card 電話卡

Prepaid phone card 預付電話卡

Bear: Do you carry any calling cards? 0_?

Clerk: Yes, we do. How much would you like? n_n

Teddy: What's the rate for calling to Taiwan? 0_?

Clerk: You can check the rate list over there to find your good deal. n_n

Bear: Thanks. May I have a 10-dollar "Great Moment" prepaid phone card? ^.^

Clerk: Sure, here you go! n_n

Find a partner for Teddy & Bear role playing game.

At the bank

Sophia: Hi! May I cash some traveler's checks here?

Clark: Yes, you may. How much would you like to cash?

Sophia: Two hundred dollars, please.

Clark: How would you like that?

Sophia: I'd like five twenties, six tens, two fives and the rest in small change.

Clark: Certainly, ma'am.

Sophia: Thanks.

Clark: (counting money) 20, 40, 60, 80, one hundred... two hundred.

Making a phone call

Ian: Excuse me. Is there a pay phone near by?

Shopkeeper: No, I'm afraid not.

Ian: Where is the nearest pay phone I can use?

Shopkeeper: There's one at the corner of 6th Avenue and Yew Street, but it will take you more than 10 minutes to walk from here.

Ian: 10 minutes? Oh! My gosh... Do you mind if I use your phone to make a local call?

Shopkeeper: No, go ahead!

Ian: Oh.... Thank you so much. It's very nice of you.

Ian: (dialing the number) Hello. May I speak with Mr. Jackson, please?

Secretary: Who's calling, please?

Ian: My name is Ian Liu, and I'm calling about the party for tomorrow night.

Secretary: I'm sorry, Mr. Jackson has gone for the day. Would you mind calling back tomorrow morning.

Ian: Can I leave a message?

Secretary: Sure. What is it?

Ian: Please tell him to call me back, and he can reach me at (604) 235-8866.

Secretary: Okay. I'll give him your message.

Ian: Thank you.

Seeing a doctor

Doctor: What's wrong with you?

Albert: I feel like vomiting.

Doctor: That's too bad. How long have you been feeling like this?

Albert: I've been feeling like this since last night.

Doctor: Do you have diarrhea also?

Albert: Yes, I've got diarrhea.

Doctor: What did you eat yesterday?

Albert: I had a seafood buffet for lunch yesterday.

Doctor: I'll take your blood pressure. Roll up your sleeve, please.

Albert: (roll up his sleeve)

Doctor: OK. You've got food poisoning. There's nothing to worry about. I'll write a prescription for you to have it filled at a pharmacy. Do you have any allergies?

Albert: No, I don't have any.

Doctor: Don't eat any oily foods and don't drink any alcohol.

Albert: Do I have to come back again?

Doctor: Only if the symptoms become worse.

At the dentist's office

Dentist: When did your toothache start?

Michael: It began when I was eating dinner last night.

Dentist: Well, let's take a look at it.

Michael: (open his mouth)

Dentist: Open your mouth as wide as you can, please.

Michael: What do you think?

Dentist: Your gums seem to be inflamed.

Michael: What are you going to have to do?

Dentist: You'll need treatment.

Michael: How bad is it?

Dentist: It's not too bad, but you'd better stop chewing gum and start taking care of your teeth.

At the beauty salon

Hairdresser: How would you like your hair done today?

Selena: I'd like my hair cut with style, shampoo, and blow dry.

Hairdresser: Sure. Here are some stylish hairstyle magazines for your reference. The hairstylists of the magazines are very cool.

Selena: Great. Um... I'd like my hair cut exactly like this one but without the bangs, please.

Hairdresser: Your hair is extremely dry. If you've got a chance, I would suggest you try our oil treatment once a month to help your hair look healthier.

Selena: How much does the treatment cost?

Hairdresser: It's from 35 dollars and up.

Selena: Can I do it today with the 35 dollars one?

Hairdresser: Sure.

Selena: Wow.... I look totally different with my new hairstyle.

Hairdresser: And your hair is shiny now.

Selena: Thank you so much for the suggestion.

Hairdresser: This is my business card and my name is Jerry. You can call

	to make an appointment next time.
Selena:	I will. Bye!

Flight confirmation

Receptionist:	Good afternoon, Teddy Bear Airlines, may I help you?
Bruce:	Yes, I am calling to reconfirm my flight.
Receptionist:	May I have your name, please?
Bruce:	It's Bruce Huang.
Receptionist:	How do you spell your last name?
Bruce:	It's H-u-a-n-g. Actually, I have a computer reservation code.
Receptionist:	Great. What is it?
Bruce:	It's TB22186F.
Receptionist:	Okay, you're on flight TB02 leaving on Aug. 15 at 2:30p.m. from New York.
Bruce:	Yes.
Receptionist:	Mr. Huang, your flight is confirmed. Please be at the airport 2 hours before departure.
Bruce:	Thank you.
Receptionist:	You're welcome. Thank you for calling TB Airlines.

1. Now is your turn to practice the dialogues with a partner.

2. Use the sentences from "Tourists Speak Up", "Doctors Speak Up", or "Teddy Bear Speak Up" to create some new dialogues.

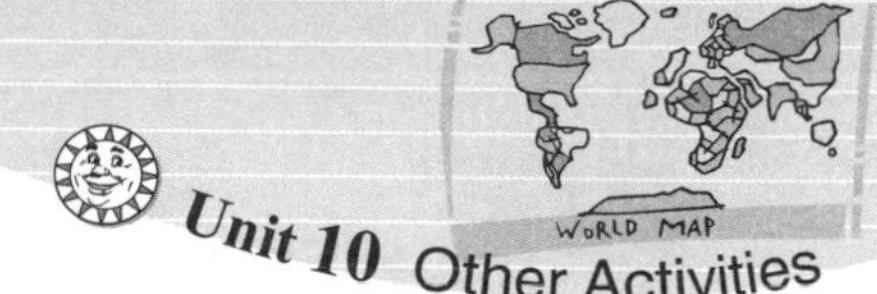

Useful Information

Spa Salon & Barber Shop

Beauty salon 美容院（女士）/ Hairdresser 美髮師

Barber shop 理髮店（男士）/ Barber 理髮師

Aesthetic services 美容

Manicure 修指甲

Pedicure 修腳趾甲

Facial treatment 臉部護理治療

Body treatment 身體護理治療

Water therapy 水療

Massage therapy 按摩療法

Hair services 1 (cut & style) 美髮 1

Cut only 只有剪髮

Shampoo + cut + blow dry 洗＋剪＋吹

Women cut and style 女士造型剪髮

Men cut and style 男士造型剪髮

Roller set 上捲子

Braids 編髮辮

Beard trim 剪修鬍鬚

Hair services 2 (chemical treatment) 美髮 2

Women perm 女士燙髮

Partial perm 挑燙

Men perm 男士燙髮

Spiral perm 螺旋燙

Japanese straighter 日式直髮燙

Highlighting 挑染

Color 染髮

Bleach 漂白

Oil treatment 護髮

Anti-dandruff treatment 抗頭皮屑療法

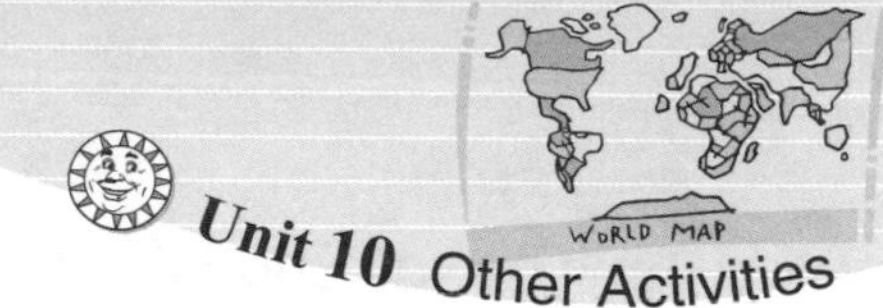

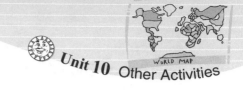

Phone Calls打電話

International direct call 國際直撥

Station to station call 叫號電話（需透過國際台的接線生）

Person to person call 叫人電話（需透過國際台的接線生）

Collect call 對方付費電話（需透過國際台的接線生）

Making a direct call using a prepaid calling card 用預付電話卡打電直撥話

1. Pick up the receiver.
   拿起電話筒。
2. Dial the prepaid calling card number and pin number.
   撥預付電話卡號碼以及識別號碼。
3. Dial the international access code.
   撥國際電話直撥碼。
4. Dial the country code.
   撥國碼。
5. Dial the area code.
   撥區域號碼。
6. Dial the local number.
   撥電話號碼。

Words & Phrases

nearest	adj.	最近的
telephone booth	ph.	電話亭

photocopy	v.	影印
traveler's check	ph.	旅行支票（美）
traveler's cheque	ph.	旅行支票（英）
exchange rate	ph.	外匯兌換率
registered mail	ph.	掛號郵件
printed matter	ph.	印刷品
postage	n.	郵資
parcel	n.	包裹
cheapest	adj.	最便宜的
by next Friday	ph.	下星期五以前
airmail	n.	航空郵件
sea mail	ph.	海運
express	adj.	快遞的
special delivery	ph.	限時專送
pay phone	ph.	收費公用電話
telephone directory	ph.	電話簿
dialing code	ph.	區域號碼（英國）
area code	ph.	區域號碼
expect	v.	預計
message	n.	口信
a headache	ph.	頭痛
a sore throat	ph.	喉嚨痛
a stomachache	ph.	胃痛
a fever	ph.	發燒
a cold	ph.	感冒
a cough	ph.	咳嗽

a toothache	ph.	牙痛
vomit	v.	嘔吐
dizzy	adj.	暈眩的
sneeze	v.	打噴嚏
a running nose	ph.	流鼻涕
a stuffed nose	ph.	鼻塞
pounding	n.	不停猛擊
heartburn	n.	胃灼熱
diarrhea	n.	腹瀉
twist	v.	扭到
ankle	n.	足踝
allergic	adj.	過敏的
penicillin	n.	盤尼西林
antibiotics	n.	抗生素
pharmacy	n.	藥房
dull pain	ph.	緩和的痛
sharp pain	ph.	強烈的痛
temperature	n.	體溫
blood pressure	ph.	血壓
roll up your sleeve	ph.	袖子捲起來
deep breath	ph.	深呼吸
flu	n.	流行感冒
food poisoning	ph.	食物中毒
gosh	int.	啊！糟了
symptom	n.	症狀
dentist	n.	牙醫

gum	n.	口香糖
inflamed	adj.	發炎的
become worse	ph.	變惡化的
stylish	adj.	時髦的
hairstyle	n.	髮型
reference	n.	參考
hairstylist	n.	髮型師
bangs	n.	瀏海
extremely dry	ph.	非常地乾
shiny	adj.	閃亮的
appointment	n.	正式約會
computer reservation code	ph.	電腦訂位代號

1. Complete the dialogue.

Sophia: ____?

Clark: Yes, you may. How much would you like to cash?

Sophia: ____.

Clark: ____?

Sophia: I'd like five twenties, six tens, two fives and the rest in small change.

Clark: ____.

Sophia: Thanks.

Clark: (counting money) 20, 40, 60, 80, one hundred... two hundred.

2. Write 5 questions that a doctor might ask you.

(1) ____?

(2) ____?

(3) ____?

(4) ____?

(5) ____?

1. Complete the dialogue.

Sophia: **Hi! May I cash some traveler's checks here?**

Clark: Yes, you may. How much would you like to cash?

Sophia: **Two hundred dollars, please.**

Clark: **How would you like that?**

Sophia: I'd like five twenties, six tens, two fives and the rest in small change.

Clark: **Certainly, ma'am**.

Sophia: Thanks.

Clark: (counting money) 20, 40, 60, 80, one hundred... two hundred.

2. Write 5 questions that a doctor might ask you.

(1) What's wrong with you?

(2) Where does it hurt?

(3) What kind of pain do you have?

(4) How long have you had this pain?

(5) How long have you feeling like this?

PART 2

Reading

Travel English

Unit 1

Announcements

Boarding announcement

Ladies and gentlemen, Teddybear Airlines flight 1060 will now be boarding at gate D68.

We invite those passengers with small children or those requiring special assistance to the boarding gate.

We now invite first class passengers to board.

We now invite those in business class to board.

We will begin boarding passengers seated in the main cabin now and will be boarding by row numbers from the back of the aircraft towards the front.

We now invite passengers from rows 50 to 62 to board.

We now invite passengers from rows 36 to 49 to board.

We now invite all remaining passengers to the boarding gate.

Welcome aboard announcement

Good morning, ladies and gentlemen,

This is your flight attendant Stephanie speaking. Welcome aboard Teddybear Airlines flight from Taipei to Amsterdam (via Bangkok). Our flying time today is 2 hours and 50 minutes. Captain Zoe Chu, Purser Kate Chang, and the entire crew are pleased to have you on board with us this morning.

May we remind you that according to CAA regulations, the operation of cellular phones, CD players, remote controls for toys, C.B. radios, and other transmitting devices are strictly prohibited in the cabin. Please make sure these are switched off at all times. For further information, kindly refer

to the "In-flight Information" section of the Teddybear in-flight magazine in your seat pocket. We appreciate your cooperation.

Now please fasten your seat belt, set your seat to an upright position, and put your footrest and tray table back in place.

We look forward to making this flight an enjoyable and comfortable experience for all of you.

Turbulence announcement

Ladies and gentlemen,

We are now experiencing turbulence. For your own safety, please return to your seat and fasten your seat belts. Kindly remain seated until the "fasten seatbelt sign" has been turned off.

Thank you.

Final approach announcement

Ladies and gentlemen,

We have begun our descent into Los Angeles. We have enjoyed serving you today. Now please return to your seat and fasten your seat belts, bring your seat upright, and put your footrest and tray table in place. Once again, please ensure all electronic devices are switched off.

Thank you for your cooperation.

Connecting flight announcement

Ladies and gentlemen,

Our passenger service agents are aware that some passengers have connecting flights and will be meeting this flight to assist you. Please

contact our agents after disembarking.

Thank you.

Chinese Translation

登機廣播詞

各位女士、先生，歡迎搭乘Teddybear航空公司班機1060的旅客請至D68號門登機。

我們首先邀請有小孩隨行及需要特別照顧的旅客請您登機。

我們現在邀請頭等艙的旅客請您登機。

我們現在邀請商務艙的旅客請您登機。

我們現在邀請一般艙的旅客登機，並將依照您座位排數由後向前的順序登機。

我們現在邀請座位排數爲50排到62排的旅客請您登機。

我們現在邀請座位排數爲36排到49排的旅客請您登機。

我們現在邀請其餘尚未登機的旅客請您登機。

歡迎登機廣播詞

各位貴賓早安，

我是空服員 Stephanie，歡迎您搭乘Teddybear航空公司由台北（經曼谷）飛往阿姆斯特丹的班機，今天我們的飛行時間是2小時50分。機長Zoe Chu、座艙長Kate Chang以及全體空勤組員很榮幸能夠在這一航段爲您服務。

我們要提醒您，根據民航局規定：在客艙內絕對不可使用行動電話、CD唱盤、電玩遙控器、個人無線電收發報機，及其他發報類電子用品，並請確定關閉電源。有關使用的詳細說明，請參閱您座位前置物袋內的Teddybear雜誌上的機上指南單元。謝謝您的合作。

現在請各位貴賓繫好安全帶，豎直椅背，收好桌子及腳踏墊。

我們希望您有一個愉快舒適的旅程。

機上遇亂流廣播詞

各位貴賓，

我們即將通過一段比較不穩定的氣流，爲了您的安全，請您留在座位上，並繫好安全帶，直到繫好安全帶的指示燈熄滅。

謝謝。

即將抵達的機上廣播詞

各位貴賓，

我們已經開始往洛杉磯的方向下降，很高興今天能爲各位服務，現在請各位貴賓回到您的座位上，繫好安全帶，豎直椅背，收好桌子及腳踏墊，並關閉所有的電子用品電源。

謝謝您的合作。

協助需要轉機旅客的廣播詞

各位貴賓，

如果您需要在此地轉機，請您下機後與我們的地勤人員聯絡，他們會很樂意爲各位辦理轉機手續。

謝謝。

Words & Phrases

announcement	n.	廣播
boarding	n.	登機；上船；上火車
invite	v.	邀請
passenger	n.	旅客
require	v.	需要
special assistance	ph.	特別照顧
boarding gate	ph.	登機門
first class	ph.	頭等艙
business class	ph.	商務艙
cabin	n.	客艙
aircraft	n.	飛機
toward	prep.	向；朝
row	n.	（一）排座位
welcome aboard	ph.	歡迎登機
Amsterdam	n.	阿姆斯特丹
via	prep.	經由
Bangkok	n.	曼谷
captain	n.	機長
purser	n.	座艙長
crew	n.	空勤組員
according to	ph.	根據
CAA (Civil Aeronautics Administration)		民航局

regulation	n.	規定
remote control	ph.	遙控器
transmitting device	ph.	發報類電子用品
strictly	adv.	嚴格地
prohibit	v.	禁止
switch off	ph.	關閉
seat pocket	ph.	座位前置物袋
appreciate	v.	感謝
cooperation	n.	合作
fasten	v.	繫緊
seat belt	ph.	安全帶
upright position	ph.	垂直的位置
footrest	n.	腳踏墊
in place	ph.	適當的地方
look forward to	ph.	盼望
turbulence	n.	亂流
final approach	ph.	即將抵達
Los Angeles	n.	洛杉磯
descent	n.	下降
disembark	v.	登陸；上岸

1. Translation (English to Chinese)

(1) We invite those passengers with small children or those requiring

special assistance to the boarding gate.

(2) We will begin boarding passengers seated in the main cabin now and will be boarding by row numbers from the back of the aircraft towards the front.

(3) May we remind you that according to CAA regulations, the operation of cellular phones, CD players, remote controls for toys, C.B. radios and other transmitting devices are strictly prohibited in the cabin. Please make sure these are switched off at all times.

(4) We are now experiencing turbulence. For your own safety, please return to your seat and fasten your seat belts.

(5) We have begun our descent into Los Angeles. We have enjoyed serving you today.

1. Translation (English to Chinese)

(1) 我們首先邀請有小孩隨行及需要特別照顧的旅客請您登機。

(2) 我們現在邀請一般艙的旅客登機，並將依照您座位排數由後向前的順序登機。

(3) 我們要提醒您，根據民航局規定：在客艙內絕對不可使用行動電話、CD唱盤、電玩遙控器、個人無線電收發報機，及其他發報類電子用品，並請確定關閉電源。

(4) 我們即將通過一段比較不穩定的氣流，爲了您的安全，請您留在座位上，並繫好安全帶。

(5) 我們已經開始往洛杉磯的方向下降，很高興今天能爲各位服務。

Unit 2

Declaration Forms & I-94

Canada customs declaration card

Welcome to Canada (Bienvenue au Canada)

Customs Declaration Card (Carte de declaration douaniere)

Part A - All travellers (must live at the same home address)

Last name, first name, and initials

Date of birth (YYYY / MM / DD)

Citizenship

Home address

Number, street

Town / city

Province or state

Country

Postal / zip code

Arriving by

Airline

Flight no.

Purpose of trip

Study

Personal

Business

Arriving from

U.S. only

Other country direct

Other country via the U.S.

I am / we are bringing into Canada:

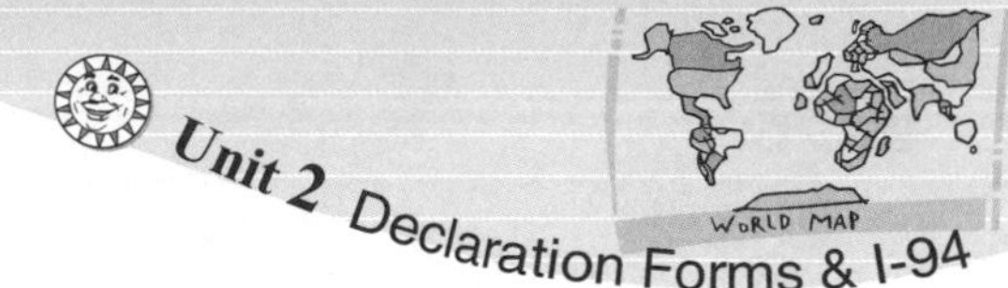

Firearms or other weapons Yes ( ) No ( )

Goods related to my / our profession and / or commercial goods, whether or not for resale (e.g., samples, tools, equipment) Yes ( ) No ( )

Food (fruits, vegetables, meats, eggs, dairy products), animals, birds, insects, plants, plant parts, soil, living organisms, vaccines Yes ( ) No ( )

Articles made or derived from endangered species Yes ( ) No ( )

I / We have shipped goods which are not accompanying me / us.

Yes ( ) No ( )

I / We will be visiting a farm or a farm show in Canada within the next 14 days. Yes ( ) No ( )

I / We have been on a farm in a country other than Canada during the last 14 days. Yes ( ) No ( )

(If your answered yes, list country / countries)

Part B - Visitors to Canada

Duration of stay in Canada (days)

Full value of each gift over CAN$60

Specify quantities: ( ) Alcohol ( ) Tobacco

Part C - Residents of Canada (Complete in the same order as Part A)

Date left Canada (Y-M-D)

Value of goods - CAN$ (including gifts, alcohol, & tobacco)

Specify quantities: ( ) Alcohol ( ) Tobacco

Part D - Signatures (age 16 and older)

U.S.A. customs declaration form

Welcome to the United States

Customs Declaration

Each arriving traveler or responsible family member must provide the following information (only ONE written declaration per family is required):

1. Family name
   First (Given)
   Middle
2. Birth date (Day / Month / Year)
3. Number of family members traveling with you
4. (a) U.S. street address (hotel name / destination)
   (b) City
   (c) State
5. Passport issued by (country)
6. Passport number
7. Country of residence
8. Countries visited on this trip prior to U.S. arrival
9. Airline / flight no. or vessel name
10. The primary purpose of this trip is business: ( ) Yes ( ) No
11. I am (We are) bring
    (a) fruits, plants, food, insects: ( ) Yes ( ) No
    (b) meats, animals, animal / wildlife products: ( ) Yes ( ) No
    (c) disease agents, cell cultures, snails: ( ) Yes ( ) No
    (d) soil or have been on a farm / ranch / pasture: ( ) Yes ( ) No
12. I have (We have) been in close proximity of (such as touching or handling) livestock: ( ) Yes ( ) No
13. I am (We are) carrying currency or monetary instruments over $ 10,000 U.S. or foreign equivalent: ( ) Yes ( ) No

(see definition of monetary instruments on reverse)

14. I have (we have) commercial merchandise: ( ) Yes ( ) No
(articles for sale, samples used for soliciting orders, or goods that are not considered personal effects)

15. Residents - the total value of all goods, including commercial merchandise I / we have purchased or acquired aboard, (including gifts for someone else, but not items mailed to the U.S.) and am / are bring to the U.S. is: $__________

Visitors - the total value of all articles that will remain in the U.S., including commercial merchandise is: $__________

Read the instructions on the back of this form. Space is provided to list all the items you must declare.

I have read the importants information on the reverse side of this form and have made a truthful declaration.

Signature

Date (day / month / year)

I-94 arrival / departure record

Welcome to the United States

I-94 Arrival / Departure Record - Instructions

This form must be completed by all persons except U.S. citizens, returning resident aliens, aliens with immigrant visas, and Canadian Citizens visiting or in transit.

Type or print legibly with pen in ALL CAPITAL LETTERS. Use English. Do not write on the back of this form.

This form is in two parts. Please complete both the Arrival Record (Items 1 through 13) and the Departure Record (Items 14 through 17).

When all items are completed, present this form to the U.S. Immigration and Naturalization Service Inspector.

Item 7 - If you are entering the United States by land, enter LAND in this space. If you are entering the United States by ship, enter SEA in this space.

I-94 Arrival record

1. Family name
2. First (given) name
3. Birth date (day / mo / yr)
4. Country of citizenship
5. Sex (male or female)
6. Passport number
7. Airline and flight number
8. Country where you live
9. City where you boarded
10. City where visa was issued
11. Date issued (day / mo / yr)
12. Address while in the United States (number and street)
13. City and state

I-94 Departure record

14. Family name
15. First (given) name
16. Birth date (day / mo / yr)
17. Country of citizenship

Chinese Translation

加拿大海關申報表

歡迎到加拿大（歡迎到加拿大—法語版）

海關申報表（海關申報表—法語版）

A—所有旅客都必須填寫（住同一個住址的一家人填寫一張）

姓、名、姓名的首字母

生日（年／月／日）

國籍

家庭的住址

　號碼、街名

　鄉鎮／城市

　省或州

　國家

　郵遞區號

到達班機

　航空公司

　班機號碼

旅行目的

　學習

　私事

　商務

從何處抵達

美國

直接從其他國家

從其他國家經美國

我（我們）帶入加拿大的物品：

手槍或是其他武器 是 ( ) 不是 ( )

與我（我們）的專業有關的或是做生意的商品，不管是否要轉售（例如：樣品、工具、裝備） 是 ( ) 不是 ( )

食物（水果、蔬菜、肉製品、蛋、奶製品）、動物、鳥類、昆蟲、植物（農作物）、植物（農作物）的部分、土壤、活的生物、疫苗

是 ( ) 不是 ( )

商品是由瀕臨絕種的動植物做成的或是來自於快絕種的動植物

是 ( ) 不是 ( )

我（我們）有物品是經由海運而來，而非跟隨我們的班機一起來

是 ( ) 不是 ( )

我（我們）在14天內將會參觀加拿大的農場或是農產品展示會

是 ( ) 不是 ( )

我（我們）在到加拿大前的14天，曾到過加拿大以外的其他國家的農場 是 ( ) 不是 ( )

（如果你回答是的話，請把那些國家名稱寫下）

B—加拿大訪客填寫

在加拿大境內停留的天數

超過加幣60元以上的禮物的價值

詳細列出數量：酒類 ( ) 香煙 ( )

C—加拿大居民填寫（依照A部分的順序）

離開加拿大的日期（年—月—日）

物品（新買的）的總價（包括禮物、酒類、香煙）

詳細列出數量：酒類( )香煙( )

D一簽名（16歲以上者）

美國海關申報表

美國海關歡迎您到美國！

海關申報表

每一位入境旅客或是家庭負責人必須提供以下資料（一個家庭只需填寫一份）

1. 姓、名、中間名字
2. 生日（日／月／年）
3. 同行的家庭成員人數
4. 在美居住地址（飯店／目的地）：(a) 街道號碼 (b) 城市 (c) 州
5. 護照發照（國家）
6. 護照號碼
7. 居住國家
8. 來美國之前，去過哪些國家（沒有則填None）
9. 航空公司／班機號碼或船名
10. 我（我們）這次旅行的目的是洽公： ( )是( )不是
11. 我（我們）有帶
    (a) 水果、植物、食品、昆蟲： ( )是( )不是
    (b) 肉製品、動物、動物／野生動物產品： ( )是( )不是
    (c) 疾病媒介、細胞培養菌、蝸牛： ( )是( )不是
    (d) 土壤，或曾到過農場或牧場： ( )是( )不是
12. 我（我們）曾緊密接近家畜（包括接觸或搬運等處理）
    ( )是( )不是
13. 我（我們）有帶超過$10,000美元或等值外幣的現金或貨幣工具（參

閱背面貨幣工具的定義）　( )是( )不是

14. 我（我們）有攜帶商品（販賣之商品、用以爭取訂單之樣品或任何不屬於私人的物品）　( )是( )不是

15. 居民—我（我們）在境外購買或獲得並帶入美國的所有物品總價值（包括送人的禮物，但不包括經由郵寄寄來的物品）：

美金 $ ___________

訪客—所有會留在美國的物品（包括商品）的總價值：

美金 $ ___________

閱讀本張表格背面的說明，將須申報的物品填入空格，如無須申報，則填「0」

我已閱讀過表格背面的重要說明，並據實申報。

簽名

日期（日／月／年）

I-94入境／出境表格

歡迎到美國！

I-94入境／出境表格—填寫說明

除了美國公民、回國僑民、有移民簽證的外國人以及加拿大公民外，所有的旅客都必須完整填寫本表格。

打字或使用原子筆，全部以大寫字母及容易辨認的印刷體來書寫。使用英文書寫。本表格背面不要填寫。

本表格包括入境記錄及出境記錄兩部分，請完整地填寫入境記錄（第1項到第13項）及出境記錄（第14項到第17項）。

完整地填完本表格後，請把它呈交給美國移民局官員。

有關第7項，如果你是由陸路進入美國，請在格子裡填上LAND字樣，如果你是乘坐船隻進入美國，請在格子裡填上SEA的字樣。

I-94入境記錄

1. 姓
2. 名
3. 生日（日／月／年）
4. 哪一國的公民
5. 性別
6. 護照號碼
7. 航空公司及班機號碼
8. 居住國家
9. 登機城市
10. 護照簽發城市
11. 護照簽發日期（日／月／年）
12. 在美地址（號碼與街道）
13. 在美地址（城市與州別）

I-94出境記錄

14. 姓
15. 名
16. 生日（日／月／年）
17. 哪一國的公民

Words & Phrases

customs declaration card	n.	海關申報表
province	n.	省
firearms	n.	槍炮

weapon	n.	武器
related to	ph.	有關
profession	n.	職業
commercial goods	ph.	商品
resale	n.	轉售
vaccine	n.	疫苗
article	n.	物品
derive	v.	得到
endangered species	ph.	瀕臨絕種的動植物
currency	n.	貨幣
monetary	adj.	金融的；貨幣的
duration	n.	持續時間
specify	v.	詳細說明
quantity	n.	量
resident	n.	居民
vessel	n.	船
disease agents	ph.	疾病媒介
cell cultures	ph.	細胞培養菌
snail	n.	蝸牛
ranch	n.	大牧場；大農場
pasture	n.	牧草地；放牧場
proximity	n.	接近；鄰近
livestock	n.	家畜類
commercial	adj.	商業的
purchase	v.	購買
acquire	v.	獲得

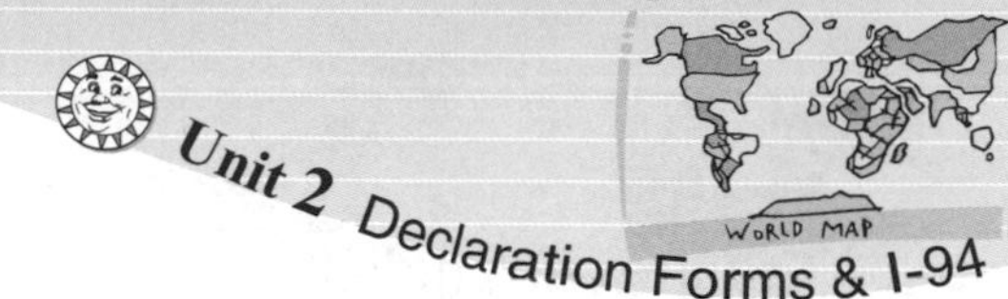

instruction	n.	填寫說明
reverse side	ph.	背面
truthful	adj.	誠實的
except	prep.	除了…之外
U.S. citizen	n.	美國公民
returning resident alien	ph.	回國僑民
aliens with immigrant visas	ph.	有移民簽證的外國人
Canadian citizen	ph.	加拿大公民
print	v.	以印刷體填寫
legibly	adv.	易讀地
capital letter	ph.	大寫字母
present	v.	呈交

1. Fill out the Canada Customs Declaration Card.

PAX | CREW IMM FR REF DIP MILT

Customs Declaration Card

Part A – All travellers (must live at the same home address)

1 Last name, first name, and initials
Date of birth Y Y M M D D Citizenship

2 Last name, first name, and initials
Date of birth Y Y M M D D Citizenship

3 Last name, first name, and initials
Date of birth Y Y M M D D Citizenship

4 Last name, first name, and initials
Date of birth Y Y M M D D Citizenship

Home address – Number, street Town/city

Province or state Country Postal/Zip Code

Arriving by	Purpose of trip	Arriving from
Airline	Study	U.S. only
Flight No.	Personal	Other country direct
	Business	Other country via the U.S.

I am/we are bringing into Canada:	Yes	No
• Firearms or other weapons		
• Goods related to my/our profession and/or commercial goods, whether or not for resale (e.g., samples, tools, equipment)		
• Food (fruits, vegetables, meats, eggs, dairy products), animals, birds, insects, plants, plant parts, soil, living organisms, vaccines		
• Articles made or derived from endangered species		
I/we have shipped goods which are not accompanying me/us.		
I/we will be visiting a farm or a farm show in Canada within the next 14 days.		
I/we have been on a farm in a country other than Canada during the last 14 days.		

(If you answered yes, list country/countries)

1 4
2 5
3 6

Detach and do not fold card

Part B – Visitors to Canada

Duration of stay in Canada (days)	Full value of each gift over CAN$60	Specify quantities Alcohol	Tobacco

Part C – Residents of Canada *(Complete in the same order as Part A)*

	Date left Canada Y M D	Value of goods – CAN$ (including gifts, alcohol, & tobacco)	Specify quantities Alcohol	Tobacco
1				
2				
3				
4				

Part D – Signatures (age 16 and older)

1		3	
2		4	

2. Fill out the U.S.A. Customs Declaration Form.

DEPARTMENT OF THE TREASURY
UNITED STATES CUSTOMS SERVICE

Customs Declaration

19 CFR 122.27, 148.12, 148.13, 148.110, 148.111, 1498; 31 CFR 5316

FORM APPROVED
OMB NO. 1515-0041

Each arriving traveler or responsible family member must provide the following information (only ONE written declaration per family is required):

1. Family **Name**
   First *(Given)* Middle
2. **Birth date** Day Month Year
3. Number of **Family members** traveling with you
4. (a) U.S. Street **Address** (hotel name/destination)
   (b) City (c) State
5. **Passport issued by** (country)
6. **Passport number**
7. Country of **Residence**
8. **Countries visited** on this trip prior to U.S. arrival
9. **Airline/Flight No.** or **Vessel Name**
10. The primary purpose of this trip is **business**: Yes No
11. I am (We are) bringing
    (a) fruits, plants, food, insects: Yes No
    (b) meats, animals, animal/wildlife products: Yes No
    (c) disease agents, cell cultures, snails: Yes No
    (d) soil or have been on a farm/ranch/pasture: Yes No
12. I have (We have) been in close proximity of (such as touching or handling) **livestock**: Yes No
13. I am (We are) carrying **currency or monetary instruments** over $10,000 U.S. or foreign equivalent: Yes No
    (see definition of monetary instruments on reverse)
14. I have (We have) **commercial merchandise:** Yes No
    (articles for sale, samples used for soliciting orders, or goods that are not considered personal effects)
15. **Residents** — the **total value of all goods,** including commercial merchandise I/we have purchased or acquired abroad, (including gifts for someone else, but not items mailed to the U.S.) and am/are bringing to the U.S. is: $
    Visitors — the **total value of all articles** that will remain in the U.S., including commercial merchandise is: $

Read the instructions on the back of this form. Space is provided to list all the items you must declare.

I HAVE READ THE IMPORTANT INFORMATION ON THE REVERSE SIDE OF THIS FORM AND HAVE MADE A TRUTHFUL DECLARATION.

X

(Signature) Date (day/month/year)

For Official Use Only

Customs Form 6059B (11/02)

The U.S. Customs Service Welcomes You to the United States

The U. S. Customs Service is responsible for protecting the United States against the illegal importation of prohibited items. Customs officers have the authority to question you and to examine you and your personal property. If you are one of the travelers selected for an examination, you will be treated in a courteous, professional, and dignified manner. Customs Supervisors and Passenger Service Representatives are available to answer your questions. Comment cards are available to compliment or provide feedback.

Important Information

U.S. Residents — declare all articles that you have acquired abroad and are bringing into the United States.

Visitors (Non-Residents) — declare the value of all articles that will remain in the United States.

Declare all articles on this declaration form and show the value in U.S. dollars. For gifts, please indicate the retail value.

Duty — Customs officers will determine duty. U.S. residents are normally entitled to a duty-free exemption of $800 on items accompanying them. Visitors (non-residents) are normally entitled to an exemption of $100. Duty will be assessed at the current rate on the first $1,000 above the exemption.

Controlled substances, obscene articles, and toxic substances are generally prohibited entry.

Thank You, and Welcome to the United States.

The transportation of currency or **monetary instruments,** regardless of the amount, is legal. However, if you bring in to or take out of the United States more than $10,000 (U.S. or foreign equivalent, or a combination of both), you are required by law to file a report on Customs Form 4790 with the U.S. Customs Service. Monetary instruments include coin, currency, travelers checks and bearer instruments such as personal or cashiers checks and stocks and bonds. If you have someone else carry the currency or monetary instrument for you, you must also file a report on Customs Form 4790. Failure to file the required report or failure to report the *total* amount that you are carrying may lead to the seizure of *all* the currency or monetary instruments, and may subject you to civil penalties and/or criminal prosecution. SIGN ON THE OPPOSITE SIDE OF THIS FORM AFTER YOU HAVE READ THE IMPORTANT INFORMATION ABOVE AND MADE A TRUTHFUL DECLARATION.

Description of Articles (List may continue on another Form 6059B)	Value	Customs Use Only
Total		

PAPERWORK REDUCTION ACT NOTICE: The Paperwork Reduction Act of 1995 says we must tell you why we are collecting this information, how we will use it, and whether you have to give it to us. The information collected on this form is needed to carry out the Customs, Agriculture, and currency laws of the United States. Customs requires the information on this form to insure that travelers are complying with these laws and to allow us to figure and collect the right amount of duty and tax. Your response is mandatory. An agency may not conduct or sponsor, and a person is not required to respond to a collection of information, unless it displays a valid OMB control number. The estimated average burden associated with this collection of information is 4 minutes per respondent or record keeper depending on individual circumstances. Comments concerning the accuracy of this burden estimate and suggestions for reducing this burden should be directed to U.S. Customs Service, Reports Clearance Officer, Information Services Branch, Washington, DC 20229, and to the Office of Management and Budget, Paperwork Reduction Project (1515-0041), Washington, DC 20503. **THIS FORM MAY NOT BE REPRODUCED WITHOUT APPROVAL FROM THE U.S. CUSTOMS FORMS MANAGER.**

Customs Form 6059B (11/02)

3. Fill out the I-94 Arrival / Departure Record

U.S. Department of Justice
Immigration and Naturalization Service

OMB 1115-0077

Admission Number

Welcome to the United States

896359961 08

I-94 Arrival/Departure Record - Instructions

This form must be completed by all persons except U.S. Citizens, returning resident aliens, aliens with immigrant visas, and Canadian Citizens visiting or in transit.

Type or print legibly with pen in ALL CAPITAL LETTERS. Use English. Do not write on the back of this form.

This form is in two parts. Please complete both the Arrival Record (Items 1 through 13) and the Departure Record (Items 14 through 17).

When all items are completed, present this form to the U.S. Immigration and Naturalization Service Inspector.

Item 7 - If you are entering the United States by land, enter **LAND** in this space. If you are entering the United States by ship, enter **SEA** in this space.

Form I-94 (04-15-86)Y

Admission Number

896359961 08

Immigration and
Naturalization Service

I-94
Arrival Record

1. Family Name
2. First (Given) Name
3. Birth Date (Day/Mo/Yr)
4. Country of Citizenship
5. Sex (Male or Female)
6. Passport Number
7. Airline and Flight Number
8. Country Where You Live
9. City Where You Boarded
10. City Where Visa Was Issued
11. Date Issued (Day/Mo/Yr)
12. Address While in the United States (Number and Street)
13. City and State

Departure Number

896359961 08

Immigration and
Naturalization Service

I-94
Departure Record

14. Family Name
15. First (Given) Name
16. Birth Date (Day/Mo/Yr)
17. Country of Citizenship

See Other Side ENGLISH **STAPLE HERE**

1. Fill out the Canada Customs Declaration Card.

PAX | CREW | IMM | FR | REF | DIP | MILT

Customs Declaration Card

Part A – All travellers (must live at the same home address)

1 Last name, first name, and initials: CHANG KATE
Date of birth: 1980 11 04 — Citizenship: TAIWAN R.O.C.

2 Last name, first name, and initials:
Date of birth: Y Y Y Y M M D D — Citizenship:

3 Last name, first name, and initials:
Date of birth: Y Y Y Y M M D D — Citizenship:

4 Last name, first name, and initials:
Date of birth: Y Y Y Y M M D D — Citizenship:

Home address – Number, street: 22, TEDDYBEAR ROAD. — Town/city: TAIPEI
Province or state: TAIWAN — Country: R.O.C. — Postal/Zip Code: 100

Arriving by	Purpose of trip	Arriving from
Airline: TB	Study	U.S. only
Flight No.: 002	Personal X	Other country direct X
	Business	Other country via the U.S.

I am/we are bringing into Canada:	Yes	No
• Firearms or other weapons		X
• Goods related to my/our profession and/or commercial goods, whether or not for resale (e.g., samples, tools, equipment)		X
• Food (fruits, vegetables, meats, eggs, dairy products), animals, birds, insects, plants, plant parts, soil, living organisms, vaccines		X
• Articles made or derived from endangered species		X
I/we have shipped goods which are not accompanying me/us.		X
I/we will be visiting a farm or a farm show in Canada within the next 14 days.		X
I/we have been on a farm in a country other than Canada during the last 14 days.		X

(If you answered yes, list country/countries)
1 / 2 / 3 / 4 / 5 / 6

Part B – Visitors to Canada

Duration of stay in Canada (days)	Full value of each gift over CAN$60	Specify quantities: Alcohol	Specify quantities: Tobacco
14 DAYS	N/A	1	0

Part C – Residents of Canada *(Complete in the same order as Part A)*

	Date left Canada Y M D	Value of goods – CAN$ (including gifts, alcohol, & tobacco)	Specify quantities: Alcohol	Specify quantities: Tobacco
1				
2				
3				
4				

Part D – Signatures (age 16 and older)

1 Kate Chang — 2 — 3 — 4

Detach and do not fold card

2. Fill out the U.S.A. Customs Declaration Form.

DEPARTMENT OF THE TREASURY
UNITED STATES CUSTOMS SERVICE

Customs Declaration
19 CFR 122.27, 148.12, 148.13, 148.110,148.111, 1498; 31 CFR 5316

FORM APPROVED
OMB NO. 1515-0041

Each arriving traveler or responsible family member must provide the following information (only ONE written declaration per family is required):

1. Family Name: CHANG
   First (*Given*): KATE Middle:
2. **Birth date** Day 04 Month 11 Year 80
3. Number of **Family members** traveling with you: NONE
4. (a) U.S. Street **Address** (hotel name/destination): HOLIDAY INN
   (b) City: LOS ANGELES (c) State: CA
5. **Passport issued by** (country): TAIWAN R.O.C.
6. **Passport number**: T2022689
7. Country of **Residence**: TAIWAN R.O.C.
8. **Countries visited** on this trip prior to U.S. arrival: NONE
9. **Airline/Flight No. or Vessel Name**: TB002
10. The primary purpose of this trip is **business**: Yes ☐ No ☒
11. I am (We are) bringing
    (a) fruits, plants, food, insects: Yes ☐ No ☒
    (b) meats, animals, animal/wildlife products: Yes ☐ No ☒
    (c) disease agents, cell cultures, snails: Yes ☐ No ☒
    (d) soil or have been on a farm/ranch/pasture: Yes ☐ No ☒
12. I have (We have) been in close proximity of (such as touching or handling) **livestock**: Yes ☐ No ☒
13. I am (We are) carrying **currency or monetary instruments** over $10,000 U.S. or foreign equivalent: (see definition of monetary instruments on reverse) Yes ☐ No ☒
14. I have (We have) **commercial merchandise:** (articles for sale, samples used for soliciting orders, or goods that are not considered personal effects) Yes ☐ No ☒
15. **Residents** — the **total value of all goods**, including commercial merchandise I/we have purchased or acquired abroad, (including gifts for someone else, but not items mailed to the U.S.) and am/are bringing to the U.S. is: $
    Visitors — the **total value of all articles** that will remain in the U.S., including commercial merchandise is: $ 100.00

Read the instructions on the back of this form. Space is provided to list all the items you must declare.

I HAVE READ THE IMPORTANT INFORMATION ON THE REVERSE SIDE OF THIS FORM AND HAVE MADE A TRUTHFUL DECLARATION.

X Kate Chang (Signature) 20, APR., 2005 Date (day/month/year)

For Official Use Only

Customs Form 6059B (11/02)

The U.S. Customs Service Welcomes You to the United States

The U. S. Customs Service is responsible for protecting the United States against the illegal importation of prohibited items. Customs officers have the authority to question you and to examine you and your personal property. If you are one of the travelers selected for an examination, you will be treated in a courteous, professional, and dignified manner. Customs Supervisors and Passenger Service Representatives are available to answer your questions. Comment cards are available to compliment or provide feedback.

Important Information

U.S. Residents — declare all articles that you have acquired abroad and are bringing into the United States.

Visitors (Non-Residents) — declare the value of all articles that will remain in the United States.

Declare all articles on this declaration form and show the value in U.S. dollars. For gifts, please indicate the retail value.

Duty — Customs officers will determine duty. U.S. residents are normally entitled to a duty-free exemption of $800 on items accompanying them. Visitors (non-residents) are normally entitled to an exemption of $100. Duty will be assessed at the current rate on the first $1,000 above the exemption.

Controlled substances, obscene articles, and toxic substances are generally prohibited entry.

Thank You, and Welcome to the United States.

The transportation of currency or **monetary instruments**, regardless of the amount, is legal. However, if you bring in to or take out of the United States more than $10,000 (U.S. or foreign equivalent, or a combination of both), you are required by law to file a report on Customs Form 4790 with the U.S. Customs Service. Monetary instruments include coin, currency, travelers checks and bearer instruments such as personal or cashiers checks and stocks and bonds. If you have someone else carry the currency or monetary instrument for you, you must also file a report on Customs Form 4790. Failure to file the required report or failure to report the *total* amount that you are carrying may lead to the seizure of *all* the currency or monetary instruments, and may subject you to civil penalties and/or criminal prosecution. SIGN ON THE OPPOSITE SIDE OF THIS FORM AFTER YOU HAVE READ THE IMPORTANT INFORMATION ABOVE AND MADE A TRUTHFUL DECLARATION.

Description of Articles (List may continue on another Form 6059B)	**Value**	**Customs Use Only**
2 shoes	$30.00	
1 hand bag	$20.00	
3 T-shirts	$15.00	
1 sun glasses	$25.00	
miscellaneous	$10.00	
Total	$100.00	

PAPERWORK REDUCTION ACT NOTICE: The Paperwork Reduction Act of 1995 says we must tell you why we are collecting this information, how we will use it, and whether you have to give it to us. The information collected on this form is needed to carry out the Customs, Agriculture, and currency laws of the United States. Customs requires the information on this form to insure that travelers are complying with these laws and to allow us to figure and collect the right amount of duty and tax. Your response is mandatory. An agency may not conduct or sponsor, and a person is not required to respond to a collection of information, unless it displays a valid OMB control number. The estimated average burden associated with this collection of information is 4 minutes per respondent or record keeper depending on individual circumstances. Comments concerning the accuracy of this burden estimate and suggestions for reducing this burden should be directed to U.S. Customs Service, Reports Clearance Officer, Information Services Branch, Washington, DC 20229, and to the Office of Management and Budget, Paperwork Reduction Project (1515-0041), Washington, DC 20503. **THIS FORM MAY NOT BE REPRODUCED WITHOUT APPROVAL FROM THE U.S. CUSTOMS FORMS MANAGER.**

Customs Form 6059B (11/02)

3. Fill out the I-94 Arrival / Departure Record.

U.S. Department of Justice
Immigration and Naturalization Service

OMB 1115-0077

Admission Number

Welcome to the United States

896359961 08

I-94 Arrival/Departure Record - Instructions

This form must be completed by all persons except U.S. Citizens, returning resident aliens, aliens with immigrant visas, and Canadian Citizens visiting or in transit.

Type or print legibly with pen in ALL CAPITAL LETTERS. Use English. Do not write on the back of this form.

This form is in two parts. Please complete both the Arrival Record (Items 1 through 13) and the Departure Record (Items 14 through 17).

When all items are completed, present this form to the U.S. Immigration and Naturalization Service Inspector.

Item 7 - If you are entering the United States by land, enter **LAND** in this space. If you are entering the United States by ship, enter **SEA** in this space.

Form I-94 (04-15-86)Y

Admission Number

896359961 08

Immigration and Naturalization Service

I-94
Arrival Record

1. Family Name: CHANG
2. First (Given) Name: KATE
3. Birth Date (Day/Mo/Yr): 04 11 80
4. Country of Citizenship: TAIWAN R.O.C.
5. Sex (Male or Female):
6. Passport Number: T2022684
7. Airline and Flight Number: TB002
8. Country Where You Live: TAIWAN
9. City Where You Boarded: TAIPEI
10. City Where Visa Was Issued: TAIPEI
11. Date Issued (Day/Mo/Yr): 02 04 05
12. Address While in the United States (Number and Street): HOLIDAY INN
13. City and State: LOS ANGELES CA

Departure Number

896359961 08

Immigration and Naturalization Service

I-94
Departure Record

14. Family Name: CHANG
15. First (Given) Name: KATE
16. Birth Date (Day/Mo/Yr): 04 11 80
17. Country of Citizenship: TAIWAN R.O.C.

See Other Side ENGLISH **STAPLE HERE**

Unit 3

It's Vegas, Baby!

Welcome to the casino Sin City of neon jungle - Las Vegas is an exciting place where people can spend time for having fun, dining, seeing a show, or gambling. All you need to have an enjoyable and unforgettable trip in Vegas is just to have a little luck pulling the handles of slot machines and shooting craps. The purpose of the city is built to part you from your money and lose your shirt.

Las Vegas is a year-round city. It remains a busy town throughout the year. It is a non-stop town also known as the city that does not sleep. When the sun goes down, the city lights up. Usually, weekdays are less crowded than weekends. It means you are most likely to get the better hotel rates on weekdays. The best time to visit is fall. Because it is still warm enough to swim, but not so hot to die. If you want some shut-eye during your trip in Vegas, you need to book your hotel room as soon as you can.

Las Vegas is an oasis located in the middle of a barren desert and surrounded by miles and miles of sand. It was a small, old-time gambling town but it has been rising to be the number-one and the hottest tourist destination in the U.S. now. Las Vegas has more hotels than any other. There are eight of the ten biggest hotels in the world in Las Vegas. To be honest, it is no piece of cake to beat this city anymore. As we know, in other cities, people build hotels near the tourist attractions. But in Vegas, hotels are the tourist attractions. The MGM Grand is the world's largest hotel & casino with over 5,000 rooms. Major hotels and attractions in Vegas are concentrated in three main areas. They are the Stripe (North Stripe, Center Stripe, and South Stripe), Paradise Road, and downtown. Everything on the Strip is within walking distance. It is roughly three miles from Circus Circus Hotel to Mandalay Bay Hotel. However, no one wants to walk that in 100-

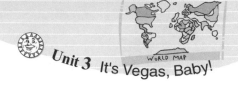

degree heat in summer or in gale-force winds in winter. Do you? And be aware that anything to buy on the Stripe costs more than anywhere else in town.

Do you know how much gambling places are there in Vegas? Can you imagine? They start at the airport and follow you all the way to your hotel. Do you know that you have to be at least 21 years old to enter a casino area? What if you happen to look younger than 21? Asian people always look younger than their real age. Be sure to carry a valid picture ID with you when enter a casino area. Don't think you are home-free to gamble if you are under 21. The casino will take away your jackpot if they find out you are a winner who is under 21.

After you have got exhausted, it is time to refuel. You will find a great variety of restaurants and some restaurants even serve food all night. There is a good variety of culinary offerings from all over the world including: American, Asian, buffets and brunches, Mexican and Southwestern, steak, seafood and international. Vegas is a very informal town. You can always see people dress in jeans at even the best restaurants. Only a few places require a formal dress code. A tip for people who wants to enjoy a more affordable meal at expensive restaurants is to eat there at lunch. Lunch menus are always cheaper than dinner.

What happen next in Vegas? Right! They are show time and nightlife. The sun goes down, and the city lights up. After dinner, explore yourself to nighttime Vegas. If you want to give your wallet some rest, and let yourself away from the slot machines and shooting craps. Here is something cool to consider: going to the shows, checking out the neon spectacle, dancing all night long, and pub or bar hopping from hotel to hotel...

Do you want to experience an unforgettable vacation in the adult's Disneyland? It goes without saying. Las Vegas is the only one in the world.

Chinese Translation

拉斯維加斯

歡迎大家來到霓虹叢林中的罪惡之城——賭城，拉斯維加斯是一個會令人感到興奮的城市，在這裡，人們可以盡情地吃喝玩樂，看熱鬧非凡的賭城秀，或是豪賭。只要是有一些好運道，隨便玩玩吃角子老虎、擲擲骰子，就可以享受一個歡樂難忘的賭城之旅。而建造拉斯維加斯這個城市的目的，主要就是要掏空賭客的口袋，直到他連自己的襯衫都輸掉爲止。

拉斯維加斯是一個一年12個月都開放的城市，也就是說這個城市一年到頭都是忙碌的。而大家都知道的，這個忙碌不停的城市也是一個不夜城，當太陽下山後，拉斯維加斯的燈火也才剛剛點亮起來，不輸白晝。一般來說平時的時候並不會像週末時那般擁擠，那也表示在平時的時候來到這裡，比較有可能得到便宜的房價。最佳來訪的季節是秋天，因爲這時的氣候還溫暖適合游泳，又不至於熱得半死。如果你想在這個不夜城旅遊時也能夠訂得到休息的飯店，那可要儘早訂房。

拉斯維加斯是一個座落於不毛沙漠中央的綠洲，她的四周都被萬哩萬哩的沙所包圍著。她以前只是一個小型、老式的賭博小鎭，一直發展到今天已成爲美國境內第一名及最熱門的觀光地。拉斯維加斯擁有的飯店房間數勝過其他城市的，在世界上排名前十名的大飯店中，拉斯維加斯就占有八間，說眞的，現在想要超越這個城市，還不是一件容易的事。我們都曉得，在其他的城市，所有飯店都蓋在觀光景點區，但是在拉斯維加斯，飯店就是她的觀光景點。MGM Grand是世界上最大的飯店，它擁有的客房超過5,000間。拉斯維加斯主要的飯店及其他觀光景點都集中於三個地方，分別爲the Stripe（分爲North Stripe, Center Stripe和South Stripe）、Paradise Road以及downtown。在Strip區，都是在可以走路的範圍內，粗略估計，從Circus Circus飯店到Mandalay Bay飯店大約只有3英哩的距離。這樣的距離雖不算太遠，但是沒有人願意在華氏100度（將近攝氏40度）的炎熱夏天或是強風吹襲的冬天走在路上吧！如果是你，你要嗎？最後我們要知道的是，在Stripe區的商店所賣的商品是全城最貴的。

你知道在拉斯維加斯有多少可以賭博的地方？可以想像得到嗎？從機場開始一路到飯店都可以有地方賭。但是你知道要進入賭場有個規定，那就是賭客至少要滿21歲才能賭博嗎？有許多東方人看起來都比實際年齡年輕，如果剛好你就是那個已滿21歲，卻看起來比21歲年輕的話該如何？請記得要隨身攜帶自己的身分證件，以便被查詢。如果你未滿21歲，不要以爲你可以把賭場當成像是在自己家裡一般自由，如果賭場知道你未滿21歲，他們會把你贏得的彩金沒收回去的。

已經玩得精疲力盡時，那是到了該充電的時候了。這裡有許多的餐廳，有些餐廳甚至整晚營業，有來自世界各國的多樣化料理可供選擇，有美式餐廳、亞洲式餐廳、自助餐及早午餐、墨西哥式餐廳、牛排、海鮮及各國料理，應有盡有。拉斯維加斯並不是一個非常正式的城市，常常可以看到穿著牛仔褲的人出入在高級餐廳，只有少數餐廳會要求客人著正式的服裝。如果有人想到高級餐廳用餐，又不想花太多錢，建議你可以到這些高級的餐廳用午餐，一般來說，午餐的菜單價位比晚餐便宜。

接下來的節目是什麼？沒錯！就是看秀及夜生活了。當太陽下山後，拉斯維加斯這個城市的燈火也才剛剛亮起來呢。晚餐過後，就讓自己遠離一下賭場吧！也好讓自己的荷包休息一下，可以去探索一下拉斯維加斯迷人的夜生活，這裡有一些很酷的選擇可以供參考喔：可以去看秀，也可以去欣賞這個城市美不勝收的霓虹燈景觀，更可以盡情地飆舞狂歡整夜或是到各飯店的酒吧、Pub去晃晃，一家接一家……

你想要體驗一次難忘的「成人迪士尼樂園」之旅嗎？不用說，拉斯維加斯是世界上獨一無二的。

Words & Phrases

casino	n.	賭場
sin	adj.	罪惡的
neon	n.	霓虹燈
jungle	n.	叢林
Las Vegas	n.	拉斯維加斯
gambling	n.	賭博
enjoyable	adj.	有樂趣的
unforgettable	adj.	難忘的
luck	n.	運氣
pull	v.	拉
handle	n.	把手
slot machine	ph.	吃角子老虎機
shooting	n.	發射
craps	n.	雙骰子賭博

part	v.	分開
year-round	adj.	整年的
non-stop	adj.	不停止的
barren	adj.	貧瘠的；不毛的
desert	n.	沙漠
surround	v.	圍繞
to be honest	ph.	老實說
piece of cake	ph.	輕鬆容易之事
beat	v.	勝過
tourist attraction	ph.	觀光勝地
paradise	n.	天堂
imagine	v.	想像
valid ID	ph.	有效的證件
home-free	adj.	像在家一樣的
jackpot	n.	賭博的獎金
exhaust	v.	使精疲力盡
refuel	v.	補給燃料
variety	n.	多樣化的
culinary	adj.	烹飪的
buffet	n.	自助餐
brunch	n.	早午餐
informal	adj.	非正式的
dress code	ph.	服裝規定
tip	n.	提示
affordable	adj.	負擔得起的
explore	v.	探索

spectacle	n.	公開展示
hop	v.	蹦跳
adult's Disneyland	ph.	成人的迪士尼樂園
goes without saying	ph.	不可言喻的

1. Translation (English to Chinese)

(1) Welcome to the casino Sin City of neon jungle一Las Vegas.

(2) The purpose of the city is built to part you from your money and lose your shirt.

(3) Las Vegas is a year-round city. It remains a busy town throughout the year.

(4) As we know, in other cities, people build hotels near the tourist attractions. But in Vegas, hotels are the tourist attractions.

(5) Vegas is a very informal town. You can always see people dress in jeans at even the best restaurants.

1. Translation (English to Chinese)

(1) 歡迎大家來到霓虹叢林中的罪惡之城——賭城，拉斯維加斯。

(2) 建造拉斯維加斯這個城市的目的，主要就是要掏空賭客的口袋，直到他連自己的襯衫都輸掉爲止。

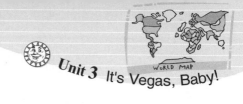

(3) 拉斯維加斯是一個一年12個月都開放的城市，也就是說這個城市一年到頭都是忙碌的。

(4) 我們都曉得，在其他的城市，所有飯店都蓋在觀光景點區，但是在拉斯維加斯，飯店就是她的觀光景點。

(5) 拉斯維加斯並不是一個非常正式的城市，常常可以看到穿著牛仔褲的人出入在高級餐廳。

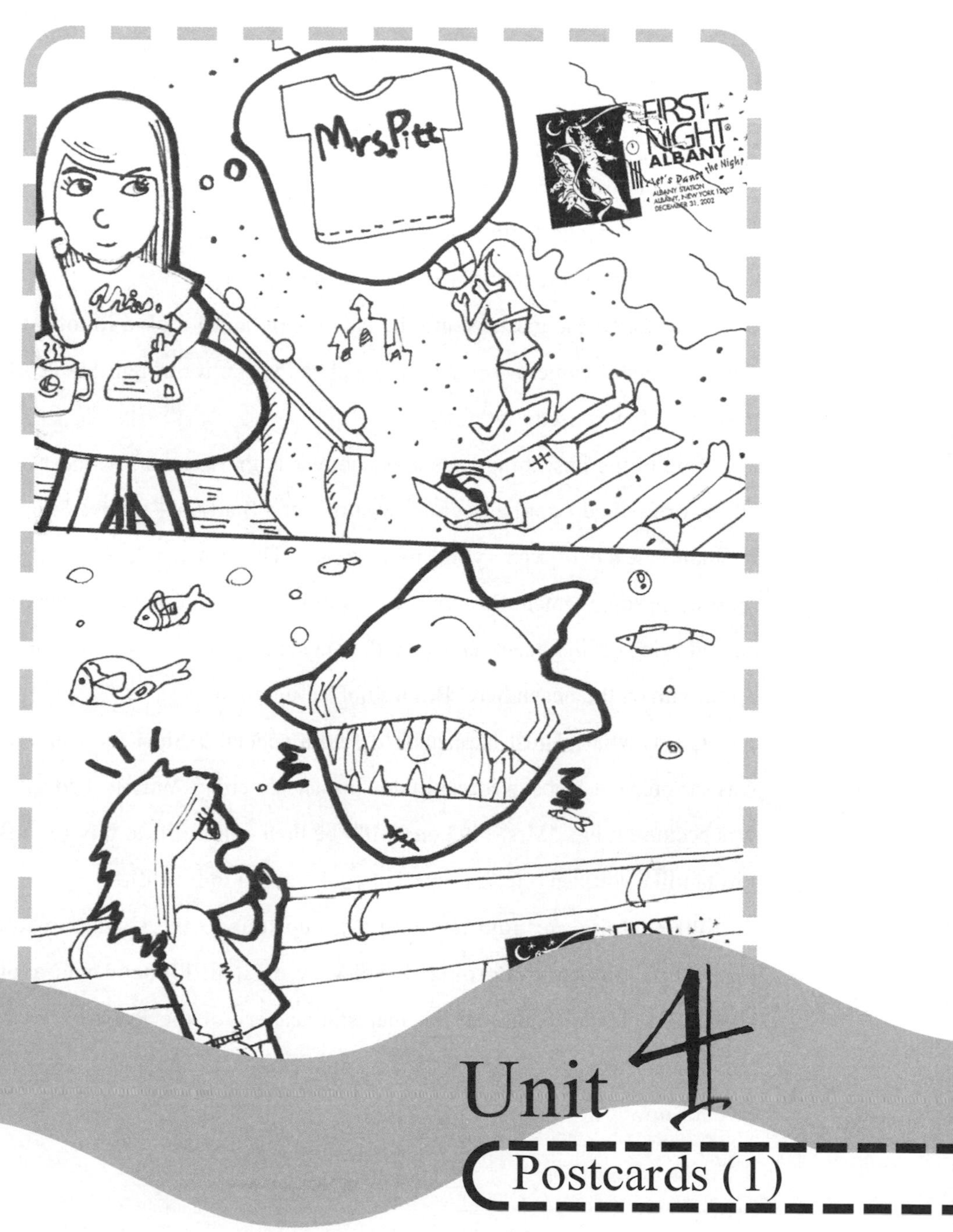

Unit 4

Postcards (1)

Greetings from Vancouver

Dear Kate,

Greetings from Vancouver.

I'm having a great time on my vacation in Canada.

Vancouver is the best place that I have been to!

I've visited the gardens and the parks here, and I took a lot of pictures with my digital camera. I rented a bicycle and rode it through Stanley Park yesterday. It was pretty interesting.

One of the best things about Vancouver is the weather. It's been sunny all the time since I got here. I'm now sitting at a Starbucks Coffee Shop near Kitsilano Beach to write you this postcard. The beach is a great place to relax and people watch. From my view through the window, I can see lots of people lying on the beach enjoying the sunshine. People really love to soak up the sun on the beach here. But it's not for me though.

Guess what? I just happened to find a special T-Shirt for you when I was shopping at Robson Street in downtown yesterday. Why is it so special? It is because it has "Mrs. Pitt" on it. It'll be the coolest gift to buy for a Brad Pitt fan like you, isn't it? I'm sure that you're going to love it!

I'll continue my journey with a group tour to the Canadian Rocky Mountains tomorrow morning. I feel very excited. I'll send you another postcard with the picture of the majestic scenery of the Rockies from the most spectacular mountains in North America.

Bye for now!

Zoe

Greetings from Singapore

Dear Stephanie,

I'm in Singapore now. I think the food is the best thing here. I've been eating a lot of different foods. The only bad thing is it's very hot here. People speak English and Chinese here, so it's very convenient to get around. I went to Sentosa Island this morning to visit the famous Underwater World. It's a wonderful place where people can watch more than 2,500 kinds of sea animals. It was a little bit scary when I walked through the long tunnel and looked at sharks swimming around.

I bought you a souvenir from Singapore, but I won't tell you what it is until you see it, because I want to give you a surprise.

I'm leaving Singapore tomorrow for Malaysia. After Malaysia I'll continue my trip to Thailand. I hope I'll have a wonderful time there in Malaysia and Thailand as well as in Singapore.

Seeya soon!

Zoe

Chinese Translation

來自溫哥華的問候

親愛的Kate，

來自溫哥華的問候。

我現在正在加拿大度假，我在此地有一個很美好的假期。

溫哥華是我到過最好的一個地方。

我已經參觀過了溫哥華的花園及公園。也用我的數位相機照了許多相片。昨天我租了腳踏車，騎著它穿越了史丹利公園，非常有趣。

溫哥華最好的一件事是她的天氣。從我到達此地一直到現在，一直都是陽光普照的好天氣。我現在正坐在一間位於Kitsilano海灘附近的星巴克咖啡店給妳寫這張明信片。這個海灘是一個可以放鬆自我以及看著人來人往的好地方。朝窗外望去，我可以看見好多人躺在海灘上享受陽光，這裡的人很喜歡在海灘上吸收陽光，而我對此則是敬謝不敏。

你知道嗎？昨天我在市中心的羅伯森街血拚時，碰巧幫妳找到一件很特殊的T恤，爲何它很特別呢？那是因爲這件T恤上面印有「彼特太太」的字樣，對於像妳這樣一個布萊德彼特迷，這將是最好不過的禮物了。我相信妳一定會愛死它的！

明兒一早，我將繼續我的旅程，跟隨旅遊團到加拿大落磯山脈觀光，我感到非常興奮。等我到了北美最壯觀的山脈後，我會再寄張有著落磯山脈雄偉照片的風景明信片給妳。

再見！

Zoe

來自新加坡的問候

親愛的Stephanie，

我現在人在新加坡，我認爲新加坡最好的事是當地的食物，我已經品嚐了各式各樣的美味了。最不好的事是這裡實在太熱了。這裡的人可說英文與中文，所以在此旅遊是很方便的。我今早參觀了聖淘沙島有名的海底世界，人們在這個很棒的地方可以看到2,500種以上的海洋動物。但是當我走在長長的隧道中看著鯊魚游來游去時，還眞的有點驚慌。我在新加坡買了一樣紀念品給妳，但在妳拿到它之前，我會先保密，因為我要給妳一個驚喜。

明天，我將離開新加坡到馬來西亞。馬來西亞之後，我將繼續我的行程到泰國，我希望在馬來西亞及泰國時也會有一個像在新加坡一樣愉快的旅程。

再見了！

Zoe

Words & Phrases

Vancouver	n.	溫哥華
digital camera	ph.	數位相機
rent	v.	租
Stanley Park	n.	溫哥華史丹利公園
Starbucks Coffee Shop	n.	星巴克咖啡店
Kitsilano Beach	ph.	溫哥華的一個海灘
people watch	ph.	看人來人往
soak up	ph.	吸收
"Mrs. Pitt"	n.	彼特太太
Brad Pitt	n.	布萊德彼特（美國影星）
fan	n.	影迷；歌迷
journey	n.	旅行
Canadian Rocky Mountains	ph.	加拿大落磯山脈
majestic	adj.	雄偉的
scenery	n.	風景

spectacular	adj.	壯觀的
North America	ph.	北美洲
Singapore	n.	新加坡
convenient	adj.	方便的
Sentosa Island	ph.	聖陶沙島
scary	adj.	引起驚慌的
tunnel	n.	隧道
souvenir	n.	紀念品
seeya		口語的再見

Write your best friend a post card from outside of the country.

Write your best friend a post card from outside of the country.

Answers will vary.

Unit 5

Postcards (2)

Greetings from Hawaii

Hi! Bear,

A-lo-ha from Hawaii!

I love Hawaii! I think it is a rich and rewarding destination to visit. And I found so many different kinds of things to do here. There are so many good things about Hawaii. But I felt sad when I visited Pear Harbor, because of its past history.

All the good things about Hawaii are: the weather is great, the food is delicious, and the white sand beaches are gorgeous. Besides, the people are friendly and kind. There are lots of Japanese. I said "Konichiwa" instead of aloha to them. It's very interesting. I ate a lot of pineapple. As you know, I really love pineapples.

Hey, Mr. Cool. Can you believe I surfed the world's biggest waves at the famous beach - Waikiki Beach yesterday? Isn't it cool? If you had been here, I would have asked you to draw me a cool surfing picture.

I also took an excursion to visit the Polynesian Cultural Center to see the authentic island arts, crafts, history, music, and a Polynesian show featuring more than 100 performers last night...

I guess I've given you all the details about my trip.

Ok! I've got to go for dinner now. It's a splendid luau feast for tonight.

Stay cool!

Zoe

Greetings from Australia

Hello! Teddy,

What's up, man?

Australia is beautiful. The best things here are the different kinds of animals. They looked so funny. I have visited the Kangaroo Island. It's a wildlife paradise and home to a breeding colony of sea lions as well as seals, kangaroos, koalas, platypus, wallabies, echidnas, and countless of bird species. I took a lot of pictures of them. I love koalas the best because they look so cute.

I spent the last week touring New Zealand. The food was great. They cooked food in hot rocks sometimes. I had a lot of kiwis. They tasted sweet. Also, I've taken some very nice walks in the beautiful woods.

I'm going to have a wonderful self drive holiday with my friends tomorrow. We're going to spend 5 days driving from Sydney to Melbourne via the coast. The total of the driving hours will be 15 hours for 1,167km (725 miles). I hope I can see some kangaroos run wild somewhere on my trip.

Bye!

P.S. Could you draw me some nice pictures of koalas when I show you the pictures I took for them here? Thanks, anyway!

Zoe

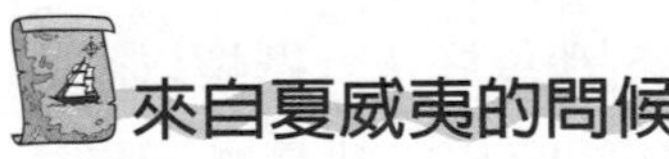

嗨！Bear，

A-lo-ha！（夏威夷語：表示歡迎、你好的打招呼語）

我好喜愛夏威夷喔！我認爲到夏威夷來參觀是很有意義且很值得的。這裡的好，說都說不完，但是當我參觀珍珠港時卻有些感傷哩。

這裡的好有：天氣晴朗、食物美味、美麗的白沙海灘眞是正點。這兒的人們都非常和善親切。這裡有好多的日本人，我和他們打招呼時都用日語的 "Konichiwa"（日安）代替Aloha，眞是有趣。我吃了好多的鳳梨，你知道的，我最喜歡吃鳳梨了！

對了！酷先生。你相信嗎？我昨天竟然在最有名的Waikiki海邊衝世上最大的浪耶？好酷喔！如果那時你也在場的話，我會請你幫我畫一張衝浪時的酷樣兒了！

還有，我昨晚參加了一個遊覽團到玻里尼西亞文化中心，看到了眞正的小島藝術、手藝、歷史、音樂，以及一場玻里尼西亞秀，演出者超過100個人……。

我想我已經把我這次的旅程全部分享給你了。

好了！我現在要準備去晚餐了。今晚的晚餐將是一頓棒極了且帶餘興節目的烤豬野宴喲。

Zoe

 來自澳洲的問候

嗨！Teddy，

怎麼樣了？

澳洲實在美極了。澳洲最好的事是動物了。牠們怎麼看怎麼好玩。我已經參觀過袋鼠島了。袋鼠島不但是個野生生物的天堂，也是個繁殖海獅、海豹、袋鼠、無尾熊、鴨嘴獸、沙袋鼠、針鼴蝟以及數不盡禽鳥種類的聚集地。我幫牠們拍了無數的照片。我最喜愛無尾熊，因爲牠們看起來最可愛。

我在上星期也拜訪了紐西蘭。那裡的食物很美味。有時紐西蘭的人也把食物放置於熱燙的石頭上煮食。我吃了許多的奇異果。這兒的奇異果吃起來很甜。此外，我也在此地漂亮的森林裡散散步。

明天，我將與我的朋友們展開自己駕車旅行的假期。我們將花5天的時間，從雪梨經由海岸線開往墨爾本。眞正的開車時間大約15個小時，開1,167公里（約725英哩）。

希望在我的旅途中可以看見到處亂跑的袋鼠。

再見了！

P.S.下次當我給你看我的旅遊照時，可不可以順便幫我畫幾張無尾熊的畫？謝了！

Zoe

Words & Phrases

a-lo-ha	ph.	夏威夷語：表示歡迎、你好的打招呼
Hawaii	n.	夏威夷
rewarding	n.	值得
destination	n.	目的地
Pear Harbor	ph.	珍珠港
white sand beach	ph.	白沙海灘
gorgeous	adj.	極好的
instead of	ph.	代替
pineapple	n.	鳳梨
surf	v.	衝浪
Waikiki Beach	ph.	夏威夷的一個海灘

Polynesian Cultural Center	ph.	玻里尼西亞文化中心
authentic	adj.	眞正的
craft	n.	手工藝
feature	v.	以…爲特色
performer	n.	表演者
splendid	adj.	傑出的
luau	n.	帶餘興節目的烤豬野宴
feast	n.	宴席
kangaroo	n.	袋鼠
wildlife	n.	野生動物
breeding	n.	繁殖
colony	n.	殖民地
sea lion	ph.	海獅
seal	n.	海豹
koala	n.	無尾熊
platypus	n.	鴨嘴獸
wallaby	n.	沙袋鼠
echidna	n.	針鼴蝟
countless	adj.	數不盡
species	n.	種類
kiwi	n.	奇異果
woods	n.	森林
self drive	ph.	自己駕車
Sydney	n.	雪梨
Melbourne	n.	墨爾本
coast	n.	海岸

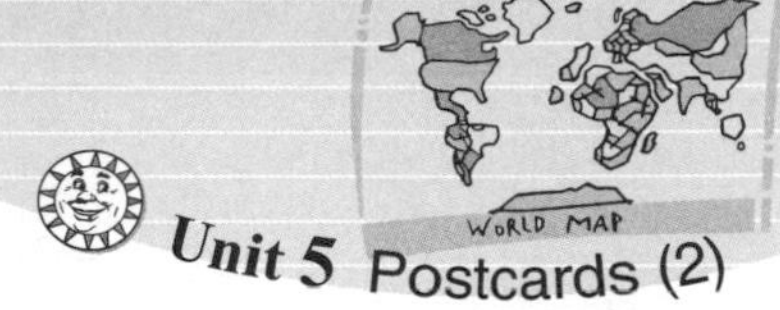

run wild ph. 失去控制的亂跑

1. What do you want to see and do if you get a chance to visit Hawaii?

2. Can you name some of Australia's animals?

1. What do you want to see and do if you get a chance to visit Hawaii?

Answers will vary.

2. Can you name some of Australia's animals?

There are sea lions as well as seals, kangaroos, koalas, platypus, wallabies, echidnas, and countless of bird species.

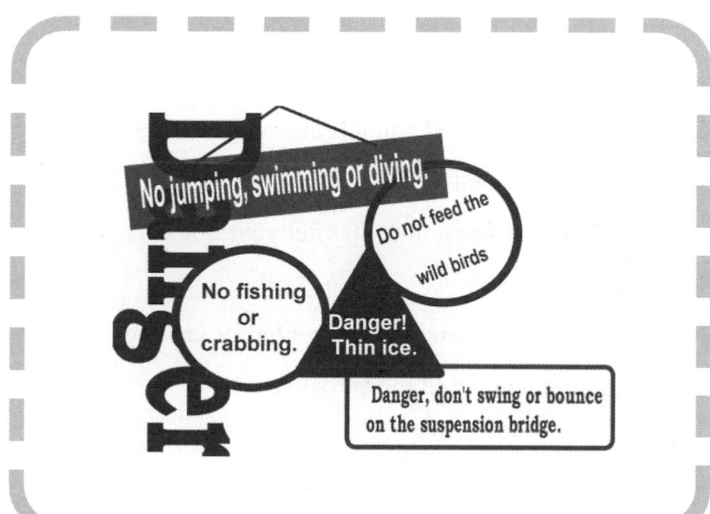
Danger
No jumping, swimming or diving.
Do not feed the wild birds
No fishing or crabbing.
Danger! Thin ice.
Danger, don't swing or bounce on the suspension bridge.

Unit 6

Signs In The Public Places

1. No jumping, swimming or diving.

2. No fishing or crabbing.

3. No skateboarding, no rollerblading, no bicycling on sidewalk.

4. Do not feed the wild birds.

5. Notice!

   No feeding allowed. Wild animals are not pets. Respect their wildness.

6. Dogs prohibited except on leash.

7. Attention dog guardians, pick up after your dogs. Thank-you.

8. Dog waste bag.

   Dog owners, please remove the problem your dog leaves behind. Close bag with a knot and put in the garbage.

9. Caution!

   Bears in area.

   Do not approach. Do not feed.

10. Warning!

    All users of Canyon Park urged to use extreme caution. The Canyon and river are extreme dangerous. Please stay on the trails and within the fenced areas. Thank-you.

11. Warning!

    Extreme Danger!

    Do not go beyond this fence. Area is extremely hazardous. And have claimed many lives. Please stay on the trails and within the fenced areas.

12. Steep cliffs!

    Stay on the trails.

13. Danger! Thin ice.

14. Caution!

Bridge is slippery when wet.

15. Danger, don't swing or bounce on the suspension bridge.

16. Pedestrian traffic only!

    All other traffic and unauthorized vehicles are prohibited.

17. Ferry traffic must line up in parking lane.

18. Please remain in gondola. You are only 1/3 of the way up.

19. Mountain bike zone. Bikers exit here, do not ride bikes in building.

20. Caution!

    Do not get on or off during boat lockage.

21. Warning!

    This park is a wilderness area.

    Weather and visibility can deteriorate:

    - Wear protective clothing and footwear.
    - Do not hike alone.
    - Register at the information kiosk.
    - Allow adequate time to return safely before dark.

    If lost, stay clam and remain in one place until help arrives.

22. Hiking Advisory!

    Sunset is at 8 pm.

    Allow enough time to return safely before dark.

23. Warning!

    Car thieves work here.

    Lock your vehicle night and day.

    Don't leave valuable in your vehicle.

    Use an anti-thief device.

24. Warning!

Please watch your children. No lifeguard on duty.

25. No lifeguard on duty.

    Swim at own risk.

    Children must be accompanied by an adult.

26. Tow away zone!

    Unauthorized vehicles will be towed at owners' expense.

Chinese Translation

標示

1. 禁止跳水、游泳或是潛水。
2. 禁止釣魚或是抓螃蟹。
3. 禁止在人行道上踩滑板、滑直排輪或騎腳踏車。
4. 禁止餵食野生鳥類。
5. 請注意！

   禁止餵食野生動物。野生動物並非寵物。請尊重牠們的野生性。

   (意指不要因爲餵食野生動物，而使其喪失原始的覓食能力)
6. 禁止帶狗進入，除非綁上狗鏈條。
7. 請狗主人注意！當您的愛犬「ㄅㄅ」後請收拾好。謝謝您的合作。
8. 免費狗狗排泄物袋。

   狗主人，請自行解決您的愛犬所留下的問題。使用後，請將袋子綁個結，再將它丟到垃圾桶。
9. 小心！

   有熊在此地出沒。

請勿靠近牠們。請勿餵食。

10. 警告！

強烈要求在峽谷公園的遊客要特別小心。公園內的峽谷以及河流是極端危險的。請走在柵欄內的人行小道上。謝謝您的合作。

11. 警告！

極危險！

禁止超過柵欄，此處是極危險的區域，已有無數人在此喪生！請走在柵欄內的人行小道上。

12. 懸崖陡坡！

請走在人行小道上。

13. 危險！薄冰。

14. 小心！

濕橋腳滑。

15. 危險！禁止在吊橋上搖晃或是彈跳。

16. 行人走道！

所有其他的交通工具或是未被授權的車輛禁止進入。

17. 搭乘渡輪的車輛必須在上渡輪的停車線道上排隊。

18. 請留在纜車內，不要外出。你目前的位置是在到達目的地的三分之一處而已。

19. 山上騎腳踏車區。腳踏車騎士請在此出站，並請不要在此建築物內騎車。

20. 小心！

當水閘升降時，不要上下船。

21. 警告！

此公園爲荒野保護區。

氣候與能見度都有可能隨時惡化。

—穿著有保護性的衣物與鞋類。

—勿獨自步行於保護區內。

—請至詢問處登記。

—預留足夠的時間於天黑前安全返回。

如果迷路了，保持冷靜並停留於定點，直到救援到達。

22. 徒步旅行的忠告！

太陽將於8點下山。

在天黑前請預留足夠的時間平安返回。

23. 警告！

偷車賊在此活動。

不管白天或晚上，請將您的車上鎖。

請勿把貴重物品留在車上。

使用防盜器。

24. 警告！

請注意看好自己的小孩，此處沒有值班的救生員。

25. 此處沒有值班的救生員。

自己要承擔游泳的風險。

小孩子們要有大人陪同。

26. 違規停車拖吊區！

違規停車將會被拖吊，拖吊費用由車主自行負擔。

Words & Phrases

skateboarding	n.	踩滑板
rollerblading	n.	滑直排輪

sidewalk	n.	人行道
pet	n.	寵物
respect	v.	尊重
wildness	n.	野蠻；原始
prohibit	v.	禁止
on leash	ph.	上鏈條
dog guardian	ph.	狗主人
knot	v.	把…打結
caution	n.	小心
approach	v.	接近
canyon	n.	峽谷
urge	v.	力勸
extreme	adj.	極端的
fenced area	ph.	有柵欄區
beyond	prep.	越出
hazardous	adj.	有危險的
steep	adj.	陡峭的
cliff	n.	懸崖
trail	n.	荒野中踏成的小道
slippery	adj.	滑的
swing	v.	搖盪
bounce	v.	跳躍
suspension bridge	ph.	吊橋
pedestrian	n.	行人
unauthorized vehicle	ph.	未授權的車輛
gondola	n.	空中纜車

lockage	n.	水閘升降
visibility	n.	能見度
deteriorate	v.	惡化
footwear	n.	鞋類
adequate	adj.	足夠的
advisory	adj.	顧問的
tow	v.	拖

1. Which of the following signs will be found at the beaches or swimming pools?

(1) No fishing or crabbing.

(2) No jumping, swimming or diving.

(3) No feeding allowed. Wild animals are not pets. Respect their wildness.

(4) Dogs prohibited except on leash.

(5) Attention dog guardians, pick up after your dogs. Thank-you.

(6) Do not feed the wild birds.

(7) Caution!

Bears in area.

Do not approach. Do not feed.

(8) Warning!

Please watch your children. No lifeguard on duty.

(9) No lifeguard on duty.

Swim at own risk.

Children must be accompanied by an adult.

(10) Tow away zone!

Unauthorized vehicles will be towed at owners' expense.

(11) Steep cliffs!

2. Which of the following signs will be found at a National Park?

(1) No jumping, swimming or diving.

(2) Notice!

No feeding allowed. Wild animals are not pets. Respect their wildness.

(3) Dogs prohibited except on leash.

(4) Attention dog guardians, pick up after your dogs. Thank-you.

(5) Caution!

Bears in area.

Do not approach. Do not feed.

(6) Warning!

All users of Canyon Park urged to use extreme caution. The Canyon and river are extreme dangerous. Please stay on the trails and within the fenced areas. Thank-you.

(7) Steep cliffs!

Stay on the trails.

(8) Danger! Thin ice.

(9) Danger, don't swing or bounce on the suspension bridge.

(10) Pedestrian traffic only!

All other traffic and unauthorized vehicles are prohibited.

(11) Ferry traffic must line up in parking lane.

(12) Caution!

Do not get on or off during boat lockage.

(13) Warning!

This park is a wilderness area.

Weather and visibility can deteriorate:

- Wear protective clothing and footwear.
- Do not hike alone.
- Register at the information kiosk.
- Allow adequate time to return safely before dark.

If lost, stay clam and remain in one place until help arrives.

(14) Hiking Advisory!

Sunset is at 8 pm.

Allow enough time to return safely before dark.

(15) Warning!

Please watch your children. No lifeguard on duty.

(16) Tow away zone!

Unauthorized vehicles will be towed at owners' expense.

1. Which of the following signs will be found at the beaches or swimming pools?

(1) No fishing or crabbing.

(2) No jumping, swimming or diving.

(8) Warning!

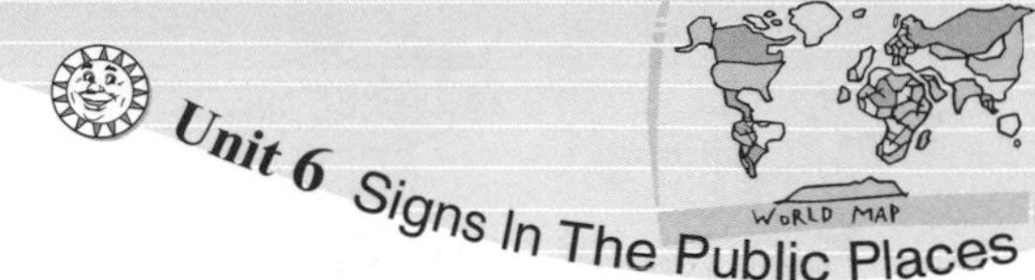

Please watch your children. No lifeguard on duty.

(9) No lifeguard on duty.

Swim at own risk.

Children must be accompanied by an adult.

2. *Which of the following signs will be found at a National Park?*

(2) Notice!

No feeding allowed. Wild animals are not pets. Respect their wildness.

(3) Dogs prohibited except on leash.

(4) Attention dog guardians, pick up after your dogs. Thank-you.

(5) Caution!

Bears in area.

Do not approach. Do not feed.

(6) Warning!

All users of Canyon Park urged to use extreme caution. The Canyon and river are extreme dangerous. Please stay on the trails and within the fenced areas. Thank-you.

(7) Steep cliffs!

Stay on the trails.

(9) Danger, don't swing or bounce on the suspension bridge.

(10) Pedestrian traffic only!

All other traffic and unauthorized vehicles are prohibited.

(13) Warning!

This park is a wilderness area.

Weather and visibility can deteriorate:

- Wear protective clothing and footwear.
- Do not hike alone.
- Register at the information kiosk.
- Allow adequate time to return safely before dark.

If lost, stay clam and remain in one place until help arrives.

(14) Hiking Advisory!

Sunset is at 8 pm.

Allow enough time to return safely before dark.

Unit 7

A Taste Of Europe (1)

Don't forget your digital camera!!

Day 1

London, England

Upon arrival in London, England, you are met at the airport and transferred to your luxurious 6 stars hotel. The rest of the day is yours after check-in. To meet your tour director and fellow travelers for a special welcome dinner at your hotel lobby about 6:30p.m.

Day 2

London, England

You'll receive a warm welcome from our professional London tour guide this morning. Morning sightseeing includes all the famous landmarks: Royal Albert Hall, Kensington Palace, the British Museums, Knightsbridge with Harrods, and Westminster Abbey. We'll also visit St. Paul's Cathedral and the changing of the Guard at Buckingham Palace. Optional excursions are available in the afternoon to the Tower of London (Big Ben), the University town of Oxford and the Windsor Castle. At night, why not just cruise on the River Thames?

Day 3

London—Calais, France—Belgium—Amsterdam, Holland

We'll depart London after breakfast. Drive through Kent to the white cliffs of Dover and then across the Channel to France. Travel through the Flanders region of Belgium to Amsterdam, Holland's 700-year-old capital. Visit Dam Square and explore the red-light district after dinner. Please keep in mind, no photos taken at the red-light district are allowed.

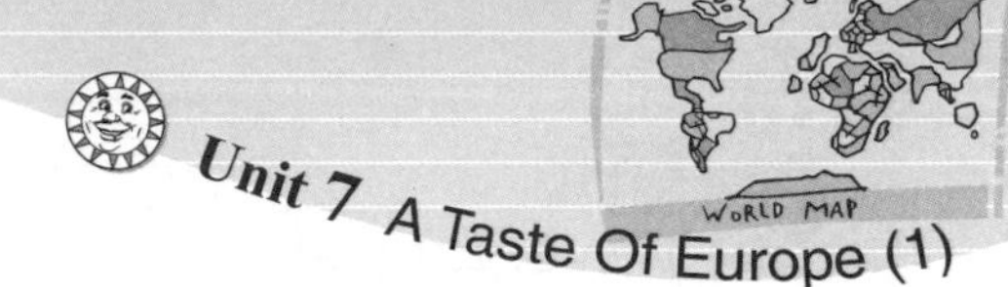

Day 4

Amsterdam, Holland—Rhineland, Germany

We'll have our morning sightseeing with a local expert to the Rijksmuseum, and take a Canal cruise to have a detailed look of the city. We also get a chance to visit a major diamond-cutting factory. After lunch, we'll drive to the German border via Arnhem and stop at Cologne to visit the awesome twin-spired Gothic Cathedral. After that, you'll enjoy a cruise on the romantic Rhine.

Day 5

Rhineland, Germany—Lucerne, Switzerland

A scenic day! You can take as many pictures as you can. A leisurely drive to the lush valleys and the Black Forest in the morning. On the way to Switzerland, we stop to admire the mighty thundering Rhine Falls and then continue driving to Lucerne.

Day 6

Lucerne, Switzerland—Liechtenstein—Innsbruck, Austria

Our first stop today is to take 360c cable car to the top of Mount Titlis for a marvelous bird's eye view. And then continue sightseeing tour to admire the Lion Monument and then a free time for shopping Swiss watches and chocolates. After that, we leave Switzerland to visit the pocket-sized principality of Liechtenstein and then take a short drive to Innsbruck, Austria.

Day 7

Innsbruck, Austria—Venice, Italy

This morning, the spectacular Brenner Pass will lead us through the barrier of the Tyrolean Alps to the water village—the magical Venice.

Day 8

Venice, Italy—Rome, Italy

In the morning, we will discover Venice, the fascination of this city built on water. Enjoy and savor this magnificent Byzantine city's unique sights and sounds on an included canal cruise to St. Mark's Square, viewing the Doges' Palace and Bridge of Sighs. Later, we head for the Apennine Mountains, a scenic drive through the vine-olive-clad Tuscan hills, home of the popular Chianti wines, which brings us to the Eternal City—Rome.

Chinese Translation

歐洲行——別忘了帶你的數位相機哦！

第1天

英國倫敦

抵達英國倫敦後，有人會在機場接您，即刻轉往您的豪華六星級飯店。辦完住房手續後，自由活動。下午6點30分時請團員在飯店大廳集合，跟隨領隊參加特別爲此團團員舉辦的歡迎晚宴。

第2天

英國倫敦

今早，您將接受我們倫敦專業的導遊熱烈歡迎，隨後的觀光行程包括所有著名地標：國會大廈、Kensington宮、大英博物館、Knightsbridge的全英最大的百貨公司Harrods、歷代英皇加冕所在地——西敏寺、聖保羅大教堂、白金漢宮前的衛兵交接儀式。下午可自由選擇參加各種短程旅行團，有：倫敦地標大笨鐘、牛津大學城，以及溫莎堡。晚上，何不搭船漫遊於泰晤士河？

第3天

英國倫敦—法國加來（法國北部海港）—比利時—荷蘭阿姆斯特丹

早餐後，我們將離開倫敦。開車越過英國肯特郡來到英法間的、有著白色懸崖峭壁的多佛海峽，穿越航道來到法國。通過比利時的法蘭德斯地區，來到荷蘭已有700年歷史的首都阿姆斯特丹。晚餐後，夜遊水霸廣場及紅燈區，請記住，在紅燈區是不准照相的。

第4天

荷蘭阿姆斯特丹—德國萊茵區

早上的觀光將由荷蘭當地導遊帶領大家參觀梵谷博物館。並乘船漫遊運河，仔細欣賞填海造地而成的水都。我們也有機會參觀一家鑽石切割工廠（阿姆斯特丹素有鑽石之都的美譽）。午餐後經由荷蘭的安恆市到德國邊界，我們將在德國的科倫稍做停留，去參觀以莊嚴宏偉、高聳入雲的雙尖塔著稱的哥德大教堂。之後，您將可以享受在羅曼蒂克的萊茵河畔漫遊的樂趣。

第5天

德國萊茵區—瑞士盧森市

今天將是沿途觀賞秀麗風景的一天。您今天可以盡情地照相。早上我們將安排參觀蒼翠繁茂的山谷，及德國西南部的著名度假勝地——黑森林地區。在前往瑞士盧森市的途中，我們將停留去欣賞澎湃洶湧、如雷貫耳的萊茵瀑布。

第6天

瑞士盧森市—列支敦斯登—奧地利英斯布魯克

今早的第一個景點將是（前往英格堡高地，自費）乘坐360度旋轉吊車登上（一萬尺高的）鐵力士大雪山，鳥瞰雪山風光。接著去參觀（由丹麥雕刻家湯華生在岩壁上雕刻的「垂死的獅子」）盧森之獅紀念碑，然後採購瑞士錶以及巧克力。之後，我們將離開瑞士前往參觀袖珍型的郵票小國——列支敦斯登公國。然後開段小路程來到奧地利的英斯布魯克。

第7天

奧地利英斯布魯克—義大利威尼斯

今早，壯觀的Brenner山道將帶領我們穿過（位於奧地利西部與義大利北部）提洛爾區居民居住的阿爾卑斯山脈屏障，來到迷人的水都——威尼斯。

第8天

義大利威尼斯—義大利羅馬

早上，我們將參訪「水都」威尼斯，它的魅力在於它是世上唯一被建立在水上的城市，到處可見水道縱橫，大小船隻穿梭往來。我們將搭乘水上巴士，享受及欣賞這個壯麗的東羅馬帝國的古城獨一無二的景觀及聲音，前往聖馬可廣場，參觀道濟斯宮以及嘆息橋。隨後，我們前往縱亙義大利半島的亞平寧山脈，一路上我們將穿越被橄欖藤蔓覆蓋，有著秀麗景觀的塔斯卡尼山，這裡也是吉安地酒的家鄉。最後我們將到達永恆之城——羅馬。

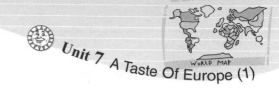

Words & Phrases

upon	prep.	在…之後立即
London	n.	倫敦
England	n.	英國
luxurious	adj.	豪華的
tour director	ph.	領隊
fellow travelers	ph.	團員
lobby	n.	飯店大廳
professional	adj.	專業的
tour guide	ph.	導遊
landmark	n.	地標
Royal Albert Hall	ph.	國會大廈
British Museum	ph.	大英博物館
Knightsbridge with Harrods	ph.	全英最大的百貨公司
Westminster Abbey	ph.	西敏寺
St. Paul's Cathedral	ph.	聖保羅大教堂
guard	n.	衛兵
Buckingham Palace	ph.	白金漢宮
optional	adj.	自由選擇的；隨意的
Tower of London (Big Ben)	ph.	大笨鐘
University town	ph.	大學城
Oxford	n.	牛津
Windsor Castle	ph.	溫莎堡

cruise	v.	搭船漫遊
River Thames	ph.	泰晤士河
France	n.	法國
Belgium	n.	比利時
Amsterdam	n.	阿姆斯特丹
Holland	n.	荷蘭
Kent	n.	肯特郡
Dover	n.	多佛海峽
Flanders	n.	比利時的法蘭德斯
Dam Square	ph.	水霸廣場
red-light district	ph.	紅燈區
Rhine	n.	萊茵河
Germany	n.	德國
Rijksmuseum.	n.	梵谷博物館
canal	n.	運河
detailed look	ph.	仔細欣賞
border	n.	邊界；國界
Arnhem	n.	荷蘭的安恆市
Cologne	n.	德國的科倫
awesome	adj.	莊嚴宏偉的
twin-spired	adj.	雙尖塔的
Gothic Cathedral	ph.	哥德大教堂
romantic	adj.	羅曼蒂克
Lucerne	n.	盧森市
Switzerland	n.	瑞士
scenic	adj.	秀麗的

leisurely	adj.	從容不迫的
lush	adj.	蒼翠繁茂的
valley	n.	山谷
Black Forest	ph.	黑森林
admire	v.	欣賞
mighty	adj.	強而有力的
thundering	adj.	如雷貫耳的
Rhine Falls	ph.	萊茵瀑布
Liechtenstein	n.	列支敦斯登
Innsbruck	n.	英斯布魯克
Austria	n.	奧地利
360c cable car	ph.	360度旋轉吊車
Mount Titlis	ph.	鐵力士大雪山
marvelous	adj.	令人驚嘆的
bird's eye view	ph.	鳥瞰
Lion Monument	ph.	盧森之獅紀念碑
pocket-sized	adj.	袖珍型的
principality	n.	公國
Venice	n.	威尼斯
Italy	n.	義大利
spectacular	adj.	壯觀的
pass	n.	山道
barrier	n.	屏障
Tyrolean	n.	提洛爾人
Alps	n.	阿爾卑斯山脈
magical	adj.	迷人的

Rome	n.	羅馬
Venice	n.	威尼斯
fascination	n.	有魅力的東西
savor	n.	氣味
magnificent	adj.	壯麗的
Byzantine	adj.	東羅馬帝國的
unique	adj.	獨一無二的
St. Mark's Square	ph.	聖馬可廣場
Doges' Palace	ph.	道濟斯宮
Bridge of Sighs	ph.	嘆息橋
Apennine	n.	亞平寧山脈
vine-olive-clad	ph.	被橄欖藤蔓覆蓋
Tuscan Mountain	n.	托斯卡尼山
Chianti	n.	吉安地酒
eternal	adj.	永恆的

1. Write an one- day tour in London.

2. What can you see in Venice?

1. Write an one-day tour in London.

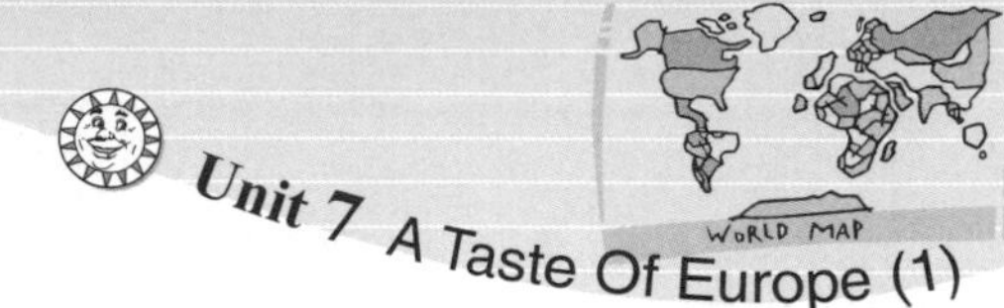

Answers will vary.

(Morning sightseeing includes all the famous landmarks: Royal Albert Hall, Kensington Palace, the British Museums, Knightsbridge with Harrods, and Westminster Abbey. We'll also visit St. Paul's Cathedral and the changing of the Guard at Buckingham Palace. Optional excursions are available in the afternoon to the Tower of London (Big Ben), the University town of Oxford and the Windsor Castle. At night, why not just cruise on the River Thames?)

2. What can you see in Venice?

(1) The fascination of this city was built on water

(2) Enjoy and savor this magnificent Byzantine city's unique sights and sounds

(3) St. Mark's Square

(4) Doges' Palace

(5) Bridge of Sighs

Unit 8

A Taste Of Europe (2)

Day 9

Rome, Italy

We'll have our morning sightseeing starts with a visit to the Vatican Museums and Sistine Chapel, world famous for Michelangelo's ceiling painting. Continue to monumental St. Peter's Square and finally visit the Colosseum.

Day 10

Rome, Italy—Florence, Italy

After breakfast, we drive back north through Tuscany to Florence, cradle of the Renaissance. This city is one of the liveliest and most creative in Europe with some of the world's greatest works of art and magnificent buildings. We will see the Cathedral, Giotto's Bell Tower, the marble Baptistery, and Signoria Square.

Day 11

Florence, Italy—Monaco—Nice, France

Today we head for Galileo's birthplace - Pisa to see the famous amazing Leaning Tower. Then we cross the border past the fashionable resorts of the French Riviera to the principality of Monaco to see the celebrated Monte Carlo casino. Before arriving in Nice, we will visit one of the perfume factories in the area. Then go sightseeing to the sophisticated holiday resort of Nice.

Day 12

Nice, France—Lyon, France

This morning is the time to enjoy the scenic landscapes. We'll drive through

the beautiful countryside of Van Gogh's beloved Provence to Avignon, an important spiritual center in the Middle Ages with its Palace of the Popes. After lunch we'll continue our way to Lyon, the second-largest city in the country.

Day 13

Lyon, France—Paris, France

On our way to Paris, the route takes us into Burgundy wine country where the road signs read like the wine list of an expensive restaurant. Then enjoy a scenic drive through the Forest of Fontainebleau to the vibrant and romantic city—Paris. After arriving in Paris, then followed by the visit of Louvre Museum. After dinner, optional Seine River cruise or a night tour is strongly recommended.

Day 14

Paris, France

Full day guided city tour visit all the most famous sights of the city including Champs Elysees, Arc de Triomphe, Concorde, and the Eiffel Tower in the morning. Optional trip to Versailles, and Notre Dame Cathedral is also available in the afternoon.

The rest of the time is at leisure to explore the world's most elegant city—Paris, shop for perfume and fancy fashion accessories, stroll through the magnificent park, or just relax.

Day 15

Paris, France—Sweet Home

All good things have to come to an end. After lunch, you can enjoy last

minute sightings of the city on our way to the airport. Bid farewell to your new friends on your return flight to your sweet home. We believe that you enjoyed your Europe trip!

Chinese Translation

第9天

義大利羅馬

早上的觀光行程將安排參觀梵諦岡宮博物館，和以米開蘭基羅的天花板圓頂畫而馳名世界的羅馬教宗西克斯圖斯的小禮拜堂。繼續到聖彼得紀念廣場，最後參觀古羅馬圓形大競技場。

第10天

義大利羅馬—義大利佛羅倫斯

早餐後，我們向北往回走穿越托斯卡尼來到義大利中部的城市——佛羅倫斯，也是文藝復興的搖籃，這個城市是歐洲最活潑生動及最有創造力的城市之一，她擁有世上最偉大的藝術品及壯麗宏偉的建築物。我們也將參觀（世界第三大教堂）「聖母之花大教堂」、Giotto的鐘塔、大理石的浸禮池，及（有露天雕塑博物館之稱的）聖日里亞廣場。

第11天

義大利佛羅倫斯—摩納哥—法國尼斯

今天我們將啓程前往（著名物理學家）伽利略的出生地——比薩，參觀世界馳名、被譽爲世界奇觀的比薩斜塔。之後，我們越過義、法邊界途經時尚的休閒度假勝地——法國的里維耶拉，來到摩納哥公國參觀著的蒙地卡羅賭場。到達尼斯之前，我們將參觀一間香水製造工

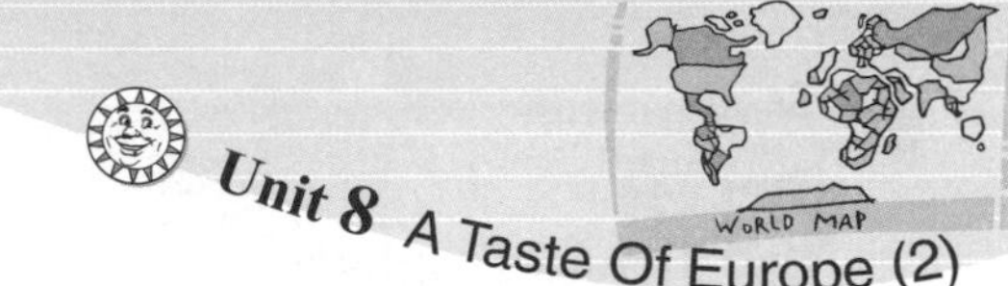

廠。之後前往著名的精緻度假勝地——尼斯。

第12天

法國尼斯—法國里昂

今早將可以享受秀麗的鄉間風景，因為我們將開車經過梵谷最喜愛的美麗鄉間——普羅旺斯，來到亞維農——在中古世紀時因教皇宮殿而成為重要的宗教中心。午餐之後將繼續我們的行程到法國的第二大城里昂。

第13天

法國里昂—法國巴黎

在我們去巴黎的路上，將會進入Burgundy勃艮地——葡萄酒之鄉，那裡的路標看起來像是高級餐廳的酒單。之後欣賞著車窗外綺麗的風景，穿越楓丹白露森林來到充滿生氣的浪漫花都——巴黎。到達巴黎之後，隨即參觀世界最大的博物館——羅浮宮。晚餐後，特別推薦自費遊塞納河，或是夜遊巴黎。

第14天

法國巴黎自由行

全天的市區觀光，早上將有當地導遊帶領我們參觀最有名的景點包括香榭大道、凱旋門、協和廣場及艾菲爾鐵塔。下午可自由選擇前往凡爾賽宮或是聖母院。

剩餘的時間是自由探索世上最優雅的城市——巴黎，可血拚香水、時髦花俏的飾品，也可以悠閒地散步在壯麗的公園中，或只是放鬆地休息。

第15天

回家

美好的事物終究也有結束的時候，午餐後在去機場的路上，您可以對巴黎做最後的巡禮。在飛往甜蜜家園的旅途中向您的新朋友道別。我們相信您有一個愉快難忘的旅程。

Words & Phrases

Vatican Museums	ph.	梵諦岡宮博物館
Sistine Chapel	ph.	教宗西克斯圖斯的小禮拜堂
Michelangelo	n.	米開蘭基羅
ceiling painting	ph.	天花板圓頂畫
monumental	adj.	紀念性的
St. Peter's Square	ph.	聖彼得紀念廣場
Colosseum	n.	羅馬圓形大競技場
Florence	n.	佛羅倫斯
Tuscany	n.	托斯卡尼
cradle	n.	搖籃
renaissance	n.	文藝復興
liveliest	adj.	最活潑的
creative	adj.	最有創造力的
magnificent	adj.	壯麗宏偉的
marble	n.	大理石
baptistery	n.	浸禮池
Signoria Square	ph.	聖日里亞廣場
Monaco	n.	摩納哥
Nice	n.	尼斯

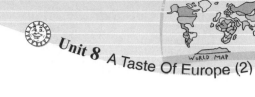

Galileo	n.	伽利略
birthplace	n.	出生地
Pisa	n.	比薩
leaning tower	ph.	斜塔
fashionable	adj.	時髦的；時尚的
resort	n.	休閒度假勝地
Riviera	n.	里維耶拉
Monte Carlo casino	ph.	蒙地卡羅賭場
perfume	n	香水
sophisticated	adj.	精緻的；老於世故的
Lyon	n.	里昂
landscape	n.	陸上的風景
Van Gogh	n.	梵谷
beloved	adj.	最喜愛的
Provence	n.	普羅旺斯
Avignon	n.	亞維農
spiritual	adj.	心靈上的
Middle Ages	ph.	中古世紀
Pope	n.	羅馬教皇
Paris	n.	巴黎
Burgundy	n.	勃艮地
wine	n.	葡萄酒
Fontainebleau	n	楓丹白露
vibrant	adj.	充滿生氣的
Louvre Museum	ph.	羅浮宮
Seine River	ph.	塞納河

Champs Elysees	ph.	香榭大道
Arc de Triomphe	ph.	凱旋門
Concorde	n.	協和廣場
Eiffel Tower	ph.	艾菲爾鐵塔
Versailles	n.	凡爾賽宮
Notre Dame Cathedral	ph.	聖母院
elegant	adj.	優雅的
fancy	adj.	花俏的
accessory	n.	飾品
stroll	v.	散步；溜達
bid	v.	向…表示
farewell	n.	告別

1. How many countries we visited in unit 7 and unit 8?

2. What can you see in France?

1. How many countries we visited in unit 7 and unit 8?

(1) England

(2) France

(3) Belgium

(4) Holland

(5) Germany

(6) Switzerland

(7) Liechtenstein

(8) Austria

(9) Italy

(10) Monaco

2. What can you see in Paris?

(1) Louvre Museum

(2) Seine River

(3) Champs Elysees

(4) Arc de Triomphe

(5) Concorde

(6) Eiffel Tower

(7) Versailles

(8) Notre Dame Cathedral

(9) Disneyland

Unit 9

Tips On Staying Safe In Foreign Countries

1. Don't open your wallet or count your cash in front of people.
2. Don't display money, jewelry or other valuable items in public.
3. Don't carry a lot of money with you. Carry only small amounts of cash on you. Almost every store takes credit cards, or traveler's checks.
4. Don't use the ATM bank machine in a lonely spot at night.
5. Always get a receipt and make sure that you have been charged for the correct amount.
6. Don't fall asleep in a public place. It is very dangerous to do so.
7. Don't let people know you are a stranger at somewhere. Be discreet when looking at map.
8. When go to a club or a bar, go with friends, don't go along.
9. Don't let people who you don't know buy you a drink or give you food. It could be drugged.
10. Drugs are common in some clubs and bars, so it is very important to be cautious.
11. If you plan to drink alcohol when going out, it is very important to arrange a way to get home in advance. Never drink and drive.
12. Do not let strangers to give you a ride home or take you to some other places.
13. Never hitchhike.
14. Always face oncoming traffic when walking.
15. Go in pairs everywhere with a friend, especially at night. Always take a friend to go with you.
16. Don't go to places where have the highest crime rates.
17. Carry a bag over your shoulder but not around your neck.
18. Always watch your belongings. Don't let your belongings unattended.

19. Lock car doors while driving and at all times.
20. Be sure to lock your car when you must leave the car, and keep your belongings in the trunk.
21. Don't drive at night when driving in an unfamiliar area.
22. If someone is bothering you on the street, just say "go away" or just walk away and go into a nearest store, a restaurant, or an business office to ask for help.
23. Stay at a safe distance away from someone who asks you for directions or some other kinds of help.
24. Keep a list of emergency telephone numbers with you all the times.
25. Always let someone you trust know where you are going and when you will be back.
26. Never leave luggage unattended in the airports.
27. Always keep your hotel doors locked.
28. Meet visitors you don't know in the lobby, and don't let them go to your room.
29. Don't leave valuables in the hotel room when you're out. You can use the hotel safe.
30. If traveling overnight on a train, lock the compartment, or takes turn sleeping if you have a traveling companion.

Chinese Translation

國外旅遊的安全告誡

1. 不要在人們面前打開錢包或是數錢。
2. 不要在公共場所顯露自己的金錢、珠寶或是其他貴重物品。
3. 不要隨身攜帶大量金錢，攜帶小額現金即可，因爲大部分的商店都接受信用卡或是旅行支票。
4. 在夜間，不要到偏僻的地方使用自動提款機。
5. 買東西時，記得向商家要收據，並確定金額是正確的。
6. 不要在公共場所睡著，這樣是很危險的。
7. 看地圖時要小心謹慎，不要引起注意，避免讓別人知道你對本地不熟悉。
8. 不要單獨前往夜總會或是酒吧，記得要跟朋友結伴同行。
9. 不要吃陌生人幫你買的飲料或食物，它們有可能被下藥。
10. 毒品在某些夜總會或是酒吧是很常見的，所以要非常小心。
11. 如果你計畫出外將會喝酒的話，事先安排好回家的方式是很重要的，千萬不要酒後駕車。
12. 不要讓陌生人開車送你回家或是到其他地方。
13. 絕對不要搭便車。
14. 走路時，要面對著迎面而來的車輛。
15. 外出時，一定要找個朋友做伴，尤其是在晚上。
16. 不要到有高犯罪率的地方。
17. 背袋子時可以斜背，但不要掛在脖子上。

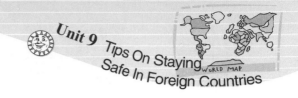

18. 隨時注意自己的隨身物品，不要讓它們離開視線。
19. 開車時一定要隨時鎖上車門。
20. 下車時記得鎖上車門，並把所有的物品、行李鎖到後行李箱。
21. 夜間時刻，最好不要在不熟悉的地方開車。
22. 如果路上有人騷擾你，直接叫他「走開」，或是遠離他，走到附近的商店、餐廳或是公司行號請求協助。
23. 如果有人向你問路或是請求幫忙之類的事，要跟那個人保持安全的距離。
24. 隨身攜帶緊急聯絡電話簿。
25. 隨時讓你信任的人知道你的去向以及回來的時間。
26. 在機場時不要讓你的行李離開視線。
27. 住旅館時，門要隨時上鎖。
28. 對於不認識的訪客，請到大廳會面，不要請他們到房間。
29. 外出時不要把貴重的物品留在飯店房內，可以使用飯店的保險箱。
30. 坐火車過夜旅行時，一定要把房間上鎖，如果有旅伴的話，可以輪流睡。

Words & Phrases

foreign countries	ph.	國外
wallet	n.	皮夾子
display	v.	顯露
valuable	adj.	貴重的
in public	ph.	公開地；當眾
ATM	n.	自動提款機

receipt	n.	收據
discreet	adj.	謹慎的
drugged	v.	被下藥
hitchhike	v.	搭便車
oncoming traffic	ph.	迎面而來的車輛
crime	n.	罪
emergency	n.	緊急情況
safe	n.	保險箱
compartment	n.	隔間
take turn	ph.	輪流
companion	n.	同伴
unfamiliar	adj.	不熟悉的

1. What are tips on protecting your property in a foreign country?

2. What are tips to ensure your personal safety in a foreign country?

1. What are tips on protecting your property in a foreign country?

(1) Don't open your wallet or count your cash in front of people.

(2) Don't display money, jewelry or other valuable items in public.

(3) Don't carry a lot of money with you. Carry only small amounts of cash

on you. Almost every store takes credit cards, or traveler's checks.

(4) Don't use the ATM bank machine in a lonely spot at night.

(5) Always get a receipt and make sure that you have been charged for the correct amount.

(6) Carry a bag over your shoulder but not around your neck.

(7) Always watch your belongings. Don't let your belongings unattended.

(8) Be sure to lock your car when you must leave the car, and keep your belongings in the trunk.

(9) Never leave luggage unattended in the airports.

(10) Don't leave valuables in the hotel room when you're out. You can use the hotel safe.

2. What are tips to ensure your personal safety in a foreign country?

(1) Don't fall asleep in a public place. It is very dangerous to do so.

(2) Don't let people know you are a stranger at somewhere. Be discreet when looking at map.

(3) When go to a club or a bar, go with friends, don't go along.

(4) Don't let people who you don't know buy you a drink or give you food. It could be drugged.

(5) Drugs are common in some clubs and bars, so it is very importment to be cautious.

(6) If you plan to drink alcohol when going out, it is very important to arrange a way to get home in advance. Never drink and drive.

(7) Do not let strangers to give you a ride home or take you to some other places.

(8) Never hitchhike.

(9) Always face oncoming traffic when walking.

(10) Go in pairs everywhere with a friend, especially at night. Always take a friend to go with you.

(11) Don't go to places where have the highest crime rates.

(12) Lock car doors while driving and at all times.

(13) Don't drive at night when driving in an unfamiliar area.

(14) If someone is bothering you on the street, just say "go away" or just walk away and go into a nearest store, a restaurant or an business office to ask for help.

(15) Stay at a safe distance away from someone who asks you for directions or some other kinds of help.

(16) Keep a list of emergency telephone numbers with you all the times.

(17) Always let someone you trust know where you are going and when you will be back.

(18) Always keep your hotel doors locked.

(19) Meet visitors you don't know in the lobby, and don't let them go to your room.

(20) If traveling overnight on a train, lock the compartment, or takes turn sleeping if you have a traveling companion.

Unit 10

People Sharing Their Trips

Melody's Asia trip

Hi! I'm Melody. I'm glad that I have this opportunity to share with you about my trip abroad. I've got a lot of things to tell you guys about my Asia trip.

First, I went to Thailand. I tried some of the great food at the local street stalls in Bangkok at the first day of my arrival. The foods were really good. The next day, I took a long tail boat along the Mae Kok River. There were also a lot of interesting things I did in Thailand such as bamboo rafting down the river, rode an elephant in the jungle, visited a number of different ethnic minority groups, stayed a night at an aboriginal village, and saw an amazing "Lady Boy Show". Everything was very inexpensive in Thailand. I had a lot of coconuts, too. They were so sweet and juicy.

After Thailand, I went to Malaysia. It's such a big and beautiful country. There were lots of Chinese people who spoke several kinds of Chinese languages.

After Malaysia, I went to Singapore. I went on a city tour of the city. Singapore is a dynamic and cosmopolitan city in the South China Sea.

I flew to Japan, the land of the rising sun after Singapore. In Tokyo, I visited the Meiji Shrine, the Imperial East Garden, and Ginza. The next day, I visited Disney Land in Tokyo. Then, I took a deluxe motor coach to the foot of Mt. Fuji and then drove halfway up to Japan's highest mountain to enjoy a spectacular view from a height of 2,300 meters.

They said that traveling by train is an ideal way to view Japan's passing mountains, forests, lakes, valleys, and the sea, as Japan has the world's most convenient and efficient railway network. However, I didn't have enough

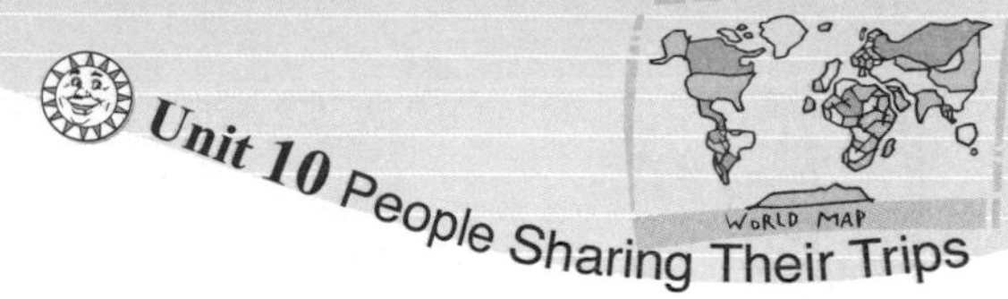

time to do it this time. I'll have to save some money and come back again next year.

If you are interested in a trip by train in Japan, you're welcome to be my companions.

Angus's African safari

Hello! My name is Angus. I'm going to tell you my unforgettable adventure of an African safari.

This safari included the best of southern and eastern Africa.

I still remember the day we departed from Cape Town and stopped at Citrusdal for the first night of our camp. This was our first time to set up and to familiarizc ourselves with the camping equipment. There were 20 people in the tour. Even though it was our first time to know each other, we had a great time that night. Everybody was so excited and enjoyed our first night.

In the second week, we stayed 2 nights at Etosha National Park, and then continued to Botswana and Okavango Delta. We explored this area by dug-out canoes and on foot. This was an incredible 1,600,000 hectares of wilderness, channels, oxbow lakes, flood plains, reed beds, and grassy islands. We saw hippos, crocodiles, and the prolific birdlife on the way.

The third week, we traveled to Chobe National Park which is the home to one of Africa's largest populations of elephants. We entered the park and took the famous "fish eagle" cruise on the Chobe river to watch elephants, buffalos, and hippos. We also traveled to Victoria Falls. The falls is one of the seven natural wonders of the world.

Week 4, we passed through Lusaka to Malawi where we made for the famed lake Malawi beaches. We had got a chance to relax beside this beautiful freshwater lake.

Week 5, we were in Zanzibar, the exotic "spice island". It's a tropical paradise with sandy beaches which has the perfect combination of culture and history. We visited the old slave markets, spice plantations, and the slave caves. One of the most interesting things to see here was the colorful mix of people: African and Arab, Christian and Moslem, and English and Swahili.

Week 6, our last week. We traveled to the Masai Mara, Kenya's best known game park. The Mara has green hills, wide horizons, and open plains containing Africa's "Big Five"—lions, leopards, elephants, rhinoceroses, and buffalos.

Africa contains the most majestic of landscapes and is filled with a remarkable diversity of people and wildlife which has given me lots of amazing memories that I'll never forget.

Chinese Translation

Melody的亞洲之行

嗨！我叫Melody，很高興能有這個機會與你們分享我的國外旅遊經驗，我將會告訴你們許多有關我這次的亞洲行。

首先，我去了泰國，第一天到達時我就品嚐了曼谷當地路邊的各種小吃攤，它們真是美味。第二天我搭乘那種有長尾巴型的船沿著眉公河駛去。在泰國還有許多好玩有趣的事，像是坐竹筏、叢林中騎大象、參觀許多不同的少數民族、在土著村度過一晚以及觀賞令人驚奇

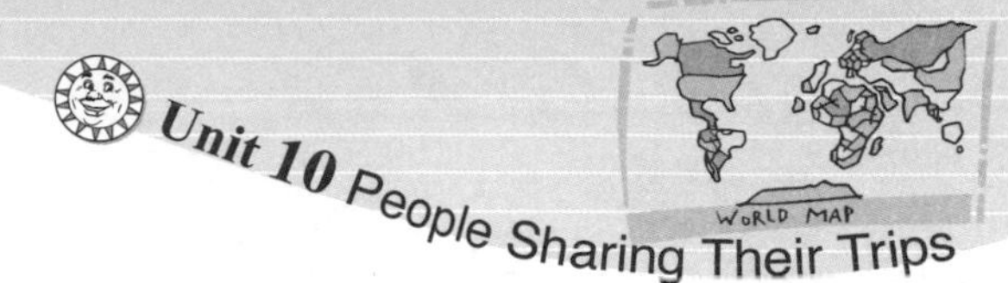

的「人妖秀」。在泰國的消費眞是便宜。我吃了許多椰子，它們又甜又多汁。

離開泰國之後，我來到了馬來西亞，她是個又大又美麗的國家。馬來西亞有許多中國人，他們說著許多種不同的中國方言。

馬來西亞之後，我到了新加坡。我在新加坡時，參加了一個市區旅遊團。新加坡是位於南中國海的一個充滿活力與生氣的國際性城市。

參觀完新加坡之後，我飛到了日升之國——日本。我在東京時參觀了明治神宮、皇居外苑以及銀座。第二天我去了東京的迪士尼樂園。之後我搭乘豪華旅遊巴士來到了富士山腳下，接著再往上開到日本第一高峰富士山的半山腰，享受從2,300公尺看去的壯麗景觀。

有人說在日本坐火車旅行是最理想的旅行方式，可以沿途欣賞高山、森林、湖泊、山谷以及海洋，因爲日本有著世界上最便捷、最有效率的鐵路系統。可惜這次我並沒有足夠的時間來趟火車之旅。我將要回家存點盤纏，明年再回來日本做趟火車旅行。

如果你對於坐火車遊日本有興趣的話，歡迎與我結伴同行。

Angus的非洲狩獵旅行

哈囉！我是Angus，我將要告訴大家我在非洲狩獵旅行的難忘冒險經驗。

那次的狩獵旅行包括了非洲南部與東部最好的地方。

我還記得那天我們從開普敦出發，第一個晚上來到Citrusdal，在此紮營，這也是我們第一次紮營，並讓我們熟悉這些設備。我們共有20個團員，雖然這是我們第一次相互認識，但大家都玩得很愉快，每一個人都很興奮地享受第一晚。

第二個星期，我們在Etosha國家公園住了兩個晚上，接著繼續前往波扎那（非洲東部的一個共和國）及Okavango三角洲。我們用乘坐獨木舟和步行來探索這裡。令人不可置信的，這裡竟有1,600,000公頃的荒野水道、U形的湖泊、氾濫平原、蘆葦塘，以及雜草叢生的島。一路上，我們看到河馬、鱷魚以及豐富的各種鳥類。

第三個星期，我們到了Chobe國家公園，這裡也是非洲數量最多動物之一的象的家鄉。我們進入國家公園，搭乘有名的「魚鷹」號航行於Chobe河，觀看大象、水牛以及河馬。我們也來到了世界七大自然奇景之一的維多利亞瀑布。

第四個星期，我們穿越路沙卡（尚比亞首都）來到馬拉威（東南非的一個共和國），朝著極富盛名的馬拉威海灘前進。我們得到一個可以在這個美麗的淡水湖旁休息的機會。

第五個星期， 我們來到了桑吉巴（非洲國家），有異國情調的「香料之島」。桑吉巴是個有著多沙海灘的熱帶天堂，有豐富的文化以及歷史。我們參觀了舊奴隸市場、香料農場，以及奴隸洞窟。還有一件有趣的事是，這裡有各種不同顏色的混血人種：非洲人與阿拉伯人的混血、基督教的與回教的混血，以及英國人與非洲斯華西里人的混血。

第六個星期，也是此行的最後一個星期，我們來到了馬塞族人（肯亞與坦尚尼亞的游牧狩獵民族）居住的Mara區，也是肯亞最有名的野生動物保護區。Mara有著蒼翠的丘陵、寬闊的地平線、開闊的大平原，包含了非洲的「五大」——獅子、美洲豹、大象、犀牛以及水牛。

非洲擁有最雄偉的風景，充滿了非凡的多樣性的人種和野生動物，給了我非常多驚奇的回憶，這些是我永遠都不會遺忘的。

Words & Phrases

opportunity	n.	機會
share	v.	分享
abroad	adv.	在國外
guy	n.	傢伙；朋友
street stall	ph.	街上的攤販
Bangkok	n.	曼谷
bamboo rafting	ph.	坐竹筏
ethnic	adj.	種族上的
minority	n.	少數
aboriginal	adj.	土著的
lady boy show	ph.	人妖秀
inexpensive	adj.	價錢低廉的
coconut	n.	椰子
juicy	adj.	多汁的
dynamic	adj.	有活力的
cosmopolitan	adj.	國際性的
South China Sea	ph.	南中國海
land of the rising sun	ph.	日升之地
Tokyo	n.	東京
Meiji Shrine	ph.	明治神宮
Imperial East Garden	ph.	皇居外苑
Ginza	n.	銀座

deluxe	adj.	豪華的
Mt. Fuji	ph.	富士山
efficient	adj.	高效率的
railway network	ph.	鐵路網
however	conj.	然而
safari	n.	非洲狩獵旅行
Africa	n.	非洲
unforgettable	adj.	難忘的
adventure	n.	冒險
southern	adj.	南部的
eastern	adj.	東部的
Cape Town	ph.	開普敦（南非首都）
camp	n.	營地
set up	ph.	著手建立
familiarize	v.	使熟悉
equipment	n.	設備
even though	ph.	雖然
national park	ph.	國家公園
Botswana	n.	波扎那（非洲東部的一個共和國）
delta	n.	三角洲
dug-out	n.	獨木舟
canoe	n.	獨木舟
on foot	ph.	步行
hectare	n.	公頃
wilderness	n.	荒野
channel	n.	水道

oxbow	n.	U字形
flood plains	ph.	氾濫平原
reed	n.	蘆葦
grassy	adj.	蓋滿草的
hippo	n.	河馬
crocodile	n.	鱷魚
prolific	adj.	豐富的
population	n.	人口
elephant	n.	大象
Victoria Falls	ph.	維多利亞瀑布
natural wonder	ph.	自然奇景
Lusaka	n.	路沙卡（尚比亞首都）
Malawi	n.	馬拉威（東南非的一個共和國）
famed	adj.	著名的
freshwater	adj.	淡水的
Zanzibar	n.	桑吉巴（非洲國家）
exotic	adj.	有異國情調的
spice	n.	香料
tropical	adj.	熱帶的
perfect	adj.	十足的
combination	n.	組合
slave	n.	奴隸
plantation	n.	農場
cave	n.	洞窟
colorful	adj.	富有色彩的
Arab	n.	阿拉伯人

English	n.	英國人
Swahili	n.	非洲的斯華西里人
Masai	n.	馬塞族人
Kenya	n.	肯亞
game park	ph.	野生動物保護區
hill	n.	丘陵
horizon	n.	地平線
plain	n.	平原
leopard	n.	美洲豹
rhinoceros	n.	犀牛
majestic	adj.	雄偉的
remarkable	adj.	非凡的
diversity	n.	多樣性

1. Share one of your trips abroad with others.

2. What did Melody do in Thailand?

(1) ______________________________.

(2) ______________________________.

(3) ______________________________.

(4) ______________________________.

(5) ______________________________.

(6) ______________________________.

(7) ____.

(8) ____.

3. What are the "Big Five" in Africa?

(1) ____.

(2) ____.

(3) ____.

(4) ____.

(5) ____.

1. Share one of your trips abroad with others.

Answers will vary.

2. What did Melody do in Thailand?

(1) She tried some of the great food at the local street stalls in Bangkok at the first day of her arrival.

(2) She took a long tail boat along the Mae Kok River.

(3) She did bamboo rafting down the river.

(4) She rode an elephant in the jungle.

(5) She visited a number of different ethnic minority groups.

(6) She stayed a night at an aboriginal village.

(7) She saw an amazing "Lady Boy Show".

(8) She had a lot of coconuts.

3. What are the "Big Five" in Africa?

(1) Lions

(2) Leopards

(3) Elephants

(4) Rhinoceroses

(5) Buffalos

觀光英語

作　　者／朱靜姿
出 版 者／揚智文化事業股份有限公司
發 行 人／葉忠賢
登 記 證／局版北市業字第 1117 號
地　　址／台北縣深坑鄉北深路三段 260 號 8 樓
電　　話／(02)8662-6826
傳　　真／(02)2664-7633
E-mail ／service@ycrc.com.tw
印　　刷／鼎易印刷事業股份有限公司
ISBN ／957-818-737-8
初版一刷／2005 年 5 月
初版三刷／2010 年 1 月
定　　價／新台幣 450 元

國家圖書館出版品預行編目資料

觀光英語 = Travel English / 朱靜姿著. — 初版. --
臺北市：揚智文化, 2005 [民94]
面；　公分.

ISBN 957-818-737-8（平裝附光碟片）

1. 觀光英語 — 會話

805.188　　　　　　　　　　94006167